He bit back a smile and the sudden impulse to take her in his arms

Instead, Justin enjoyed the warm glow that permeated his being and had nothing to do with the sun beating through the car windows.

Lilah cocked her head and stared at him.

Justin held his breath.

She wet her lips.

The only noise was the whizzing of traffic outside and the occasional honk of a car horn. Not to mention the violent thumping of his own heart.

This would be it...their first kiss. Finally.

Dear Reader,

I live in a small college town. Every spring, the azaleas bloom in candy cane colors, the daffodils and tulips blanket the lawns and flowerbeds and the spirited alumni return for their class reunions. These annual rituals bring together the bittersweet memories of past joys and disappointments as well as the promise of beautiful and fulfilling things to come—all the elements of a great romance, in my opinion. Is it any wonder that I had to write a series of stories set during Grantham University's reunions? I hope you enjoy reading this first installment as much as I took pleasure in writing it.

Let me mention the inspiration for my heroine, Lilah Evans. I happened to read an op-ed piece by *New York Times* columnist Nicholas Kristof on the organization Run for Congo Women and its founder, Lisa Shannon. As a woman and a mother, I couldn't help but be moved by Ms. Shannon's valiant efforts, and I knew I wanted to create a heroine who embodied her spirit. While I was influenced by elements of her story, the characters and events in my book are, of course, strictly fictional.

As always, I love to hear from my readers. Email me at tracyk@tracykelleher.com.

Tracy Kelleher

On Common Ground
Tracy Kelleher

TORONTO NEW YORK LONDON
AMSTERDAM PARIS SYDNEY HAMBURG
STOCKHOLM ATHENS TOKYO MILAN MADRID
PRAGUE WARSAW BUDAPEST AUCKLAND

Recycling programs
for this product may
not exist in your area.

ISBN-13: 978-0-373-71762-0

ON COMMON GROUND

ABOUT THE AUTHOR

Tracy sold her first story to a children's magazine when she was ten years old. Writing was clearly in her blood, though fiction was put on hold while she received degrees from Yale and Cornell, traveled the world, worked in advertising, became a staff reporter and later a magazine editor. She also managed to raise a family. Is it any surprise she escapes to the world of fiction?

Books by Tracy Kelleher

HARLEQUIN SUPERROMANCE
1613—FALLING FOR THE TEACHER
1678—FAMILY BE MINE
1721—INVITATION TO ITALIAN

Other titles by this author available in ebook format

Many thanks to Renée Dinnerstein,
an inspired teacher. You're a good sport.
For her insights into early childhood education,
see Renée's blog, Investigating Choice Time: Inquiry,
Exploration, and Play, at investigatingchoicetime.com.

This book is dedicated to Peter and James:
two great guys who are generous, smart and funny.
Plus you give the best hugs!

CHAPTER ONE

March

THE VILLAGE WOMEN STOMPED their bare feet to the rhythm of the drums. They kicked up dirt that collected on the hems of their long cotton dresses, making an earthen border of red clay. The bright, bold patterns of their bandannas created a swirl of color. And the joyous sounds they intoned combined in a song in celebration.

To say the least, Lilah Evans was a long way from home.

You couldn't get much farther from Orcas Island, off the coast of Washington State, than the remote jungle of the Democratic Republic of Congo. But whatever the distance—indeed, whatever the differences—the primal African beat had a universal appeal. And a special one for Lilah.

Because the women who sang and danced? They were singing and dancing for *her*.

It was a gift from the hearts of women who owned almost nothing and had lost so much—husbands and children and homes in the ongoing civil war.

Growing up on an idyllic island, surrounded by fishermen, artists and executive escapees from Seattle, Lilah wouldn't have been able to imagine that people were capable of such cruelty. After her schoolteacher mother had read her Grimm's fairy tales, she'd had nightmares for weeks. To this day, she never looked at gingerbread quite the same way.

So when Esther, her good friend among the Congolese women, had told her what had happened to her, her soft voice mingling with the smoke from the kitchen fire in her small hut, Lilah had cringed.

"Lilah, they came one day—this was after they had raided the village and killed my husband and the other men. And taken my oldest son," Esther had explained. Her tone was flat, but raw emotion cut the sentences into staccato clips. "They were crazy. The militiamen— crazy on drugs. They went from hut to hut. They raped the women, young daughters no more than children, grandmothers—toothless grandmothers. Then they came to me." Her voice faltered. "They took me, too, in ways not normal. They made sure that my children were watching. It was a game, a sport, *n'est-ce pas?* When they were done, they laughed. Then they started to talk among themselves. I knew there was more to come. I tried not to show any fear. That was what they wanted of course."

"You don't have to say any more," Lilah remembered telling her friend. She was too old to hide under the covers, but that was what she wished to do. Barring that, she wished she could cover her ears with her hands. But she didn't. She owed it to Esther to listen, to be brave in any way she could be.

And her friend finished the story, a story so horrific that now, after the fact, Lilah still blotted out the details of how Ester came to lose her leg and what had happened to the rest of the family. What she did recall vividly was her own reaction—crying and reaching out to her friend. Her own words, thinking back now, seemed so self-centered. "I don't think I would have been able to withstand that. I don't know if I am strong enough," she had said.

And Esther had placed her thin hand, as light as a bird's, on Lilah's arm and replied, "You do it because you have to. You have to think of tomorrow. There is no choice."

But for Lilah, there had been a choice. Back in her senior year of college, suffering from the flu, she'd wrapped herself in a quilt on her couch and killed off a dozen boxes of Kleenex, while flipping through the channels on the TV. By chance she landed on this day-time talk show, the sort that she would have never admitted to watching. It carried a heart-wrenching report on the plight of Congolese women.

By the time the program broke away for a commercial for a new women's deodorant, Lilah had made that choice. She decided to enlist other women to help provide health care to women and children in the remote areas of Congo—places where medical providers were practically unheard of.

And so Sisters for Sisters was born.

It was one thing to find a cause. It was another to carry it out. First had come the efforts to establish a base of operations in the capital of Kinshasa, staffed with a part-time office manager and a nurse who volunteered when she wasn't working at the hospital. One year later, Lilah got the first traveling clinic up and running. Equipped with medical supplies and a portable lab, that team of two nurses and a female doctor set out to war-torn villages in eastern Congo. After three years, the organization was finally able to pay the nurse in the main office and had added another two clinics, then two more. In total, five traveling clinics were making the rounds—

true, often on a shoestring budget and understaffed, but at least they were providing services.

Through her own outreach efforts, Lilah had also co-ordinated field operations with a group of volunteer doctors, and this partnership helped increase much-needed manpower and opened up Sisters for Sisters to larger funded studies. Now ten years later, her organization had seen both ups and downs—plenty of downs—but she was still unwilling to give up when there were good people like Esther suffering. But there were times when Lilah found it almost impossible to follow Esther's credo and "think of tomorrow."

Lilah shook her head. Tomorrow could wait, especially when this moment in time was perfect. Today, Esther was dancing joyfully with a prosthetic leg thanks to Lilah's efforts.

The music ended. The performers and villagers erupted in a chorus of cheers.

Esther approached Lilah, her gait awkward but confident. She hugged her. *"C'est pour toi."* "It's for you."

"C'est fantastique!" Lilah exclaimed in French. The language was a vestige of colonialism, but it was still the common language spoken in Congo. *"Tu m'as donné un cadeau énorme! Merci bien."* "You've given me a wonderful gift. Thank you so much," she said in her less than fluent French.

"But it is we who are thanking you, *ma petite soeur,* my little sister," Esther said. "We are all sisters helping each other, *mais non?*" She smiled and her voice held a hint of teasing.

That was another of Lilah's choices—the whole sibling concept.

Her idea for raising money was to hold 5K road races for women where each participant or "sister" sponsored a "sister" in Congo. The idea had taken off. Now her non-profit organization had more than twenty local affiliates that sponsored fun runs and competitive races almost every month, all across America. Plans were already set to branch out to Europe and Australia.

But while these runs remained the backbone of Sisters for Sisters's funding and a way for women to "actively" participate in the organization, Lilah recognized the limitations of races as the sole source of revenue. As a result, much of her time was spent writing grant proposals to funding agencies and foundations. This had led to a collaboration with a Doctors Without Borders type of operation to provide cell phones to women in rural villages, thus allowing them to obtain long-distance medical help. Similar programs in other countries, using towers and satellites that the military or World Health Organization had put in place, were already up and running.

Here at last was a way to supplement Sisters for Sisters's meager staffing. So far only a pilot program in a few locales, including Esther's village, had been funded, and if they were going to expand, they'd need more money. Lilah figured she'd have to give up on sleep altogether to get out more grant applications.

As if that weren't enough to worry about, after a race two months ago in Poughkeepsie, New York, a woman had approached her who was a senior VP at a large investment house. She wanted to help set up a local banking system so that women could establish savings accounts to better the lives of their children.

Lilah felt overwhelmed. What did she know about banking? Microfinancing sounded like a good idea, but was it something Sisters for Sisters should be affiliated with? They always had been associated strictly with medical care. On the other hand, if she said no, would she be turning down an opportunity too good to miss? After all, the link between improved standards of health and financial well-being, not to mention better education, was well documented.

But all these questions would simply have to wait. Now she reveled in the warmth radiating from Esther's skin as Lilah embraced her "sister." A late-afternoon shower started to fall, heightening the smells of the village and the jungle.

Esther broke away from their hug and looked to the skies. "It's time for the feast. It is good we have the school to keep us dry." That was something of an exaggeration. Made of sticks, the school consisted of a thatched roof and dirt floor.

Esther clapped for her three remaining children to come, and with her head held high she clumped along on her artificial leg. She nodded for Lilah to follow.

Lilah joined the procession, smiling with the thought that she resembled one of the baby ducks following their mother in the children's book *Make Way for Ducklings*.

A cell phone rang.

All the women reached into the deep folds of their dresses. Lilah had to laugh. It was a sign of progress that the towers were functioning, and that women were growing familiar with the equipment even though the likelihood of receiving calls was remote. Still, given the loudness of the ring tone, Lilah knew it was for her. She held her phone aloft to let the other women know, then rushed through the raindrops into Esther's mud hut. "Hello," she answered. Very few people outside her organization and her family had her number.

"Lilah, it's Mimi." The voice on the other end of the line belonged to Mimi Lodge, Lilah's roommate from college. Always outspoken and very smart—some might say too smart for her own good—Mimi had gone on to be a television news correspondent.

"Talk about a voice out of the blue. Where are you calling from this time? Chechnya? Afghanistan?" Lilah asked. If there was a hot spot in the world, chances were that Mimi was there.

"Close. Waziristan."

Lilah cringed. People sometimes questioned her sanity about traveling to Congo, but Waziristan? The northwest region of Pakistan was a known stronghold of terrorists. "Promise me you're calling to tell me you're safe," Lilah implored.

"Not to worry about me. I'm in my element. It's you I'm calling about—with news."

"Don't tell me—actually do tell me—that someone has decided to give Sisters for Sisters millions of dollars after seeing your piece on TV?" she asked.

"No, but there's the possibility."

"I'm always open to possibilities, long shots, even highly unlikely probabilities."

"It's like this. Seeing as you're such a hard woman to track down, the alumni office of our illustrious alma mater, Grantham University, contacted me through my television network. They were hoping I could hunt you down directly."

"Oh, please, there is no way I'm making a contribution to Annual Giving. I barely make enough money to pay the rent on my hovel of an apartment—and I use the term *hovel* generously," Lilah decried. After college, she'd landed in Brooklyn, and for some mysterious reason that only the gods of real estate understood, her block had defiantly escaped the rampant gentrification that had swept the rest of the outer borough.

"Actually, it's the other way around. They want to give you something."

"You're kidding me, right?" Lilah ran her hand through her chestnut-brown hair, which despite the practical clip holding it back in a ponytail, was frizzing madly in the rain and humidity.

"I kid you not. Apparently, the feature I did on you actually penetrated the mostly deaf ears of the ivory tower powers-that-be. Now the university wants to honor you with a big alumni award at Reunions this June. Who'd a thunk it, heh?"

Lilah knew that Mimi didn't harbor any great fondness for Grantham despite her family's long history of involvement and support for the Ivy League institution. Nor was Lilah particularly the Reunions "type." What was the point of rehashing your college days? Or seeing people from your past you really could do without? She could think of one person in particular—boy, could she ever. Then there was the more fundamental anxiety. Ten years out—had she measured up to her own expectations? And the more troubling thought, *If I accept the award, will they figure out I'm no longer some sterling idealist?*

But those doubts were for her ears alone—something she'd have to work out. So Lilah retorted with the slick sarcasm that so often substituted for wit and intelligence among her fellow Grantham alumni.

"So why exactly would I want to wax poetic about my time at that dyed-in-the-wool chauvinist bastion?" she asked, using Mimi's withering expression for Grantham. "I mean, can't I just accept the award without showing up to Reunions? 'Cause I'm not totally convinced I can stand there with a straight face, listening to the university president give some rah-rah speech about all my good works somehow being an outgrowth of that special Grantham spirit. And the thought of rubber chicken served under a tent by the boathouse? Please. Is there anything worse? Oh, right—sleeping in a dorm room all over again."

Truth was, she'd die for a dorm room right now. Tonight Lilah would be sleeping on the dirt floor on a thin straw mat. Not that she was complaining, mind you, when she had so much compared to the villagers around her.

Speaking of which, Lilah angled to the side to let one of Esther's daughters carry an earthen platter of *baton di manioc,* boiled palm leaves filled with a paste made from starchy manioc tubers.

"I feel your pain, really I do," Mimi responded from thousands of miles away. She, too, had mastered the glib speak. "But look at it this way. Does Miss America get her cr-own in absen-tia?" The satellite line had a slight delay, and the transmission sputtered.

"I get your point. I get your point," Lilah replied. "But aren't Reunions in June? That's…that's not going to work out. Our first major fundraising race in Europe is at the beginning of that month—in Barcelona. I couldn't possibly miss that."

"I'm pretty sure they're at the end of June, but, c'mon. This is Mimi here. Your bosom buddy? You and I both know you're manufacturing excuses. The real reason you don't want to go back to Reunions and accept this award is Stephen."

Lilah hadn't spoken her ex-fiancé's name in almost ten years. And she wasn't about to start now. And why bother to rail against the cruelty of love when her friend flat out didn't believe in love? Or so she had claimed many a time over. Too many times over, Lilah some-times thought.

"From your silence, I presume I hit the nail on the head. Well, let me tell you. I have just one thing to say in response."

"Grin and bear it?" Lilah offered.

"Oh, please. What do you take me for? A leader of a Girl Scout troop? My kind of pep talk is…" She pro-ceeded to string together several swearwords in a highly creative and visually interesting fashion.

Crude, but effective, Lilah couldn't help thinking. "So you really think I should go, then?" she asked.

"Yes, of course I think you should go. Not only do you deserve all the praise in the world for what you're doing, you'll have those old coots eating out of your hand. They'll see this brilliant, cute young woman, and they'll immediately feel the need to help. The next thing you know, they'll be writing monster-size checks to sup-port your work. You might even think about upping your own salary from near poverty line to something where you could afford to go to a decent hair salon."

"Hair salons? They still have them?" Lilah asked face-tiously. Reflexively she fingered her bangs, slowly grow-ing out from her last feeble attempt at giving herself a cut.

The light shower had turned into a thick curtain of rain, and the sound of drops hitting against the thatched roof formed a steady rumble. The red dirt on the floor was already transforming into a rusty-colored slime, the same mud that coated the soles of her hiking boots.

From her position in the doorway of the hut she could see Esther, along with two other women from the village, cooking rice, beans, bananas and more manioc. Through the haze of smoke she noticed two large cauldrons cooking meat—probably chicken and goat. Today had to be special if meat was on the menu.

These women who had suffered so much were unfailingly generous. Who was she to balk at attending some awkward ceremony and meeting a few strangers at Reunions if it meant helping them out?

Lilah rubbed her sticky palm down her sundress. The outfit was a concession to the festivities, but she'd paired it with her usual hiking boots because there were too many poisonous snakes for her to consider wearing sandals. Not a great look but always practical.

She exhaled through her mouth with resignation. "All right. I hear the wisdom of your words. Just tell me whom to contact about setting up my triumphal return to our beloved alma mater. And in the name of a good cause—and good people—I promise to show the proper humility and speak about the urgency of the problem." She paused, her mind working on overdrive. "But I have one condition."

"Hey, I gave you prime time network exposure. Don't expect me to open my meager checkbook, as well," Mimi protested.

"I wouldn't think of it. I know the prices at the salon you frequent. No, my request—no, my ultimatum is this. I'll go provided you come, too. If I'm going to give a convincing performance for a day—"

"We're talking days, bubby," Mimi interrupted.

Lilah groaned. Oh, yeah. Grantham University never did anything by half measures. Their Reunions lasted three days and were scheduled immediately before commencement ceremonies, thus cementing a lifelong hold on graduating students.

Lilah cleared her throat. "Okay, but if I am going through with this charade, I think it's only right and proper that I have moral support. And nothing says moral support like a forceful female friend close at hand."

The metaphorical clock ticked away in silence until Lilah heard a sigh. "All right," Mimi agreed. "Only for you will I set foot on Grantham, New Jersey, soil. I suppose that also means I won't be able to avoid putting in an appearance at the family manse, will I?"

"I'll make it up to you. I promise. Besides, once my parents get wind of the award, I'm sure at least one of them will insist on making an appearance, and then you'll have a parental buffer."

"If you mean that having a critical mass of people will in any way be enough to preserve my sani—"

Mimi's voice was drowned out by a decisive rat-tat-tat. It had to be the sound of gunfire.

"Mimi? Mimi? Are you all right?" Lilah asked.

"Never better. This is what I live for, right?" Her words were upbeat, but they couldn't camouflage the underlying edge. "Listen. Gotta go. I'll text you the contact numbers at Grantham. Promise." The call ended abruptly.

Lilah held the phone away from her ear. Her concern didn't stop just because the conversation was cut short. She shifted her gaze toward the encroaching jungle. Danger from natural predators and roaming militias was never far away here, either. For now, at least, there didn't appear to be any imminent threats to be fearful of.

But sometimes the bigger fears came from within oneself.

CHAPTER TWO

June

JUSTIN BIGELOW STOOD in the international arrivals area of Newark Liberty Airport with a sign dangling from one hand and wondered if he was making a big mistake. A seriously big mistake.

It wouldn't be the first one, as his father, a professor of classics at Grantham University, would no doubt have reminded him. Growing up, this pronouncement traditionally came during dinner, where conversational topics were limited to his father's research on the ancient Greek Punic Wars, with possible digressions into stories from the day's headlines in the *New York Times* that were of particular interest to him.

This arrangement, with Stanfield Bigelow as the central star around which all family members orbited, had seemed to please his mother and sister. Naturally. His mother happily trekked over the remains of archaeological sites in Sicily and North Africa while painting watercolors of the landscapes—very well, as it happened. Her book, *A Companion's Guide to Sicilian Wildflowers,* was a classic among aficionados.

Justin's older sister, Penelope—named for Odysseus's devoted wife—was equally sympathetic to their father's passion for ancient Roman history and Latin historical authors. She had dutifully followed in his footsteps, graduating first from Grantham University before going to graduate school at Oxford on a Marshall Scholarship, then winning a Prix de Rome, and now an appointment as an assistant professor at the University of Chicago—not quite the Ivy League, but somehow more so.

On the other hand, Justin—short for the Byzantine emperor Justinian, a fact that no one, and Justin made sure ab-so-lutely *no one,* knew about—had been left completely out of the conversation. Sports, his passion growing up and something he excelled at, held no interest for his father. And the only show on National Public Radio that Justin listened to—"Car Talk," the humorous call-in car repair broadcast—didn't count as highbrow fare. A real shame, since Justin had been more than handy when it came to keeping his father's ancient Volvo station wagon up and running. In recognition of which his father would nod silently, turn back to his books and then add while he flipped a page, "Make sure you wash your hands before you touch anything in the house."

It used to be that statements like that hurt Justin's feelings, and he would lash out. Now he didn't bother. What good would it do anyway? People didn't change. They were who they were, for better or for worse.

Justin smiled at the thought of someone better, lots better. And with that smile still on his face, he stared up at the arrivals screen.

Her plane had just landed.

Justin glanced at his watch, an inexpensive Timex with large numbers. Given the water and sand he came into contact with daily on his job, there was no point in spending more—not that he was into status-y stuff anyway. It was an international flight, so he figured it would be another twenty minutes or so before she'd appear. Enough time to check his messages.

He tucked the sign under his arm and pulled out his smart phone, juggling it with the bouquet of flowers in his hand. He had left work early to drive to the airport, and he wanted to make sure that everyone got home. Then he set about methodically answering anything that required an immediate response. As he did so, he wandered a few steps to a large rectangular pillar, tucked the flowers and sign under his arm.

"Lilah? Lilah Evans?" a female voice called out from behind a few minutes later.

Justin held up a hand and quickly finished replying to a message. "I'm sorry. I just needed to send that."

"Is that sign for Lilah Evans?"

A woman pointed to the words on his sign. A cascade of sun-streaked brown hair fell across her face, blocking her features.

"Can I help you?" he asked, bending over to address her eye to eye.

She stood up. The hair fell away. She indicated the sign again. "Did you mean Lilah Evans?"

His mouth opened. She looked very familiar, even though he didn't recognize her immediately.

The Lilah Evans he remembered had that kind of fresh-faced milkmaid appeal—all rosy cheeks and rosy attitude to life—an apple dumpling with a heart of gold, to mix metaphors in a really, really awful way. She'd been rounded, maybe even a little pudgy, not that Justin ever complained about a few extra pounds. If anything, they only served to enhance her womanly appeal. Anyway, she'd always seemed supremely unaware of her own attractiveness. It hadn't mattered if she had on a sweatshirt and had her hair pulled up and anchored by a pencil, or was wearing some slinky dress and high heels, the woman had invariably produced a catch in his throat even though she'd only thought of him as a friend. Was there anything worse?

Back in college, Lilah was his roommate's girlfriend. That made her strictly off-limits.

And now? Now that same woman—who was *not* the same at all—was staring at him with a critical frown. She looked older. There were lines in her forehead and around her mouth, too, and she'd tucked a pair of reading glasses into the neckband of her drab olive T-shirt. Gone were the pillowy-soft curves, replaced by a delicate frame with sinewy muscles and minimal body fat. And instead of that wide-eyed, can-do outlook, she conveyed a weary, been-there-done-that air.

He cleared his throat. "Lilah? Is that really you?" He pointed between her name on the sign and herself in person.

"Well, yes, I'm Lilah Evans, spelled *L-I-L-A-H,* not *L-I-L-L-A.*" She hooked a thumb under the strap on her backpack. "You *are* waiting for the *L-I-L-A-H* version, right?"

He shrugged off a laugh. "I never could spell. And as to waiting for the *L-I-L-A-H* version? To tell you the truth, it seemed like I've been waiting for a large portion of my adult life."

CHAPTER THREE

"OH, DON'T TELL ME." Lilah covered her mouth before slowly dropping her hand. "Justin? Justin Bigelow? From college?" Her voice ended in a high squeak, the kind of girlie sound that Lilah hadn't emitted since…well… since college.

"In the flesh," he admitted sheepishly.

Though what he had to be ashamed about Lilah wasn't quite sure. No, check that. If Justin's behavior was still consistent with his days in college, he had a lot to apologize for. Which, Lilah reflected, had only made him that much more attractive.

What was it about bad boys? Lilah wondered. Every woman knew they were poison, but that didn't stop them from wanting to take a bite out of the apple.

Back in college, Lilah had found Justin incredibly attractive. Maybe it was his cherubic blond curls that should have made him seem like Harpo Marx, but somehow they just turned up the sex-appeal quotient instead? Maybe it was the long, loose-limbed body, the kind that never seemed to put on a pound despite an enormous consumption of beer and pizza? But then, he had been a lightweight rower, Lilah reminded herself—all those calories burned away in killer practices. Or maybe it was the way he didn't mind shooting the breeze with her in the dorm rooms he shared with Stephen. Or when Stephen was off editing the *Daily Granthamite,* the college newspaper, the way he listened to her worry that her Junior Paper wasn't original enough, or about the interview she was sure she had messed up for a summer internship at the Guggenheim Museum. She hadn't, he'd assured her, and sure enough she'd gotten the job.

She studied him now. Gone were the curls. Instead, his hair was close-cropped. He still appeared trim and fit, but he seemed to have lost the red-rimmed and bleary-eyed gaze of someone who burned the candle at both ends.

I guess even a party boy has to know when to quit sometime, she thought. But talk about parties! Much of the social life at Grantham University centered around social clubs, basically coed fraternities, each with its own personality. Stephen had belonged to Contract—the elitist club for political aspirants. Their parties involved a lot of sherry. Justin had joined Lion Inn, the ultimate jock hangout where beer was the beverage of choice. Lilah, on the other hand, had declined to rush any club, claiming the Grantham experience for her was more centered around her studies, her job in the art history library and her position on the board of the film society. But the truth was, she hadn't gone that route because she'd been afraid she'd be turned down.

Anyway, Justin. There was never any doubt that he would join Lion Inn. Or that he would have just about every woman flocking after him. And since she was Justin's roommate's girlfriend, she was somehow supposed to know his every personal detail for all those other women to mine.

"Is it true he's having an affair with the dean's wife?" they'd ask.

To which she answered, "She's old enough to be his mother—not that that would stop him."

Then there was, "Does he really quote one particular sonnet by Shakespeare to all the women?"

"It may be the same one over and over, but can you beat, 'Shall I compare thee to a summer's day?'"

Or her favorite: "Does he compose songs on his guitar for every woman he sleeps with?" To which she answered, "No one has a repertoire that big."

But what they all really wanted to ask was, "Do you think he likes me?" "Does he want to go out with me?" "Does he want to sleep with me?"

Lilah didn't worry whether Justin liked her. She wasn't sure why, but she had always felt that he liked her in the no-pressure kind of way. As friends *without* benefits. Besides, she had Stephen.

Stephen. Just the thought of her ex-fiancé made her suddenly suspicious. She looked around but didn't see him. Then she narrowed her eyes at Justin. "Someone we both know didn't send you to get me, did he?"

"No, you can rest assured. I'm here on my own accord as your official welcoming party."

"An official welcoming party that's busy texting instead of keeping an eye out for me? That's some kind of welcome."

"This is New Jersey. Give me a break. Though in my defense, I wasn't expecting you through the doors so fast. But to make up for my grievous faux pas, these are for you." He reached for the bouquet and handed it to her.

As Lilah reached for the flowers their fingers brushed. She felt the roughness of the pads of his fingers. She wondered if he still rowed, recalling the thick calluses he had built up in college. Then she pulled apart the patterned paper and stopped. Tulips—dozens of Rembrandt tulips, the striated, white-and-red, white-and-orange, and white-and-purple flowers depicted by the Flemish master.

"They're your favorites, right?" he asked.

She looked up. "I'm amazed. How did you remember?"

"You didn't think Stephen kept track of those kinds of things, did you? I may not have graduated *magna* like some people I know—" he tipped his chin down as he eyed her "—but I've got a pretty good memory for details."

Lilah pressed her nose to the flowers. The waxy petals were just starting to open, and their faint perfume was intensely fresh. She closed her eyes for a moment, and felt transported back to a simpler time when her worries consisted of studying Old Masters, not worrying whether she could help yet another woman get proper obstetrical care rather than risk death in childbirth.

She opened her tired eyes. "You always did remember the details—especially when it involved women." Irony was the only emotion she seemed able to muster.

"I'm not sure that's entirely a compliment, but I'll just assume it is." He looked around, then pointed to her backpack. "Is that all you've got?"

"That and my laptop." She held up the case for him to see. "I prefer to travel light. It's just easier, faster. I'm all about streamlining."

He nodded uncertainly. "I can imagine the advantages. Well, let me take your pack." He didn't bother to wait and moved to take it off her shoulders. He slipped his long fingers between the padded strap and the thin cotton of her T-shirt.

Lilah felt her skin prickle. She blinked. *I really must be tired after the flight from Spain, not to mention the*

hard work getting the race all sorted out. The race...
That's right. Her muscles were still sore.

Yes, she was tired, but even Lilah couldn't deny the ego boost of having a good-looking male in his absolute prime touching her body—even if it was strictly on a practical level and wasn't by any stretch of the imagination accompanied by smoldering looks. Ah, the imagination...

Lilah watched Justin sling her pack over one shoulder as if it contained only a fistful of Ping-Pong balls instead of the forty-pounds-plus of clothing and paperwork stuffed into its bulging sides. Relieved of the weight, she felt as if her spine had decompressed and she'd grown an inch. And she would have felt even more relieved if she didn't still feel the residual tingle of Justin's touch.

"Shall we go find the car, then?" he asked with a nod of his head.

That tingle she was feeling just got even more annoying because it appeared that Justin was totally oblivious to the same hypersensitivity. Lilah frowned. The decision to return to Grantham appeared to promise additional obstacles. At least, maybe she could find out about the obvious one that had been bugging her ever since she'd heard about the award. "I was wondering. I know you said you weren't Stephen's emissary, but do you know if he's planning on coming this weekend?" She tried to sound oh-so-casual. She practically had to hop to keep up with Justin's long strides.

"As far as I know, he's not coming to Reunions. So you're safe," he said, waiting for her to go through the revolving door first.

Lilah stopped. "Safe? I think the embarrassment factor is still pretty high. I can't begin to remember the number of times I poured out my soul to you. About the only thing I *do* remember is that it was way more than to Stephen."

"And you never thought that was one of the problems with your relationship?" He scooted in behind her into the slowly turning segment of the revolving door.

She was conscious of his legs coming perilously close to the back of her thighs. Lilah cleared her throat. "Let's leave that evaluation aside for now, okay? I don't need you to lecture me on how I wronged your good buddy. Besides, for all I know, as soon as you're alone, you'll immediately contact him to let him know my rear end is bigger than ever."

Finally, the slowly revolving door deposited them on the sidewalk, and she stumbled out on the pavement. The fresh air should have been a relief, but this was Newark, and fresh air was a relative concept given the bus and taxi fumes.

Justin followed closely behind. "I won't text, let alone communicate with Stephen in any form. I should let you know, I haven't kept up with him since graduation."

Lilah raised her eyebrows. "You're kidding me."

"So you've nothing to worry about on that score." He held his arm out toward the street. "We need to cross here. I'm parked in the lot across the way."

"But you two were practically joined at the hip in college."

"Except where you were concerned," he reminded her. "And by the way, I don't know where you get off saying your butt is too big. Anyone can see you're incredibly fit and trim." He started to cross the street when the light changed. "In fact, if anything, you could probably afford to gain a few pounds."

She shouldn't have felt pleased, but she was. It was the inner-anorexic in all women who were once overweight.

"Well, I run a lot these days—the job kind of requires it. So, it's hard to gain weight."

"You could try eating more."

"Eating? Who has time for eating?"

"Lots of folks do. It's called three square meals a day."

"I know. It's something we try to make happen in the villages."

He slanted her a glance. "And you don't practice what you preach?" He kept up a steady pace as they passed the rows of cars.

Lilah frowned. Why did he seem angry with her? She took a few giant strides to catch up. "Wait a minute. I don't get it," she called out after him.

Justin stopped. He fished some keys out of his pocket and waited.

She jogged to his side. "Tell me this. If you're not here because Stephen sent you to escort me, why *are* you here?"

A giant SUV pulled out of the row near them, and the driver gunned the engine as he raced off.

"Why am I here?" he repeated. "To tell you the truth, I don't usually get too involved with Reunions stuff." He wet his top lip. "I'm here because of you."

"Me?" Lilah stopped while Justin opened the trunk of a green sports car. She looked down. "And this…this… little car is yours?"

"This is not just a little car. It's a fully restored…well, partially restored—I still have some body work to do— Triumph TR4, a British classic." He gazed at it lovingly.

The rust around the back fender didn't exactly induce confidence. "Is it roadworthy?" she asked.

He narrowed his eyes. "Careful, or I'll change my mind." He shut the trunk lid and gave it an extra push to make sure it closed. Then he turned to her. "I was the one who recommended you for the Paine Prize, and as a result, I have the enviable task of serving as your personal chaperone for the duration of the Reunions festivities. How can I put this?" He rubbed his chin philosophically. "We'll be like two peas in a pod."

"In this thing we will, that's for sure," she joked, then from his silence, realized she may have gone too far. "That's very nice of you," she said quickly to make up for her insensitivity, "but you know, it's really not necessary. I'm sure I can find my way around."

Justin walked over to the passenger-side door and held it open. "You'd deny me the pleasure of your company? Besides, if you don't toe the line, *I'll* be the one to get in trouble. And who knows, on top of all the trouble I caused in my undergraduate days, they might just take away my diploma retroactively."

Lilah had to laugh. "You didn't get in that much trouble—okay, you did. But it wasn't as if you ever flunked a single course—even if I never saw you study."

"Ah, I had my secret ways." He pointed to the open door. "Are you going to get in?"

"Are you changing the subject?"

His smile was a little too charming.

"Okay, we'll let that pass—for now." She slipped into the seat without further complaining. Until it collapsed under her weight. "I think you need to do some internal renovation in addition to the bodywork," she said, watching him circle the car.

He slipped into the driver's side. "Be careful of the loose spring on the right side."

Lilah shifted closer to the gearshift. "Now you tell me." The bucket seats were really quite close and the gap separating them, not that wide.

"I've been concentrating on working under the hood so far."

"So you fix cars for a living?"

"It's just a hobby. And my work is nothing nearly as exciting as yours, that's for sure." He turned the key in the ignition and put the car in Reverse, looking over his shoulder before he pulled out.

"No, I'm curious. I mean, what does someone end up doing who spent most of his college years seducing every woman in sight and giving parties that are possibly still talked about in some quarters."

Justin grinned slyly. "Not possibly. Definitely."

He still had terrific dimples, Lilah noticed.

"And I didn't seduce every woman, as you personally can attest to." He reached across, his forearm almost skimming the front of her shirt. "Excuse me."

Lilah swallowed with difficulty.

He flipped down the glove box and pulled out a ticket. "Your job is to guard this with your life," he said and held it out for her.

"And if I don't?"

"You don't want to know what the Port Authority will do to you," he joked.

"Oh, for a minute, I thought you had plans."

He swung into the lane that led to the payment booths. "Oh, I have plans, but they've got nothing to do with parking fees."

Lilah rolled her eyes. "So what *do* you do if you're not in the business of fixing cars? Provide escort service, because I gotta tell you, your pickup lines are getting a bit old."

He pulled to a stop behind a Cadillac Escalade. "You think? No one's been complaining lately."

"Then the women where you live have pretty low standards. Where do you live anyway?"

"In Grantham." He put the car in first and inched his way up to the booth.

"In Grantham! You're joking?"

He shook his head. "Ticket, please." He held out his hand.

Lilah slowly placed the stub in it, careful to avoid skin-to-skin contact. "So you work at the university? Doing what? Coaching crew?"

He paid for the parking and pulled away, smoothly shifting up to second. "No, I gave up rowing a year out of college. I teach."

Lilah leaned away from him to get a broader view. "You're kidding me?"

He shook his head and concentrated on the signs.

"You mean at the university?" she asked.

"I have a much higher caliber student." He deftly avoided a semi crossing three lanes at once. "The turn-off for the turnpike comes up sooner than you think, so I need to get in the far lane."

"I don't get it. Higher caliber? What do you mean?"

"Ah, ha! There it is." He put on his signal and took the sharp exit to the right. "I told you it came up quickly." He glanced over, obviously pleased with himself. "What do I mean? Isn't it obvious?"

She shook her head.

"I teach kindergarten."

CHAPTER FOUR

MIMI HAD HER HEAD BURIED in the refrigerator at her father's house when she announced loudly, "Well, I for one wouldn't mind having Justin Bigelow pick me up from the airport—or any place, for that matter." She shut the stainless-steel door. "Dah, da-ah!" She held a jar of peanut butter triumphantly aloft. Then she spied the label and her enthusiasm diminished. "Wouldn't you know it? Organic peanut butter with no salt and no sugar. No wonder it was in the fridge."

"Since when has your dad become all health food conscious?" Lilah asked. She sat on a stool in the Lodge's sprawling kitchen. Her entire studio apartment could have fit into the center island—with room to spare. The surface gleamed with acres of polished granite.

"It's not Daddy. People who raid beleaguered companies don't do organic, or so I've been told. It's the preoccupation of his latest wife, the lovely Noreen, by way of Limerick. It seems no processed food is allowed to touch the lips of my little stepsister Brigid. Noreen even sent Cook to a health food cooking school for further instruction."

Mimi seemed to think nothing of having "Cook" as part of the household. *Ah, the prerogatives of privilege,* Lilah thought. Not something that had been part of her upbringing, that was for sure

She watched Mimi unscrew the lid to the peanut butter

and stick her finger in. Then she swallowed a glob and gagged. "Oh, yuck," Mimi howled. "It's like having sex without an orgasm."

It had been way too long since Lilah had had sex, let alone an orgasm, for her to comment. Which probably also explained why her next thought was of Justin. She cleared her throat and moved on to the obvious—not about sex. "Noreen? Last I heard your father was married to Adele."

Adele had originally been Mimi's nanny before she pushed aside Mimi's mother to become the second Mrs. Lodge. That was also before Mimi's mother had committed suicide, a forbidden subject at all times.

"Boy, are you behind the times. After Adele and Daddy had a son, they hired Noreen as a nanny. That son would be my half brother, Conrad Prescott Lodge IV, known to one and all, yourself included, as Press."

"Which would not have been my first choice for a nickname," Lilah quipped.

"Be that as it may, Noreen then replaced Adele in the wife department. Daddy, as you may have gathered, seems to focus on the household help when he's looking for a new mate. It doesn't require too much legwork, I guess."

"Look on the bright side. At least he marries them," Lilah reflected. "Hey, how old is Press now? Last I saw him, he was obsessed with Magic Cards and some little medieval action figures or other."

"Warhammer figures—the holy grail of prepubescent boys with unwanted blackheads and extensive imaginations."

"I hope he's gotten out of that phase—the blackhead part, I mean."

"Oh, he's turned out all right, our Press—quite a

handsome man-boy. He's very nice, actually, no thanks to either my father or Adele. I mean, how can you relate to a mother who looks like a boiled prune from playing tennis all day or a father who's never there? Come to think of it, maybe that's why he turned out so well?"

"So he's how old?" Lilah asked.

"He's just finished up his junior year at Grantham, a biology major but focusing on paleontology. I think he also plays on the tennis team. Anyway, he mentioned that he's working Reunions, but I don't know what exactly."

Mimi abandoned the jar of peanut butter on the counter and wandered over to the adjoining walk-in butler's pantry. Lilah, being Lilah, screwed the lid back on the jar and put it away in the fridge. Then she followed Mimi, leaning against one of the old-fashioned cabinet drawers that held linens. On one wall, glass-faced cabinets displayed massive amounts of silver serving pieces and glassware. On the others, shelves held neatly arranged packages and jars of whole-wheat flour, honey and granola. Lilah took in the jars of dried beans and legumes of varying dull colors.

"I can see that Noreen has had a major influence on this room, as well," she said. "When I think back to college, these shelves had the biggest supply of Pop-Tarts I'd ever seen—it just makes me want to cry."

Mimi let out a dramatic sigh. "You're right. It's the fall of civilization as we know it." She shook her head and marched out of the pantry. "Never mind. There's still the liquor cabinet."

Lilah tripped along behind her into the dining room, where drop cloths covered furniture, rugs were rolled up and bundled in plastic, and the walls were denuded of paintings. "So what's going on? A garage sale?" she said.

Mimi lifted a spattered sheet covering the side-board. "No, it's protection from the dust, all part of the current-wife-renovations phenomenon. First comes the new master bedroom—for all the obvious reasons. Then they work their way around the house imprinting their own unique personality. When Adele became the official Number Two, she had the kitchen redone, a wine cellar built and a new pool house put in the back. Now that Noreen rules the roost, she's converting my old bedroom into a yoga room and turning the library into a screening room. They'll probably sit around and watch documentaries about eating local."

Lilah watched Mimi study the labels of various bottles of liquor. "So where are you staying, then?"

Mimi grabbed a bottle by the neck and straightened up. "Why, the pool house of course. It's my version of the stepdaughter's revenge. I'm co-opting something that really mattered to that money-grubbing bitch who usurped my mother's rightful place." She marched back to the kitchen. "C'mon, I've made the unilateral decision that we're going to have gin and tonics. I think I noticed some designer tonic water in the back of the pantry."

"And I'm sure there's organic limes in the fruit bowl." Lilah yawned. In Spain, where she'd just come from, it was already well after midnight. Between jet lag and the time difference, she was fading fast. "Dare I ask where the 'money grubbing bitch' is now?" she asked, trying to keep up with the conversation.

"Oh, in the center of town, ensconced in the new town house development on Grantham Square. It's supposed to look oldie and charming—all brick Georgian and stately. But of course the places have elevators and the latest in stainless-steel appliances and jetted spa baths. But get this. According to Noreen, they're asking more than a million for the places, and you still have to pay parking on top. Can you believe it?" After a quick pit stop to the pantry, she marched back in the kitchen and placed the bottles on the counter. She opened a cabinet and took down two highball glasses.

Lilah covered her mouth and stifled another yawn. "Sounds better than the dorm where I'm staying. Mind you, I haven't seen it yet. I asked Justin to bring me here first."

"And he didn't stay for a chat? I'm offended."

"I offered, but when we pulled up to the house he checked his email, and said that something had come up that he needed to follow up on right away."

"Ooh! *Quel mystère.* I can just imagine the type of emergencies Justin Bigelow must have."

Lilah was about to explain that the Justin of today didn't totally resemble the Justin of yore, but Mimi had already moved on.

"I don't know why you want to stay in the dorms when you can bunk here with me." She didn't bother with a jigger and instead poured generous amounts of gin in the glasses, stopped, eyed the levels and added more. Then she picked up the glasses and ambled over to the refrigerator. "I'm sure the pool house is bigger than the room they'll put you in." The automatic ice maker made a racket when she pressed one glass and then the other against the lever. "I mean, really, a girl could start to feel rejected," she shouted over it.

Lilah waited for her to finish. "I haven't looked at my information packet yet. It's in my knapsack. But like I already told you, I'll be running around doing my official best, so I figure it'll be more convenient."

Mimi poured in the tonic water and added a lime before handing Lilah her drink. "Cheers."

They clinked glasses. Lilah took a sip, and then coughed. "Whoa. I'm barely standing as it is. After drinking this, I'm not sure I'll make it to dinner."

"Not to worry. I already placed an order for takeaway. I thought we'd trip the light fantastic and dine on our favorite Grantham food." Mimi smiled slyly.

Lilah blinked. "Don't tell me. Hoagies from Hoagie Palace?" She patted her heart.

Mimi tipped her glass and gulped a generous mouthful. "What else? I ordered a tuna melt for you and a Cheese Steak-Fried Egg Special for me with extra mozzarella cheese sticks and hot sauce. And did I mention the two orders of fries with Ranch dressing?"

"Please, you're killing me—and that's before all the cholesterol."

"Not only that. I bribed Press to pick it all up. I say, what are half brothers for after all, if not to run errands? Plus, I figure that if we're totally blitzed when it's time for you to crash, he can give you a lift back to campus."

"I wouldn't want to put him out. I can always call a taxi or, really, walk from here. What is it to campus? Half a mile? A mile at most? Heck, I could run that in under five minutes." The mammoth, yellow stucco house was located on Singleton Street, one of the main arteries leading into town from the west—the fancy side of town. White pillars flanked the front portico. Twelve-foot-high rhododendrons lined the circular drive. The Historical Society of Grantham held their gala under a tent in the gardens every spring.

"Walk? Oh, please. Drink some more." She followed her own advice.

Lilah took another sip and felt the alcohol go directly to her bones. The nagging ache in her right Achilles tendon from overtraining seemed to magically disappear.

Mimi smacked her half-empty glass on the counter. The ice rattled. "So, let's get back to the really important things. Like Justin Bigelow. How does he look? Still incredible?"

Lilah took another slow sip and leaned her elbow against the center island. She used her other hand to brace herself from taking an inelegant nosedive into the fruit bowl containing an artful display of limes, lemons and pomegranates.

Pomegranates? Lilah couldn't help thinking. *What real person has pomegranates in their fruit bowl?* The answer came to her quickly. She was not among "real" people.

She decided to hold off on her drink. And instead narrowed her eyes, trying to picture Justin driving his little sports car, the windows open to the breeze, the light dancing off the polished wood steering wheel and the tips of his clipped curls. "What can I say? He looked like a god—all sun-kissed and good enough to eat." She sighed.

"You make him sound like a Florida orange."

Lilah stared at her. "Vitamin C was the last thing on my mind when he picked me up earlier today."

Mimi rubbed her chin. "You know, I always wondered how he got into Grantham. I mean, I know he was a terrific athlete, captain of the lightweight crew, right?"

"Uh-huh." Lilah eyed her drink and went for another sip. Why not? She wasn't driving.

Mimi, way ahead of her, drained what was left of hers and took that as a cue to make another. She held up the bottle of gin to Lilah.

She shook her head. "I'm not there yet."

"I am." Mimi fixed herself another drink. "Somehow I kind of figured that he got special dispensation being a faculty kid," she said, her back to Lilah. "I mean, it wasn't as if I ever heard him engage in an intellectual discussion."

"No, that's not true. I remember staying up late one night in his and Stephen's suite. I was haranguing him about how the French Impressionists were overhyped, and that it was their German counterparts who really deserved the attention. He might not have known his Monets from Manets, but we had a real conversation and he made me think."

"And what did Stephen say?"

Lilah waved her hand dismissively. "Oh, he wasn't there, as usual—debating or editing or something." She frowned in thought. "No, Justin wasn't dumb, not by a long shot. It's just that for some reason he liked to give the impression that he never studied. I don't know why. And I'm pretty sure he was a double major—economics and music. So how dumb could he be?"

"Cheers." Mimi clinked her refreshed glass against Lilah's. They both took healthy sips. "So maybe I'm wrong. It's just I always pictured him as this sexy golden retriever—great hair, sunny personality, always willing to roll over and expose his privates—adding a brain to the equation kind of dulls the fantasy."

Lilah laughed so hard the liquid squirted out her nostrils.

"So he's remained gorgeous."

If Mimi only knew how gorgeous, Lilah thought and reflexively put the cool glass to her lips.

"But what else? Did you find out what's happened to him since college? Wasn't he working to make the national team or something?" Mimi asked.

Lilah removed her glass and blinked at it, surprised that somehow she'd managed to finish it. "What's he been up to? Well, let me tell you, you'll never, *ever* guess." She leaned forward with her chin to emphasize her words, grabbing the edge of the countertop at the last minute.

"A challenge." Mimi closed her eyes. "What *is* he doing? What does your typical ex–Ivy Leaguer do once he lands in the real world? Let's see. Investment banker?"

Lilah coughed. "Did I say Justin was typical?"

Mimi opened her eyes wide. "Lawyer?"

Lilah rolled her eyes. "Where are your vaunted investigative reporter instincts?"

"Pole dancer?"

Lilah laughed. "An interesting career choice, but no."

"I don't know. Dog trainer? I'm running out of ideas here."

"Told you you'd never guess." She raised an eyebrow. "He teaches kindergarten."

"You're kidding me. Mr. Sexy Labrador teaches little kids?"

The door to the mudroom off the kitchen opened. A high-pitched squeal and hushing adult tones could be heard. Then a gauzy pink tutu came whirling through the kitchen.

Lilah looked baffled as a young girl wearing a rhinestone tiara—at least, Lilah hoped it was rhinestone—with the word *Princess* spelled out in large loopy letters on the front of her leotard twirled around them, anointing them with a feathered wand as she did so.

Lilah looked askance at Mimi. "I take it this is not the amazing transformation that Press has undergone over the years?"

Mimi shook her head. "No, this is not Press. Lilah, allow me to introduce my six-year-old half sister, Brigid." Mimi cocked her head to the mudroom. The sound of steps grew nearer. "And my newest stepmother, Brigid's mom, Noreen. Noreen, this is Lilah Evans, who's being honored at Reunions."

Noreen was a striking woman with a shock of tamed red hair and pale skin with the texture of clotted cream. She circled the island, transferring the BMW key fob to her left hand, and held out her right. The nails had a perfect French manicure. "Of course. What an honor to have you here. I've followed your work closely ever since I saw Mimi's story on you on television." With her drawn-out vowels and slightly singsong cadence, her voice betrayed the remnants of an Irish accent.

"I'm trying to interest Conrad in giving money to your organization, and in fact, I'd love to talk to you about organizing a run here in Grantham." She deposited her oversize Prada bag on the counter. "I know all the women in my book group and Pilates class would love to participate, and since I'm active in the PTA at Brigid's school, I'm sure I can generate interest from other moms."

Brigid meanwhile continued to twirl around the room, stopping periodically to touch various objects, including the bottle of gin and exclaim, "I hereby pronounce you a knight of the realm."

Lilah looked at the woman who, on close inspection, was somewhat older than she. Whatever else the birth of a child had affected, it didn't appear to have altered her twenty-two-inch waist, judging from the way her wide leather belt cinched the top of her pencil skirt. Normally, Lilah would have jumped to conclusions and immediately hated Noreen—her obvious self-indulgence, her unabashed display of wealth. Lilah had never seen a canary-yellow diamond before, and Noreen's was hard to miss. And she should have hated her on principle because she was Mimi's stepmother, and Mimi always hated her stepmothers.

But she couldn't. Not when Noreen stuck out her hand and shook Lilah's with the force of a longshoreman. The woman had spirit, life, enthusiasm, and clearly a seriously good manicurist.

"Sure, sure. I'm happy to talk about it," Lilah answered, worried that she sounded less-than-professional after the G and T. "Why don't we say sometime over the weekend? Right now I'm totally jet-lagged and a little worse for wear after letting Mimi ply me with alcohol." She indicated her glass.

"Of course. That would be wonderful. You must be exhausted, and as to a drink—I could use a wee dram myself, as they would say in the Old Country." Her eyes twinkled as she made fun of herself. "I deserve one anyway. Cook has tonight off so she could visit her sister in Moorestown—such a quaint place—and Conrad, as usual, is late in the City, so I took Brigid to Sustenance, the new fusion restaurant in town. All very organic and locavore. I've become fanatic about not allowing a single processed bit of food to pass her lips."

Lilah nodded blankly and out of the corner of her eye saw Mimi push the gin in her direction.

Noreen glanced at the alcohol but shook her head. "I probably shouldn't. I have yoga first thing in the morning, and I like to feel fresh even before I start." She glanced over at her daughter who was counting the door pulls on the cupboards and smiled. "Now what was I talking about before? Oh, yes, so there we were in Sustenance, and I started remembering how I grew up on a solid diet of fish and chips, and somehow I managed to survive. That's when I decided to let Brigid have a hot-fudge sundae."

Lilah noticed Brigid's tutu fan over her head as she did a series of somersaults across the kitchen. Ah, yes, signs of a sugar high. Then she glanced back to Noreen, who was nervously strumming her fingers on the granite. "I take it you shared?" she asked.

"Why, yes, how did you know?" She became aware of her strumming. "I'm not usually this much of a motormouth, either. I swear on my grandmother's Bible." Then she hooked her arm through her bag. "Brigid, dear, why don't you give your sister, Mimi, a kiss good-night before we go upstairs for your bath and a bedtime story?"

Brigid closed her eyes and fluttered her arms.

"Brigid O'Reilley Lodge. There will be no bedtime story if you don't stop that and come now." Noreen's voice was firm.

The little girl opened her eyes and inhaled loudly. Then she swiveled on the toe of her Mary Janes and tromped inelegantly to Mimi.

Mimi abandoned her drink and bent down, awkwardly offering her cheek.

Brigid gave her a loud smack, then twirled around to Lilah. "You, too," she announced. She walked over and raised her chin.

Lilah knelt down, her Achilles tendon smarting despite the infusion of gin, and reached out and gave the six-year-old a hug and kiss. She smelled of ketchup, hazelnuts and baby powder.

Brigid seemed very pleased. She looked at her mother. "I want *her* to read to me," she said, pointing with her wand. "You're beautiful, you know."

Lilah blinked, amazed at the self-possessed child. "No, I didn't know. Thank you."

"But your sneakers are dirty. You should get Mommy to buy you new ones."

Noreen shook her head. "The scourge of living in an affluent community like Grantham, I'm afraid."

Lilah laughed. "We should all have such problems." She looked seriously at Brigid. "I don't need new ones. I can just wash these."

"Your next lesson will be how to use the washing machine," Mimi cracked.

Lilah glanced over. Mimi would never admit it, but Lilah thought she looked jealous. "And I'm sure your big sister, Mimi, will be happy to show you."

"A worthy idea." Noreen pried her daughter from Lilah. "Lilah will read to you another night, maybe. Tonight she's seeing her best friend, Mimi, who she hasn't seen in a long time."

"I don't mind," Lilah said, painfully standing up.

Noreen clasped Brigid's small hand. "Don't be silly. She gets a story every night, so there are plenty of opportunities another time. In fact, because of her fantastic teacher, she won't go to bed without one. It's just amazing—to have someone who's a real proponent of the Reggio Emilia model of early childhood education."

Lilah and Mimi nodded with a complete lack of comprehension.

"I'm sure my mother would be very intrigued. She's an elementary school principal," Lilah said.

"How interesting," Noreen said and she actually appeared to mean it.

"Anyway, in addition to understanding the importance of play, they read the most wonderful books, lots of the old classics. And then they start doing other things because of the reading. Like building castles after hearing chapters from *The Wizard of Oz*."

Brigid wrapped an arm around one of her mother's

legs, clinging to the tight black leggings. The effects of the sugar seemed to be wearing off.

"Naturally there're those parents who are skeptical because they're so used to the emphasis on testing even at such a young age. It's so competitive out there now." Noreen ruffled Brigid's fine hair, removing the tiara that was already slipping over one ear. "But I believe that the Reggio Emilia system works better in the long run, producing natural readers and ones with fewer social problems. And even the critics can't deny that the teacher is good at picking up any learning disability."

She shook her daughter's hand playfully. "C'mon, munchkin. Time for bed. It's late for a school night. You want to be up bright and early for Mr. B tomorrow, don't you?"

"The early bird catches the worm. But I don't like worms. I want to catch butterflies."

"Well, your bird can catch butterflies," her mother announced and guided her to the door.

"Wait a minute. This Mr. B?" Lilah called out.

"Mr. B, Tweedle B. Tweedle B and Tweedle Bum," Brigid recited bowing her head back and forth. She pulled on her mother's arm.

"That's right, dear." Noreen didn't bother to correct her.

"How many six-year-olds know Lewis Carroll?" Mimi asked.

Lilah was almost convinced she detected some sisterly pride.

"Oh, that's par for the course in Mr. B's class," Noreen said over her shoulder. "I'll catch you later this weekend, then." She waved.

Lilah pushed away from the island. "Before you go.

One question—Brigid's teacher? Mr. B? His full name wouldn't be…"

"Justin Bigelow." Mimi supplied the answer.

"How did you know?" Noreen bent down to pick up Brigid and carried her upstairs.

Left alone in the kitchen, Mimi lowered her chin and looked over her nose at Lilah. "You think she's in love with him?"

"Brigid or Noreen?" Lilah asked.

"Either one. Both."

Lilah pursed her lips. "Maybe I will have another drink." She reached for her glass, and asked casually, a little too casually, "This love thing? You think it's contagious?"

Mimi raised her eyebrows. "Why? You think you feel symptoms coming on?"

CHAPTER FIVE

"So, TELL ME AGAIN WHO we're picking the food up for?" Matt Brown asked as he opened the drinks case at Hoagie Palace. It was a Thursday evening, and the Grantham take-out institution was packed with high school and college students, and Matt, a local kid home for summer vacation after his freshman year at Yale, fit the profile. The smell of hot sauce, fried saturated fat and hormonal imbalance hung in the air.

"My half sister Mimi and a friend of hers from college," Press Lodge explained as he held out money to the cashier. "She's this woman named Lilah Evans—the head of a nonprofit in Africa or something." As he waited for his change, he spoke to Angie, the woman behind the counter who owned the popular food spot with her husband, Sal. "Hey, Angie, I gotta satisfy the hoagie fix for the returning alums in the family. Otherwise they get ornery."

"That's what we count on," Angie said with a laugh and passed the coins and bills to Press. "But if anyone gets ornery with you, hon, you send 'em to me. You're like family." Angie beamed over her shoulder at a wall of photographs. Press followed her gaze. Front and center was one from Press's graduation from his prep school in Connecticut.

He'd invited Angie and Sal, never expecting they'd make the trip. Not only had they come, Sal had handed him an envelope on the side. "If you ever need any-thing, you know who to call," Sal had offered with a swift handshake. "We're proud of you." Then he'd taken the picture of Angie with her arm around Press, a proud smile on her face, a dopey one on his. In the corner of the photo, slightly out of focus, stood his mother, glancing down at the Rolex on her wrist, probably checking how much time she had before her tennis match. His father—surprise, surprise—was nowhere in sight.

Press blew a kiss to Angie and led the way through the organized throng, asserting himself with one of his wide shoulders. His father had been disappointed that he hadn't gone out for football at Grantham—he'd been heavily recruited. Just another disappointment in a long line, Press figured. Anyway, practices interfered with his job as a research assistant in his advisor's lab, and he wasn't about to give that up.

He waited outside of the store for Matt. The two of them had worked together at Apple Farm Country Club last summer, Matt manning the cash register in the pro shop and Press as a teaching pro for kids. Sometimes when they got in early and before the kids' Swedish and French au pairs swarmed around Press, they'd go to the driving range and hit a bucket of balls. Matt was hope-less, but Press was a natural, hitting three hundred yards every time. It didn't matter much because the point was really just to talk—about school, music, their parents, life. A bond had formed, and the two kept up on Face-book during the school year when Matt started Yale and Press finished up his junior year at Grantham.

Press watched as Matt stumbled out the front step and onto the sidewalk. He had tried to open his can of Arnold Palmer iced tea and walk at the same time. "Focus, Matt

Brown, focus. How many times do I have to tell you," he ribbed his friend.

Matt managed to stop next to him without tripping. "I know. I'm pathetic. But before I forget. I gotta ask you. Did you say Lilah Evans?"

"I THINK YOU LI-IKE HIM," Mimi taunted Lilah.

"Oh, please. This isn't junior high school. And I'm too old to have crushes," Lilah replied. She let her eyes wander around the kitchen, anywhere but on Mimi. *How often did someone use two dishwashers?* she wondered.

"I don't know what you're so defensive about. What's the big deal about being forced to stay close to a man who is drop-dead gorgeous—and as we now have personal proof of—gentle and gifted and loves children?"

"You don't understand."

"What don't I understand?" Mimi grabbed for the gin bottle again. "Don't tell me you still have a thing for Stephen?" She poured two fingers and didn't bother with the tonic water.

"No, of course not. Not anymore." Lilah eased herself onto a stool. The night was growing longer by the minute. "You know, I looked him up on Google when I decided to come back."

"As anyone rightly would." Mimi took a swallow.

"Seems he's a partner in a big law firm in Cleveland. They even had a picture up on the website—he's gotten fat. Which is kind of ironic when you consider how he always used to be on me about my weight."

"*And* he's married with two children and a third on the way."

"You're kidding? How did you find out?" She realized she experienced a glimmer of jealousy—but not for Stephen. Her breakup, which was once so heart-wrenching, now only held a faint "what if?" No, the pang she felt was for the idea of children. Lilah rested her chin on her hand.

"Excuse me. I'm a reporter. I'm supposed to get that kind of information."

"Well, did you also find out that he's not coming to Reunions?"

"That I don't know. It seems you have your own sources. Speaking of sources—" She glanced down at her watch. "Where is that little brother of mine? I'm beginning to think he didn't turn out so well after all." Then she looked back at Lilah. "Hey, no pooping out yet. The night is still young—especially because we still haven't cleared up this matter."

"What matter?" Lilah stifled a yawn.

"About Justin? You and Justin? C'mon. Let's wait outside by the pool. We'll spot Press sooner that way."

Lilah took the remnants of her second drink and dutifully followed Mimi. "There is no me and Justin." Lilah settled into one of the deck chairs around the pool. Tiled dolphins cavorted as in some Roman mosaic. For all she knew, it *was* a Roman mosaic. She squinted and peered more closely. *No, it couldn't be, could it?* "You know, maybe I shouldn't have had this second drink."

Mimi settled into the chaise next to her. She flicked off her sandals and ran her bare feet up and down the cedar slats. "Don't tell me there's no you and Justin. I mean, in the face of overwhelming positive attributes, can't you let go for at least a long weekend? No one is expecting you to find true love, after all. But even you, especially you, you little saint, deserve to fall off your pedestal every once in a while."

"You don't understand," Lilah protested. "Every time I look at Justin I'm reminded not only what a total creep

Stephen was, but I also unfortunately remember how incredibly self-centered I was, too."

"Self-centered? That's the last thing I'd describe you as, Ms. I Don't Have A Dime To My Name, but go ahead and please take the shirt off my back. Hey, maybe you can use that line on Justin?"

Lilah placed her drink on the side table between them. "Feel free to laugh."

"Who said I was laughing?"

"Listen, admit in retrospect that Stephen was a creep. But even though he called off the engagement, I really didn't give him any alternative. Up until then, I had always gone along with his plans. He always seemed so goal-oriented, so focused on our future."

"His future, with you in tow," Mimi cracked. "The future corporate attorney with the good little academic wife standing steadfastly at his side."

"Excuse me. It was my idea to go to graduate school at NYU while he was in law school at Columbia," Lilah argued.

Mimi threw up her hands. "I don't even know how you can justify his actions. As far as I remember—and I have a pretty good memory—when you decided on a change in career, it didn't go down well with him. And when you wouldn't change your mind, he dumped you and broke your heart."

Lilah dropped her head. "I'd always been such a good girl up until then," she said softly.

"Lilah, we were all good girls once upon a time, you especially."

"I'm still a good girl," Lilah said despondently.

"Well, get over it. And I can't think of a better way than with someone warm and sexy by your side. And really. You can't tell me that you think all these depressing thoughts *every* time you look at Justin Bigelow?"

Lilah pictured Justin driving again, one hand comfortably on the wheel, the other on his thigh, his fingers tapping out a lazy rhythm on his faded jeans that fit his legs perfectly…. *No, not every time.*

"Because if that's the case, why not reintroduce him to me?"

Lilah bit down on her bottom lip. If the Justin she had met today was still the old Justin Bigelow, the one embedded in Lilah's memory, then there'd be no problem about her having a simple romp with a scrumptious good-time guy. *Plus* it'd be a snub to an ex. What more could a girl ask for?

But the *new* Justin Bigelow was…well…new. He seemed much more than the old one. And the voice of her overly developed good-girl conscience told her that was exactly the problem.

CHAPTER SIX

"LILAH EVAN AS IN SISTERS for Sisters Lilah Evans?" Matt asked.

"I don't know about this Sisters thing, but I guess so. I didn't know she was such a big deal. I mean, Mimi said something about her getting some alumni award, but I figured it was because she gave big bucks to Grantham." Press shifted the large bag of food to one arm and fished the car keys out of his jeans. His dad had given him his old BMW convertible when he graduated from high school. He'd left the keys with a card that his secretary had written.

"I don't think it was for giving money, dude," Matt said. "She came and gave a talk at Yale last fall at the Political Union. She founded this group that helps women in Congo. You know about the civil war going on there, right?"

"Sorry. If it happened after the Mesozoic era, I'm pretty ignorant," Press answered. He stepped off the curb, and like most students, didn't bother to look either way before heading out into traffic. A Lexus SUV screeched to a halt and let him cross. "C'mon, the smell of all this food is reminding me just how starved I am. Let's head home."

Matt chugged along beside, holding his can at his side. "Why I'm even friends with such an ignoramus is beyond me."

"It's so you have someone to freely lecture." He beeped open the car and settled the bag in the backseat.

Matt got in the front passenger seat, and before he even put his seat belt on, twisted around and fished out a take-out container of French fries. "So you're telling me you don't want to hear all about the warring factions and about how everyone—*and* his little brother—is trying to get ahold of the diamonds and gold and other metals in the country?"

Press started up the car. "Not really." He grabbed a French fry. "Hey, crack your window, would you? The smell of this stuff stays around for days otherwise."

Matt shook his head, but turned to press the window lever. "How you can worry about the smell in your car when millions are being killed is beyond me, and believe me, it's mostly women who are being brutalized. And besides, didn't your mother give you Febreze when you went off to college?"

Press slanted him a skeptical look. "My mother?"

"You're right. What was I thinking? Maybe you could give her some to use with all her tennis shoes? A handy travel size for her sports bag?"

Press didn't bother to laugh as he pulled out of the parking lot and into Main Street. Some people, like Matt, had good parents and some people didn't. It was less painful to discuss the state of world politics. "So where does Lilah Evans fit into the whole scenario?"

And naturally Matt was off and running, summarizing Lilah's work.

Press stopped at the traffic light on the corner of Adams Road. The university library was on the left and the town's only movie theater on the right. He recognized some friends from school and honked the horn. Then he glanced over at Matt. "Well, I'm glad someone thinks she can save the world. And I have even greater respect for her because given all the culinary delights possible in our fair city, she had the wisdom to choose Hoagie Palace."

"Laugh all you want. I'd give anything to ask her about an internship." Matt took a swig of his drink.

"But I thought you said the name of her organization was something like Sisters for Sisters? Is having a sex change operation part of the price to pay for an internship?" He made the remainder of the lights on Main Street, and they passed without incident through the center of town.

Matt rolled his eyes. "It'd almost be worth it, but I'm not sure Babička would approve," he said, referring to his great-grandmother, who lived in town.

"Not to mention your dad and Katarina," Press said, slowing down the car, just barely, to pass over the speed bumps.

"Yeah, my dad," Matt grumbled. "He's giving me so much grief about not having a job yet this summer that I'm almost thinking of moving in with Babička," he said.

Press knew that Matt's childhood hadn't been the easiest, what with his single mother dying of breast cancer when he was still in high school and only discovering who his dad was at the reading of her will. The truth of the matter was it had come as a shock to Matt's father, as well. The two had butted heads early on, but the relationship had smoothed out pretty well thanks in large part to Katarina, his stepmom, and Katarina's grandmother. Babička's baking also played a major role, in Press's opinion.

"You don't think your great-grandmother would have any cookies on hand, do you?"

Matt took another sip. "Maybe later. For now I really want to get this food to your house before it gets cold."

"If I didn't know you to be this bleeding heart do-gooder, I'd say you just want a summer job with this Evans woman so you can get your parents off your back and pad your résumé."

"Okay, Mr. Professional Cynic, you're so worldly. How do you think it'll go down if I introduce myself to Lilah Evans on bended knee with her hoagie in hand—" Matt made the appropriate gestures, spraying some of his drink in the process "—all the while running through my stellar freshman-year grades, my majoring in political science with a concentration in foreign affairs, and that I have a fantastic way to broaden the appeal of her outstanding organization by expanding her concept to Sisters *and* Brothers for Sisters."

"I think I need another French fry."

Matt growled.

"One thing. The 'bended knee' bit?"

"Yeah?" Matt asked hopefully as Press pulled into the driveway to his dad's house.

"Definitely use it. No matter what women say, they're suckers for the big, romantic gesture. Just hold on to something while you do it. Knowing you, you'll fall flat on your face otherwise, and we need you in one piece if you're going to save the world."

CHAPTER SEVEN

LILAH FELT SOMEONE KICK her foot. Half-asleep, she decided to ignore it, and let her foot flop over the edge of the chaise longue and stay there.

Next came a shaking of her shoulder. She groaned and scrunched her eyes more tightly shut.

Then someone had the nerve to blow in her ear—hard.

This time, Lilah yelped and practically bounced off the chair.

Mimi turned to Press and Matt. "Works every time," she said triumphantly. "She's awake now, trust me. What can I say? Two drinks, and she's out like a light."

Press turned to Matt. "I wouldn't worry about the bended knee. Probably the two-armed boost-up would be more effective in this case." He rested the bag of food on the patio table.

Lilah opened one eye. "I'm not that far gone that I need help getting up. And it's not the alcohol. It's the jet lag that leveled me." She hoisted herself to an upright position and rubbed her eyes, daring to open both in narrow slits. "Are these two Wise Men bearing gifts?"

"I don't know how wise they are, but that's my half brother, Press, and his friend whose name I don't remember—"

"Matt."

"And Matt, apparently, who've brought your hoagie and fries."

Lilah made some noise.

"Is that a sound of joy or disgust?" Mimi asked.

Lilah yawned. "Neither. I'm afraid I'm too tired to eat anything." She shook her head and studied Press and Matt with only the barest of insight. "I may be wrong, but you both seem to be growing boys. I'm sure you can figure out what to do with my share of the food." She rose, a little wobbly on her feet. "I don't mean to break up the party, but if it's not too much trouble, I'd really appreciate it if someone could drive me to campus."

Mimi crossed her arms. "What a party pooper. Here you force me to come back to Grantham and attend Reunions and act as your bodyguard, and what do you do but crap out on the first night. Is that fair?" She pouted.

Lilah pushed her bangs out of her eyes and felt the back of her head, realizing that her barrette had fallen out. She searched around her chair, then ducking her head underneath, she responded, "There will be other nights, I promise." She righted herself, barrette in hand. "Tomorrow night, in fact. That's when my dad comes in. You're having dinner with us, remember?" She frowned as she looked around the patio. "I wonder where I left my backpack? It's got all the information about where I'm staying on campus."

"Where were you besides here? If you were making drinks, maybe the kitchen?" Matt suggested.

"Clever boy. Why don't you hustle on in there and see if you can find it?" Mimi said. Matt did as he was told.

Press breathed in slowly. "Do you have to be so imperious? I know you think coming back here is a real effort on your part, but how about toning it down a notch where my friend is concerned?"

Mimi rolled her eyes. "Mr. Sensitivity. But all right. I promise to act nice."

Lilah winced. Even in her half-awake, mildly inebriated state, she recognized the bitter undertones. Mimi's dysfunctional family had always seemed amusing from afar, and her renditions of the latest family gossip were always bitingly witty. But up close, what had seemed amusing now just appeared mean.

Still, she didn't want to think badly of her friend—her only old friend, for that matter. But that didn't mean that Lilah was ignorant of Mimi's shortcomings.

She heard the sound of the screen door from the kitchen banging shut, and she knew relief was in sight. "Great, my stuff. You're a lifesaver…ah…what is your name again?"

"Matt," he said enthusiastically and placed Lilah's backpack on the table next to the food. His thin shoulders noticeably straightened up when he was relieved of the weight. "And can I tell you what an honor it is to meet you. I've read all about your work. You're so inspiring."

Lilah offered a trembling smile. "Thank you. I don't feel very inspiring at the moment, but it's nice to hear that people your age are still interested in social causes."

"Oh, he's interested all right," Press added. He looked at his friend, who was eyeing him with embarrassment. Then he leaned closer and whispered, "Are you going to ask her about a job, or what?"

"Not now, dude. She's half-asleep," Matt said out of the side of his mouth.

Lilah was vaguely aware of their conversation, but she needed all of her concentration just to unzip an outside pocket. "Finally."

She slipped out a legal-size envelope and sifted through the contents. "Somewhere in here should be directions." She pushed aside a map of the university campus and her name tag and unfolded a sheaf of bright orange papers. She squinted at the pages. "Did they have to use such a tiny font?" She held the paper closer to her nose, then tried backing it away. "This is hopeless. I'll have to dig out my reading glasses." She rifled through a side pocket.

"If you want, I can read it for you?" Matt suggested eagerly.

Lilah studied him. He seemed a nice, polite boy. *What was his name again?* "How good are you at deciphering mouse-type?" She handed over the piece of paper.

Matt eagerly skimmed over the information. "Let's see, it's got your schedule here."

"I'll deal with that tomorrow," Lilah interrupted. "Just go to the part where it tells me which dorm I'm staying in."

Matt nodded and flipped to the second page. "It says here that you're staying in Griswold College."

"That's my college," Press explained. Grantham grouped dorms around quadrangles and referred to these larger units as residential colleges. "No air-conditioning, I'm afraid."

"That's okay. She wouldn't know what to do with AC," Mimi said. "Forget the name of the college. Just tell her which dorm."

"It says here," Matt read on, "that you're in Bayard Hall, room 421." He looked up.

Lilah blinked once. "Could you repeat that again?"

Matt reread the location.

Mimi looked at Lilah. "Why does that sound familiar?"

"Because that was where Stephen and Justin lived senior year. They've gone and put me up in their old suite," Lilah squeaked.

Mimi whistled.

Press and Matt looked at each other, obviously unsure of the importance of the information.

"Is that kismet or what?" Mimi asked.

Lilah was still shaking her head. "The question is, is it good fate or bad or what?" She pursed her lips. "You know, maybe I will have that hoagie, after all."

CHAPTER EIGHT

AFTER DIALING THE PHONE the next morning, Justin switched it to speaker mode so he could look in the mirror to check to see if his tie was straight. The noise of the dial tone permeated the sunny one-bedroom apartment. It was early enough—around eight on a Friday morning—so the sound of commuting traffic was still at a minimum.

Justin lived in a large clapboard Victorian with a wraparound front porch, which in its original state had housed a single upper-middle-class family and their devoted household servant. All very Andy Hardy with Mickey Rooney and Judy Garland ready to put on a show in the barn. Now the house was broken up into three separate apartments, one on each floor, with Justin occupying the top floor. And the "barn" out back held his vintage sports car, a Toyota Prius from the first-floor tenant—an assistant professor in the chemical engineering department—and an artificial Christmas tree of unknown ownership.

The best thing about the place in Justin's view—besides all the light and the relatively modest rent—was the fact that it was located directly downtown in Grantham, a stone's throw from the cemetery, where he could stroll among the burial plots of Revolutionary War heroes and former U.S. Presidents, and across the street from the public library.

Justin realized all too well the irony of this last convenience since any place with books had once been a source of frustration and embarrassment during his childhood. Now, however, he could think of nothing better than heading out on a Saturday morning, first to get coffee at Bean World, Grantham's ever-so-chic coffeehouse, before heading to the library to scout out the bestsellers and laze away a few hours reading magazines and newspapers from all over the world.

Justin stared in the mirror and gave his half Windsor knot a tug to the right. He rarely wore a tie, so it took a few tries to get it right. It was important to look properly attired for the luncheon. The university president would be there, after all.

And so would Lilah.

Truth be told, the reason he had debated wearing a blue shirt or a white shirt with his blazer and gray trousers—he'd finally gone with white—was because he wanted to look good, not just proper—good. For Lilah. Even though he was still trying to figure out who *this* Lilah was.

The Lilah he had remembered from college had been serious about her studies and what she thought was important, but she'd also been bubbly—quick to laugh— an effervescent personality. The new Lilah, the one he had picked up from the airport yesterday, seemed older, wiser. Well, they were both older and hopefully wiser, he thought. And she was probably exhausted from the long flight and the killer schedule she put herself through. And if she lacked the kind of cuddly, rounded body she once had, who was he—a man, after all—to complain about how she'd been transformed into this fit, sinewy presence? Except, he kind of missed the old Lilah, the one who never seemed to judge him, the one he could tease and she could tease back without either ever taking offence. She'd been a pal. More than a pal. Undemanding, yet never taking him for granted. Unavailable, yet constantly alluring. The ripe fruit that begged to be picked but was always out of reach.

In short, a fantasy. And now?

"Hello?" The familiar female voice with a distinct Brooklyn accent answered.

Justin smiled. It was a voice that invariably wrapped around him with the comforting warmth of a favorite afghan. "Roberta," he answered and picked up the cell, switching back to regular Talk mode. "I just wanted to touch base with you again after our conversation last night."

"So are you still smarting from the principal calling you into his office yesterday?" she asked good-naturedly. Roberta Zimmerman had been Justin's professor and guiding light at Bank Street College of Education, where he'd gotten his degree in early education.

"I'm much better. That's what I wanted to let you know. Besides, there're only a few weeks left to the school year for public schools in New Jersey, so I might as well chill out—especially since I've got a sub covering for me for these few days. I mean, I know that I overreacted last night. Geez, you'd have thought after all the trouble that I'd gotten into as a kid I would have been better prepared. It was just the tone of his email—demanding that I see him as soon as possible and that he'd wait around his office specifically for me. To say the least, it kind of shook me. I mean, I know there'll always be some parents who'll grumble about my teaching methods—"

"That's because you do things differently. Anyway, I don't understand all the emphasis on testing, testing, testing these days—even before kids get to kindergarten!

If I have one more parent ask me if her child is ready for kindergarten, I'm going to scream. I'm not surprised you were upset."

"I guess it kind of blindsided me because the day before in class had been so terrific."

"Tell me."

Justin could practically hear her rub her hands together. That's what he loved about Roberta—her enthusiasm, her heart. Things he always used to find so great in Lilah...

He smiled and then remembered he was still on the phone. "After I read them a book about the Brooklyn Bridge, there were whole groups of kids building bridges of blocks. They even labeled the tollbooths and made money for the cars to hand in. You should have seen it. There's even one kid making a GPS system to help drivers get over the bridge back to Grantham. And they did it all on their own."

"They wouldn't have done it without you. And that's because you're a terrific teacher, Justin. So don't doubt your abilities just because a new administrator comes through who's got his own agenda about how to teach. Besides, your kids score very well on these standardized tests—am I right?"

"Are you ever wrong?"

Roberta chuckled. "Whatever you do, don't ask Oscar that question." Oscar was her husband.

"Oscar would probably agree that you're always right."

"True, but then he is a good man. He married me, after all, but then he always said I was quite a babe back in those days."

Justin grinned. He remembered seeing photos of the two of them taken at Coney Island. Oscar was indeed a lucky man. "Okay, okay. What can I say?" Justin replied.

"You're right. It's just that the way he told me, saying there'd been complaints, just threw me for a loop—especially when he wouldn't say who'd been complaining. He claimed confidentiality or something, making me smell a setup."

"Now you're being paranoid."

"Am I?" Justin frowned. "Maybe you're right. It's just that when someone questions my abilities, my old insecurities rise to the forefront."

"Justin," Roberta said firmly over the line.

"I know, I know. No whining." He laughed, then looked in the mirror again, pleased that his tie was indeed straight.

"Now, tell me something."

"Yes?" Justin immediately turned away from his reflection. He had a feeling that Roberta was peering over his shoulder.

"You're calling on a Friday morning, when you would normally be teaching. You haven't told me something else that I should know about?"

Justin sighed, knowing he would have to come up with an answer. "I'm taking a personal day. As it turns out, I'm hosting a prizewinning alum for Reunions weekend at Grantham."

There was a slight pause. "Is that alumnus or alumna?" Roberta asked, differentiating between the male and female varieties.

Justin laughed. "Alumna. And my classics professor father would be proud of you."

"It's you he should be proud of."

"Let's not go there," Justin said.

"Tell me, the reason you're hosting this prizewinning person is because…?"

"Because I was the one who nominated her for the prize."

"And you did that because...?"

"Because she does fantastic work in Africa and is totally self-sacrificing."

"I get the picture. She's a saint. So why do I get the impression that there's something more than what you're telling me?"

"Well, this is purely coincidental..."

"Excuse me, Dr. Freud. Nothing is coincidental."

Justin didn't bother to refute her statement. "She also happens to have been the ex-fiancée of my senior year roommate."

"Ex? Now this I got to hear more of. Have you seen her yet? Is she everything you'd hoped for?"

Cupping the phone under his chin, Justin strapped on his watch and looked at the time. He hurriedly slipped his wallet into the back packet of his trousers and grabbed his blue blazer off his unmade bed. "Listen, I don't have much time because, as a matter of fact, I'm just on my way to do some errands, then pick her up to take her to lunch with the university president."

"Did you clean out your car?"

If his father had asked the same question, Justin would have lost it. But because it was Roberta, Justin took it as a matter of course. "Okay, now. I have just enough time to answer one question. You want it to be about the car or the woman?"

"Which do you think?"

"Okay, I was going to vacuum—"

Justin heard a groan from the other end of the line.

"She's done all these amazing things, and I think she may be more beautiful than ever...."

"Why do I feel a 'but' is about to follow."

"But," Justin continued, "she's not the woman I remember."

There was silence from the other end of the line. Finally, Roberta cleared her throat. "So she's not the same woman. Heaven knows I'm not the same person I was ten years ago—as my bathroom scale unfortunately tells me far too often. But so what? You think my husband loves me any less?"

"How did we get to talking about love? I called about my teaching. And as far as that goes, thanks for the reassurances."

"It's not my words that count. You're the one who needs to reassure himself that he's doing the right thing."

"About teaching or about love?" he asked, making light of their conversation.

"You tell me. You're the teacher," she answered.

He didn't laugh.

CHAPTER NINE

"LILAH, IF ANYONE EMBODIES Grantham University's motto of duty to society, it's you." Grantham University's president, Theodore "call me Ted" Forsgate greeted Lilah at the entrance to Edinburgh House, Grantham's faculty club.

The Italianate mansion, surrounded by a lush formal garden—with its own endowment no less—once served as the on-campus home for the university's presidents. Then the sixties came, and even though student protests at Grantham University were mild compared to other locales, the then-president thought it wise to decamp to an equally imposing abode about a mile down the road. The protestors' loss was the professors' gain. Lunch and dinner were served regularly, and the university frequently used the rooms for official functions.

"Thank you, President Forsgate," Lilah said, bowled over by the sincerity of his double-handed shake—almost literally, since President Forsgate was a large man and took a full-blooded approach to shaking hands. "It's very rewarding to be back in an environment that puts a premium on public service. I must confess, I feel a little overwhelmed by the recognition," she added. This was the first time she had met Forsgate, an astrophysicist who had apparently discovered a distant galaxy.

Then she turned to her left and attempted to extract

her hand. "I think I owe all the attention in large part to Justin. You've met of course, Justin Bigelow?"

Justin nodded.

"Of course. One of our premier varsity athletes. Always a pleasure. You're also Stanfield Bigelow's son, correct?"

"You have a good memory, but really, I'm just here as a chaperone and bodyguard to keep Lilah's adoring fans at bay. This weekend is about her, after all."

"You're right, of course," the president replied. "Shall we?" He ushered Lilah into the rotunda with its soaring cupola. The interior had been restored to its former glory and the woodwork and walls were painted with period-appropriate faux marbling.

"Your parents must be very proud," he said.

"I think they certainly respect my work, and they were delighted to hear about the award—especially from Grantham. I'm an only child, and to have their daughter not only get in but be honored by the university is like a dream come true for them. I'm the first person in my family ever to go to college outside the state, let alone an Ivy League institution. In fact, my dad's coming in later today for the ceremony on Saturday."

"Not both your parents? I thought—" the president said, looking momentarily baffled.

"No, my mother is unable to come. She's the principal of the elementary school on Orcas Island, and they still have another week to go, including their own little graduation. It wouldn't do for the principal to miss that."

Out of the corner of her eye, she noticed that Justin's eyebrows seemed raised to new heights as he gazed at the university president. And that the president, after less than a moment's hesitation, seemed to respond to some telepathic communication.

He refocused on her. "Yes. It would be a long way to come from Washington State for such a short period of time," he said with what sounded like genuine understanding. Then he held out his arm to guide her through the hallway to the smaller dining room. "We go this way," he said with extreme largesse. The Queen couldn't have been treated more royally.

Lilah stepped across the dark-stained wood floors under the watchful gaze of nineteenth-century portraits of old white men and then hesitated slightly. The only other time she'd been in Edinburgh House had been as a freshman when there was a welcoming reception for new students. Actually, to be technically correct, she'd never been in the house, only the terraced garden in the back. She, along with the other nervous newcomers, had formed a serpentine line along the gravel paths that bisected the formal beds of perennials. The then-president had been Eleanor Henrietta Nesmith, an expert on Victorian literature who the alums adored for her devotion to the football team. She had held forth in front of the bubbling fountain, greeting each new Grantham student with a sturdy handshake as twin carved-stone fish spouted water playfully from their bounteous lips.

"You all right?" Justin whispered behind her and touched the small of her back.

The feel of his fingertips through her loose-fitting black jacket didn't help her regain her bearings one bit. But at least the jolt of contact helped her avoid turning into the cloakroom by mistake.

"Here we are," Ted announced and waited as she passed through tall double doors—to a whole throng of people.

Lilah gulped. "I thought this was a private lunch?" She had been anticipating that the three of them would sit at a small table discussing world politics, or baseball or the annual alumni fund drive or whatever it was one talked to university presidents about.

"I thought you'd enjoy meeting some of the university trustees. They're in for one of their regular meetings, of course."

"Of course." She felt like a broken record.

"And I knew there were several who were interested in meeting you," Ted said, encouraging her to go in. "I hope you don't mind?"

"Mind?" Lilah asked. Sure, she was used to talking to individuals to raise money for her foundation, but they were usually like-minded women who already knew about her work. But a bunch of middle-aged banker types or insurance execs who held a soft spot for the old orange-and-black of Grantham University? She was not exactly in her element.

Justin leaned closer. "Don't worry. They'll love you," he whispered.

She knew he meant to make her feel better. But if only she didn't feel the flutter of his breath on the sensitive skin of her neck. She closed her eyes a moment to re-group, and out of nowhere, the mental image appeared of him placing his lips right where the molecules of air tickled her epidermis.

Her eyes flashed open. Just in time to see a moderately tall woman in a very expensive-looking suit—Lilah didn't know designers, but she figured it was one of the best, given the way it hugged her form—and a humongous strand of pearls, immediately descended on her. She had her hand outstretched. A hand with a giant diamond ring, Lilah noticed.

"Vivian Pierpoint," she announced, her first and last names coming out in a rapid staccato. She took an equally swift gulp from her champagne glass. "I can't tell you how delighted I am that you won the alumni award instead of some banker from Biloxi." She punctuated her words with a ringing laugh and an insider's wink.

Lilah put out her hand, but found herself leaning forward in order to catch every syllable.

"Vivian is the CEO of eSales, the successful online auction company, and member of the class of '82," Justin said by way of identification. He held out his hand as well, introducing himself.

Vivian smiled, her lips close to the rim of her glass. "That's right. You were the genius who nominated Lilah."

"I like to think I was merely recognizing Lilah's genius," he said diplomatically.

Vivian waggled her perfectly arched eyebrows. "How delightful."

Lilah was ready for them to exchange phone numbers. "He always was a charmer."

Justin looked at her. "When you have limited capabilities—"

"Here we go again. I know, I know. You work with what you have." She finished his sentence.

Vivian glanced from one to the other. "So you two are…ah…close?"

Lilah cleared her throat. "I wouldn't necessarily say that."

"We just go back a ways," Justin explained.

"Classmates," Lilah said.

"Friends," Justin added.

"More, friends of friends."

"More friend of a friend," Justin specified.

Vivian opened her mouth, but didn't say anything.

At least Lilah didn't think she said anything, but it was

quite possibly because a waiter strolled by with drinks, distracting her for a few moments. Lilah took the sparkling water. She had to drive to the airport to pick up her dad later in the afternoon, and she wanted to be clear-headed.

"Do you still keep up with any of your classmates from Grantham, besides Justin here?" Vivian deposited her empty flute on the tray and took a full one.

"I really don't keep up with Justin."

"It's more an accident of circumstances," Justin explained.

"Just my kind of accident." Vivian smiled. "Any other college friends then—accidental or otherwise?"

"I guess the only person I see on a regular basis is Mimi Lodge, my old roommate. The television news correspondent?"

"Certainly. I remember the piece she did on your organization. I can't tell you how inspiring it was. But then if you're friends with Mimi, you obviously know Noreen Lodge then, too," she added without missing a beat.

Lilah processed her rapid speech as best as possible. "Mimi's stepmother, you mean? Actually, I just met her. You know her through Mimi's dad, Conrad, her husband, then? The Grantham University connection?"

"Not through Conrad, though I have met him. Business at certain levels is a fairly small world, if you know what I mean."

Lilah was beginning to realize this more and more.

"Noreen and I met at Trinity College in Dublin," Vivian explained. "I spent my junior year abroad there."

"Really? That must have been a wonderful experience." In hindsight, Lilah wished she had done something similar, but at the time she would never have considered being away from Stephen for so long. What an idiot.

"Yes, it opened my eyes to art and architecture, not to mention Irish whiskey." Vivian cleared her throat. "But of course what you really remember from experiences like that is the people you meet."

"I know what you mean. My friend Esther in Congo has completely revolutionized the way I look at that country," Lilah said. She turned to Justin, who she realized was being left out. "Wouldn't you agree about the importance of people connections?"

"Totally. I wouldn't be in early education if I didn't value the importance of socializing. But I don't want to interrupt Vivian while she was telling us about Noreen."

Vivian mugged to Lilah. "He's so sweet, and indulgent," she said. "Now, where was I? Oh, right." She happily rattled on. "Noreen. An interesting person—far more so than meets the eye. Back in university she had a double degree—economics and public health. Got a first, you know."

"No, I didn't." Lilah figured Vivian was referring to a degree with top honors. "I just know she was the Lodge's nanny—not that there's anything wrong with that—before she married Mimi's father. And she definitely has a certain fashion sense that I envy but could never personally carry off."

Vivian threw back her head in laughter. "I know what you mean. Noreen has this compulsive-perfectionist side to her that comes out in whatever she's doing—whether it's being the perfectly groomed trophy wife or the most organized mother in a child-centric privileged community like Grantham. To me, her current phase, while genuine, is also a sign of boredom. No, let me tell you more about the Noreen I know."

Vivian sat back in her chair. "Just before Noreen was supposed to graduate, her father died suddenly. He'd been a source of inspiration her whole life. A poor boy from a coal mining town made good—scholarship to university, medical degree, the whole bit. Yet despite the fact that he could have had a much more affluent life-style, he insisted on going back to his childhood home in the poorer neighborhoods of Belfast and caring for the locals. As if that wasn't enough of a sacrifice, he packed up the family one month a year to go to Africa, where he volunteered at a clinic in Zimbabwe. Noreen always claimed the experience was transformative. So it wasn't any surprise, given her sterling academic record and her personal connection, that she was considering various offers from places like the World Health Organization for work when she graduated—not to mention various financial institutions with interests in development in Africa."

Lilah shook her head. "I don't understand. If that was the case, how on earth did she become a nanny in the U.S.?"

"Actually, the whole nanny thing was my idea," Vivian confessed. "Her father's death devastated her—totally. Still, after graduation, she started working for the International Monetary Fund on their African desk, but after a little more than a year, she decided to take a leave of absence. It was all too much. Well-meaning but inter-fering friend that I am, that's when I convinced her that what she needed was a complete change of scenery—to regroup and stop punishing herself for not somehow living up to the memory of her sainted father."

She lowered her chin. "Naturally, I didn't use those exact words. Anyway, I encouraged her to come to the States since she'd never traveled here before. I told her that the easiest kind of job to get was as a nanny—that an agency could work out her visa status. I thought it would be perfect—no confining office, no frantic deadlines. Although, neither she nor I ever counted on it being more than a year's break before she went back to Ireland or points beyond. Let me tell you, the jobs were still waiting for her. But—" Vivian held up her hands "—the rest, in particular her marriage to Conrad, is, as they say, history."

"Well, after all that, I hope she's happy," Lilah responded. "And now that I know more about her, I'm less—how can I put this—confused. I mean, I understand there's more to her than meets the eye…"

"Excuse me, there may be more to her, but as tacky as this sounds, most men would say that Noreen more than fulfills all the necessary requirements in the meets-the-eye department." Justin jerked his head back and forth. "What? I've met her at parent-teacher conferences, okay?" he said.

Lilah slanted him a frown. He shrugged.

Vivian accepted his comment, though, with a sly laugh. "You're right. Conrad, the old coot, is very lucky to have her. That's all I can say. And between you and me—" she leaned forward "—he'll be lucky to keep her."

As opposed to the usual turn of events with Mimi's dad, Lilah thought, but she kept this evaluation to herself.

"I hope you don't mind, but I insisted that we sit together for lunch. I wanted to hear more about your plans," Vivian went on, changing the subject swiftly. She waved behind her at the cluster of round tables laden with silverware and draped in white damask. "Naturally, I couldn't shake President Forsgate. But he's not a bad sort really. Who would have thought astrophysicists could be so charming?"

"They must be somewhat romantic if they spend their days looking at the stars," Justin observed. "At least he doesn't pretend to be a longtime fan of Grantham football."

Vivian laughed and studied him slyly. "Like someone we could mention from our days. I like that. Anyway, you know what they say about choosing an Ivy League president?"

"No, I can't say it comes up in conversation on a regular basis," Lilah admitted. She let her eyes wander to the intricately braided frog closures on Vivian's suit, and silently wondered how many months' rent it would take to buy the outfit.

Vivian looked at Justin. "Any thoughts?"

"This sounds suspiciously like a question that requires a drink first. Are you sure I can't get you something stronger?" he asked Lilah, and when she shook her head, he headed off to corral the strolling waiter.

Lilah watched him from behind, admired, really. She couldn't help it.

Vivian did, too. "This is a terribly sexist thing to say and probably very inappropriate, but just between you and me—beneath that ill-fitting blazer, he does appear to have a very nice butt, don't you think?" She sighed and turned to Lilah. "Now, where were we?"

"Ivy League presidents?" Lilah prompted. Was that a pang of jealousy she felt?

"Yes, well, here's someone who can answer the question, I have no doubt." She hooked one of her long arms into the elbow of a passing gentleman who was slightly bent over, either from the first signs of osteoporosis or from sitting at a desk all day.

"Professor," Vivian chirped, and after pinning him to her side, planted a large kiss on his sallow cheek. "I'm so happy you could make it. I insisted that you be at my table."

She turned to Lilah. "The professor here was my advisor on my senior paper. Who knew a thesis on Helen of Troy would be such good training for business leadership? But tell me. I'm sure you know the answer to my riddle. What should an Ivy League president always be?" she asked.

"The person needs to be an alumnus *or* alumna of that particular institution. Otherwise they just don't understand the ethos. They are doomed to feel inferior, hence the need to overcompensate," he said with the unquestioned wisdom of the Oracle of Delphi.

"You see." Vivian pointed a finger and her by-now empty glass at Lilah. "The classics, and a classic professor, are always relevant."

"The classics are timeless, regardless of funding and the dwindling number of majors," he agreed with the utmost sincerity. "As I keep trying to tell our new president," he added with a hint of criticism. He straightened his wire-rimmed glasses, the smudged lenses only partially concealing a pair of watery blue eyes.

There was something strangely familiar about the man that Lilah couldn't put her finger on. Maybe a ten-year-old memory of him, a distant figure traipsing across the campus, books and notes under one arm, head bent, mouth moving in silent, scholastic muttering?

"But surely Ted understands that? He did get a degree from Grantham after all. He understands the value of a liberal-arts education—there's no question about that."

"His PhD is from Grantham. His undergraduate

degree is from Dartmouth." The pronouncement seemed to say it all as far as the professor was concerned.

"But everyone seems so enthusiastic about his appointment, myself included," Vivian countered.

"Don't be won over by the lure of large government grants for scientific research. *Cave pecuniam,*" he added knowingly.

"Beware of money?" Lilah asked, frowning.

"Exactly. You studied Latin, young lady?" The professor peered at Lilah with sudden interest.

"Unfortunately, no. I just know some French," she said modestly.

Vivian put a hand on Lilah's shoulder. "How rude of me. Lilah Evans, our alumna of the year, may I introduce you to a fellow Granthamite, class of '68, and the Vivian Pierpont Distinguished Professor of Classics—Stanfield Bigelow."

"Bigelow?" Lilah asked.

Justin skirted in behind her. "Did I hear someone page me?"

Lilah stared at him and then rotated toward the older man to her right. "Actually, I was just being introduced to—"

Justin narrowed his eyes. "Hello, Father. Fancy meeting you here."

CHAPTER TEN

JUSTIN SAT AT THE SMALL TABLE silently nodding and smiling only when necessary. Inside, he was having a regular hissy fit. But immature anger wasn't the only emotion. Insecurity. Inferiority. All those lovely juvenile neuroses that you were supposed to grow out of sometime after the advent of facial hair.

Justin stared at the tiramisu parfait confronting him and decided to pass in favor of two cups of tepid black coffee.

After his phone conversation with Roberta, he had actually been feeling pretty good about himself. Convinced that the run-in with his principal was nothing to stew about. He reminded himself that, after all, he was free for a few days, free to forget about work and teaching. He could concentrate on what had been his plan all along—to rekindle…no, that was the wrong word… *kindle* was more accurate—yes, kindle a relationship of some sort with the engaging and enthusiastic woman he had remembered so clearly. In fact, he could have described her in detail with his eyes shut.

Now his eyes were open. And even though Lilah sat across from him at the round table, she wasn't the woman of his memories. The politely attentive Lilah that he now saw sat ramrod-straight in a charcoal-gray suit and had both feet, shod in leather flats, firmly on the floor. He could overhear as she forcefully articulated stories about her work, but gone were the wild hand motions of her younger, more passionately involved days, replaced instead by the occasional open palm a discreet inch away from her water glass.

Still, he couldn't let go of that memory. Surely it was buried beneath the professional demeanor just waiting to burst forth. Maybe if she could loosen up? He could tell she was under a lot of pressure to make things happen for her foundation. She had already made it clear that that was the only reason she'd come back to Grantham. And coming back, well, it probably brought back her own memories of Stephen. What a shnook. Didn't he know that in Lilah he'd lost the best thing to ever happen to him?

Well, if there was one thing Justin knew, it was how to make a woman relax and enjoy herself. Sure, he was a bit rusty. But how different could it be from getting five-year-olds to stand in line without kicking each other or fighting over exchanging the latest Silly Bandz? Reaching for his water glass gave him an excuse to lean forward to try to catch what Lilah was saying to Vivian and the university president so that he might enter the conversation with some witty rejoinder.

That's when he noticed that he still had a few of the brightly colored rubber bracelets, or Silly Bandz, stretched around one wrist. His usual solution to fighting over "nonsharing" as he euphemistically called it, was to temporarily confiscate the materials until both parties apologized. As surreptitiously as possible he slipped them off.

"Part of your new fashion statement?" the critical-sounding voice to his left asked him.

Justin looked across to his father as he stuffed the bracelets in his jacket pocket. "Just something left over from school," he said. There was no point in trying to explain about the latest children's fad because his father's idea of fun was limited to memorizing reams of ancient texts.

"Frankly, I'm surprised to find you here at lunch," his father said.

"Almost as surprised as I was to see you, too," Justin replied. "I thought you and Mother were on sabbatical in Rome now that the Vatican Library had reopened after renovations. And I was working under that miconception when the alumni office told me that Lilah's parents were planning on coming to the ceremonies, but that there were no more hotel rooms available. Given the desperate circumstances, I volunteered to let them stay at your house—my place is so small. But now that you're back, I can change the arrangements."

They shared a silence while the chatter went on at the other side of the table.

"Don't be silly. I am only back for a few days at the invitation of Vivian. The development office is anticipating a large donation on her part, and they wanted a show of hands, so to speak. In any case, we will return in late July after a small side trip to Oxford. At that time, I'm sure your mother would love to see you for dinner," Stanfield said. He dug his spoon into the Italian dessert, spearing a large piece of ladyfinger and a mound of cocoa and creamy pudding center. Swallowing with relish, he dug in for another bite. Dinners at the Bigelow manse were never a relaxed occasion.

Justin debated telling his father that a bit of custard had caught on the corner of his mouth. The recalcitrant child in him—there seemed to be no limit to his childishness today—had him holding his tongue. "I'll be sure to call Mother," he said instead, knowing he'd probably forget.

"I spoke to your sister, Penelope, last week on Skype. Amazing this new technology and how it simplifies overseas communication."

Justin interpreted that tidbit of information as veiled criticism of his own lack of communication with his parents. "I'm glad to know she stays in touch." His sister and father probably traded insights into their latest research into Plutarch or Thucydides. Penelope had followed in their father's footsteps and was an assistant professor of classics at the University of Chicago. He debated whether a third cup of coffee was overkill.

"How's the…ah…t-t-time you spend with our local youngsters going?" Stanfield asked. His one-year postdoctoral appointment at Oxford had left him with the rarified stutter that characterized the dons and students from that esteemed place of higher learning.

Justin viewed that statement as *less*-than-veiled criticism. Anyone who was involved with learning at a preuniversity level simply didn't make the grade in his father's opinion, he figured. "You're not working hard enough, not concentrating. Anyone should be able to read," Stanfield used to lecture Justin when he was in elementary school.

Even back then Justin knew "anyone" meant "anyone who is a son of mine."

"If you spent half the time you do biking up to Antonelli's Garage in Easton and hanging out with those grease monkeys…"

Justin knew his father would have denied all accusations that he was a social snob.

"If you gave the same effort to your books as you do to the rowing club…"

His father's idea of athletic exertion was to pull out the push lawn mower on arbitrary occasions, and mow their patch of front lawn wearing dark socks with old blue sneakers.

"I don't understand it. Your teachers claim that you are of above-average intelligence, but as far as I can tell…"

What do mere elementary school teachers know? was the underlying translation.

And by inference now, what did he know in his current job as a kindergarten teacher?

Justin finally responded to his father's question about his work. "It's called teaching, Father," he said simply.

Across the table, Justin became immediately aware of Lilah folding her napkin.

"You must understand that I didn't—"

Then he saw her push back her chair. "Hold it, Father," Justin said out of the side of his mouth.

His father lifted his spoon. "But I wanted to pass on some information about Penelope."

Justin looked down at his father, pleased with the vantage point. "I tell you what, Father. When you get back to Rome, Skype me. You're such a fan of it. In the meantime, duty—and Lilah—calls."

LILAH SLIPPED HER BAG OFF the back of her chair and stood. The luncheon had not been nearly as painful as she had anticipated. Vivian was larger than life, literally—but in a good way, full of enthusiasm for Sisters for Sisters and brimming with suggestions for potential donors. Lilah should have felt pumped. She didn't.

She felt overwhelmed and guilty—guilty at being overwhelmed. Guilty that she was letting down Esther and all the other Congolese women she'd met or who needed her help.

And right now they probably deserved someone better and less jaded than she was.

Oh, she was a good girl. She always had been—doing all her homework on time, standing when older people came into the room and paying all her bills on time—when she had the cash, that is. She hated to think about the balance on her credit card at the moment.

So, no matter how deep her funk, she would trudge on and do the right thing. Write the grants, fight the good fight, not let on to her daily fears that the job was just too big for her and that she would fail her parents, all the Esthers of the world, and never meet the expectations of others, like Vivian, who believed in her.

If only they knew…

"You're not going to have your tiramisu?" Professor Bigelow waggled an index finger toward her untouched portion.

"Unfortunately, I really have to get going. I'm supposed to pick up my dad at Newark Airport. But it's a shame to have it go to waste." She picked up the saucer with the parfait cup and passed it in his direction. "Surely, I can tempt you."

"I'll go with you then," Justin offered.

Lilah glanced over the centerpiece of orange gerberas and saw him standing. She noticed for the first time that the tiny repeated pattern on Justin's tie was orange flowers, too. What kind of a man wore ties with flowers on them and still looked so…so…manly? She averted her eyes from his tie and concentrated on his chin. She saw he had a tiny nick on the underside from shaving. It was a very nice chin, slightly indented, firm jawline….

"I'd take the tiramisu, if I were you," Vivian announced to Stanfield.

Lilah shook her head. "No need to come. I've made arrangements for a rental car already."

"Then at least let me drive you to the agency," he insisted.

Vivian liberated the plate from Lilah's hand to pass to Justin's father.

"I could almost do with a second helping myself," President Forsgate said with a chortle.

Lilah refocused on Justin. And noticed for the first time that his eyes were a smudged, smoky gray, the color of pussy willows. She opened her mouth, closed it, then started to speak again. "There's no need for you to go out of your way. I'll just get—"

"A taxi? Don't even think about it. As your host—" Justin added.

"You've already provided—" she continued.

"On second tasting, interestingly, it makes me think this dessert may actually be zuppa inglese, the Tuscan dessert as opposed to a tiramisu, which is a Venetian confection," Stanfield said, studying his spoon.

"Not nearly enough assistance," Justin finished her words.

"I always wondered what the etymology of zuppa inglese was," Vivian admitted with a frown.

Lilah looked around the table. President Forsgate, Vivian and Justin's father all seemed deep in conversation while peering at their dessert cups. She saw Justin take in the scene, as well.

"I didn't touch mine, either, if you're still hungry?" he offered.

The other three looked up. "What does this mean when neither of the young folk eat dessert?" his father asked.

"Or is it just these two particular young folks? After

all, we don't have a statistical sampling," President Forsgate noted.

"Trust a scientist to make that observation. You're right, of course," Stanfield had to agree.

"Well, I'm happy to have it." Vivian held out her hand. "And as to their similar habits, I can add further information. You see, he's a friend of a friend," she explained, pointing her spoon from one to the other.

The president tilted his head. "And here I thought there might be something more."

It was all getting too confusing. Lilah quickly offered her hand to say goodbye. "Not in the least. And you can tell there's nothing between us because he didn't even clean out his car before picking me up."

Justin's father looked up from dissecting his second dessert. "On the contrary. It's quite significant that he let you *in* his car at all."

CHAPTER ELEVEN

"ARE YOU SURE YOUR FRIEND there can lift a full keg?" Tony, the manager of the Lion Inn asked skeptically. Like the other social clubs at Grantham University, Lion Inn was located on the edge of campus, but it was actually an independent organization open to student members and run by a board of alumni members. Members, alumni who were members as undergraduates and their guests were welcome at all events.

Press and Matt had joined Tony by the club's side entrance next to the basement keg room. It was around two o'clock in the afternoon, and they were there to get their instructions for working at Reunions, starting that night.

"Sure, no problem," Press assured him with an easy smile. "He may look puny, but he's tough. You wouldn't know it, but he wrestles for Yale at the one-hundred-thirty-two-pound weight class."

Tony smiled with a look of incredulity. "You're right. I wouldn't know it. But, hey, if you say he's okay, then that's good enough for me." Tony stamped out his cigarette butt on the pavement, and like the good manager that he was, he picked up the butt and deposited it in a plastic baggy that he carried in the back pocket of his jeans along with his trusty Bic lighter. "So, why don't you come inside now, and I'll show you where to stow the kegs." Since the two were nominally only shifting the supplies around and not manning the open taps, the club didn't need a special license for them to work.

They tromped in through the side door off the driveway while Tony lectured them on putting kegs in the cooler, bringing them out at the right time and working the taps. "So, is that all clear now?"

Both boys nodded.

"We didn't get into college on our good looks alone, Tony," Press reminded him.

"I think you got in on your silvery tongue," Tony wisecracked back. "And how you work the taps is clear?"

"No problem. It's easier than milking a cow."

"Which you do about as frequently as your buddy here goes ten rounds on a mat, I'll wager." Tony searched the top of the bar. "I thought I had left the order forms here, but they must be in my office. You'll need them to keep track of deliveries. Listen, I'll be right back." He lifted the flap to the bar top and headed upstairs.

Matt watched him go, and then nudged Press. "Hey, why'd you make up all that stuff about me being a wrestler? You didn't need to do that?"

Press ignored Matt and prowled the wood-paneled, dark room. Once upon a time, the keg room had been a bastion of good ol' boy camaraderie, its wooden countertop scratched with the engraved initials of future male captains of industry and government leaders. Then Grantham had gone coed in the seventies, and Lion Inn's women members had added their names to the handiwork. Coed or single sex, by now the place could best be described as beloved shabby chic—with the emphasis on *shabby*.

"I'm really stoked about working Reunions," Press said in between checking the flood of text messages on his phone. "It will be great just to relax after busting my butt all school year. Plus I could really use the cash."

"You? Need cash? Can't you just borrow from your dad?"

"I'm not sure my father would recognize me if he saw me. We don't cross paths that often."

"Maybe you could send him your résumé to refresh his memory? There's always your mother I suppose."

"I don't think Mother's in town. I think she might have mentioned something about going to La Quinta to work on her backhand. Or maybe it was Pebble Beach, to perfect her putting. Besides, the way she's spending her alimony, she'll be the one hard up for cash pretty soon. Oh, goody-goody—perhaps I'll have a new stepfather."

"At least you've got Noreen."

"Yeah, she's pretty cool besides being ama-zing-look-ing."

"Is it me, or is there something wrong to think your stepmother is hot?" Matt asked.

"It's you. Anyway, you got to hand it to Noreen. I figure she's the first woman to ever have my father by the balls. He'd do anything for her. Heck, he might even make it to my graduation next year—keep up the old family ties and everything."

"Does that mean he goes to his class Reunions, too?" Matt wandered from the taproom to the basement hall-way and peered up the stairway, waiting for Tony to come down again.

"Yeah, I think so. I'm pretty sure he still marches in The Parade—when I was little and he and my mom were still getting along, we all marched one year." Grantham alums and family members were famous for their annual parade during Reunions through the campus and down Main Street, complete with marching bands, a few flimsy floats and everyone decked out in gaudy class outfits—special orange-and-black costumes that screamed big fashion mistake.

Finally, the sound of footsteps and someone talking on a cell phone could be heard.

"At least if I'm working, I shouldn't run into him. Besides, Lion Inn is the locale this year for the Tenth Reunion parties. So I doubt he'll show up here."

"Isn't the Tenth your sister's reunion year?"

"That's right."

"So it's Lilah Evans's, too? Maybe I'll still have another chance to get to talk to her, then?"

Press approached his friend and, pointing his index finger, he looked him squarely in the eyes. "The question is, are you man enough to talk to her, or are you just going to stammer and get all nervous when you come face-to-face while drawing her a tall glass of Yuengling?"

Matt balled his fist. "I'll do it. I promise."

"If you don't, I will personally beat up that one-hundred-and-thirty-two-pound puny body of yours." Press playfully pounded his friend on his back and shoulders. What he didn't say was that he figured he could always talk to Mimi on Matt's behalf. Talk about scary! But, hey, he'd risk it for his friend.

Tony stepped back into the room and flipped his phone shut. "Okay, sorry to keep you guys waiting. That was the liquor store on the phone. They want to pick up the empty kegs tonight and not wait until tomorrow morning since there's so much stuff going on on campus. That means you guys need to stay here until closing— normally 2:00 a.m., but you never know. You got it?"

"Since when have I ever left before a party was over?" Press boasted.

Matt nodded earnestly. "I got it. But listen, Tony. There's something I gotta tell you. About this whole wrestling thing?" Matt had a concerned, I-need-to-confess look on his face.

Tony dismissed him. "Don't worry, kid. I know Press is full of it. That's part of his charm. Besides, I also know that whatever the job is, he'll pull his end *and* yours. Press always comes through—in spite of himself."

CHAPTER TWELVE

AFTER FIDDLING WITH THE dials at the stoplight, Lilah ended up turning off the radio in the rental car. All she'd wanted was a little classical music to soothe her brittle nerves. But with all the stop-and-go traffic on Route 206, she needed to keep both hands on the wheel and eyes forward instead of being tied up with distractions.

Talk about distractions. Justin had insisted on standing in line with her at the Enterprise office.

"This is boring, trust me. I'm sure you must have other things to do," she had tried politely. Being around Justin was just too confusing at the moment, too unsettling. And, really, was she supposed to make a move in a car rental agency? Then again, did she really want to?

"Besides, we'll see each other tomorrow at the ceremony in the afternoon, not to mention all the wining and dining through the night, right?" she added, attempting to send him on his way.

"Actually, tomorrow's festivities begin in the morning with The Parade. *And* it's not just tomorrow that you're stuck with me. We're scheduled to be together for the annual Reunions softball game this afternoon, followed by the pig roast."

"Softball? But I'm supposed to pick up my father. Then I'm going out to dinner with him and Mimi," she protested.

"You didn't read your schedule, did you? The game

doesn't start until around five, five-thirty, so you should have plenty of time to make it back."

Lilah gritted her teeth. "Well, I guess I'll try to make it, but if my father's plane is late, I can't guarantee anything." Really, the last thing she wanted to do was run around a softball field.

Justin pulled his iPhone from his pocket and tapped on the screen. "Not to worry. I have this handy app, keeps me completely up-to-date on flights. See—your father's plane is actually scheduled to come in a few minutes early." He held the screen up to her face.

Lilah squinted to read the unwelcome news. She nodded, and Justin hit the Sleep button. She saw a photo of a bunch of kids, probably his class, she guessed. Her first impulse was to say, "Aw-w," but she swallowed it. If she reacted emotionally like that, would he take that as an offer of interest? And was he interested? She thought so, but her antennae were not exactly functioning at top speed. Argh-h.

"Well, that's good to know," she said instead. "But I think it would be kind of rude just to drop my dad off where he's staying and then rush out to play some softball game, especially when I haven't seen him for months, almost a year even."

"This is not just some softball game!" Justin said with the right amount of righteous indignation. "Besides, when I told him about it, he was all excited about playing. I didn't realize that he played baseball for the University of Washington?"

Lilah took one step closer to the car rental counter. She hung her head, accepting the inevitable. "Yeah, Dad played center field. He was the batting champ for two years running. What was I thinking? Obviously he would want to play. He'll probably bring his mitt." She stopped and turned to Justin. "Hey, wait a minute. You talked to my father?"

The man in front of her in black shorts and an orange T-shirt moved to the side, fumbling with his rental form and keys. A picture-perfect family of one blonde wife with toned upper arms and two perfect towheaded children—the boy with a cowlick and the girl with pigtails and a missing front tooth—swarmed around him.

That could have been me—me and Stephen, Lilah thought ungrammatically. But what made her wistful was not the thought of Stephen but the two kids and the toned arms. Yes, her memory of Stephen seemed to be rapidly dimming in the reality of Justin.

"Sure, I called your father. Since you're my responsibility, he's mine, as well—for the weekend, that is," Justin answered her.

"Do you have your rental confirmation number?" the perky woman behind the desk asked. Her white teeth sparkled and matched the high-gloss sign hanging behind her.

Lilah narrowed her eyes. "So you two talked about me?" She waved off her own question. "Never mind. I don't want to know." Then she turned and dealt with the tedious process of renting her car.

And now as she inched along Route 206, she glanced to the right at the tiny strip mall with its row of small shops—a tae kwon do academy, a high-end marble and tile store, and a fresh pasta shop. *So Grantham, isn't it?* she thought and she told herself she had been right to practically push Justin into that ridiculous little car of his. *It was cute, wasn't it?* And she had been right to insist that, no, she wasn't too tired to drive to the airport and that she would meet him at the baseball field by the university football stadium. "Yes, I remember where it is," she had said, not bothering to mask the irritation in her voice. "After all, how hard is it to miss a football stadium?"

"But there's a new physics building blocking it from Adams Road as you cut across campus," he had tried to explain as he reluctantly eased his way into his car.

He'd looked up, all puppy-dog eager—she could picture what he must have looked like as a young child.

And then she'd slammed the door in his face and inserted the keys into the late-model Hyundai sedan that she'd rented.

She'd been right, definitely, she told herself, creeping forward as the cars crawled in the end-of-lunch hour traffic. She had needed space, distance, to decide just what she was going to do with Justin Bigelow. She eased her foot off the brake, letting the car roll forward.

"What's stopping you?" she asked out loud. "You're thirty-two, a free woman. Why not enjoy yourself for a change? There's nothing wrong with feeling good or having a good time. People do it all the time—feeling good and having sex."

Lilah glanced at the clock on the dashboard. If the traffic kept up like this, she would be cutting it close. She tried not to feel anxious. So she was late. It wasn't like her father would disown her—unlike her mother for whom punctuality superceded godliness. Besides, she could always text him. Now that he had acquired his iPhone—in addition to his iPad—he had officially become a techie.

And just like that, thoughts of smart phones had her thinking about a certain cuter-than-cute photo on someone else's phone that she had recently seen. Justin. He had been so proud, so engaged, so geeky so... Her thoughts turned decidedly away from geeky....

She slammed on the brakes as the traffic abruptly came to a halt. Then she saw the reason. Two cars up, a minivan put on its turning signal to take a left onto a side road.

"So what if Justin and I—this weekend—kind of...?" she asked herself out loud, barely able to form the words yet somehow wanting an answer.

She got it.

A violent jolt from behind. A crunch of metal. Her car lurched forward. Her head snapped back against the headrest. Her chest pressed against the seat belt.

Her first thought was thank goodness she'd taken full insurance coverage on the rental. Her second was to look in her rearview mirror. She saw a lightweight truck, a man at the wheel—older, and a woman in the passenger seat—talking, no, yelling at each other.

She turned off the car engine and located the emergency flashers. Watching for traffic in her side-view mirror—this being New Jersey, the cars insisted on passing around her without bothering to stop—she carefully inched open her door and stepped out. Well, it might have been a lightweight truck, but it had a giant bumper that had managed to dent every panel in the back of her gray sedan. Luckily, it looked as if the structure had survived unscathed, no doubt due to the low speed of the truck on impact. That would explain why the airbag hadn't triggered.

The inspection over, she walked back to the truck. The driver, a diminutive man, sat there shell-shocked behind the wheel, blinking rapidly as his wife loudly complained to him. Then when Lilah came into view, she turned her complaints on her. She rifled in her purse and pulled out a cell phone, punched in a number and proceeded to complain to the person on the other end.

The driver got out and circled the front of his truck. He stared at his bumper, then her car before looking up guiltily at Lilah. Not a word passed his lips.

"I think we better share insurance information," Lilah said.

His back hunched, he retreated silently to the truck and leaned over his wife to open the glove compartment.

His wife pushed him aside and clambered out of the truck. With a melodramatic heave, she began patting her chest. "My heart, my heart. I can't take this."

"Is there something I can do?" Lilah asked.

"My heart! I was just at the doctor. I have pain. Something terrible. Why did you keep going and stopping and going and stopping?"

"Well, it *was* stop-and-go traffic," Lilah replied. She watched the husband come to his wife's side, and the older woman let him guide her to sit on the curb. She adjusted the keyhole opening of her navy T-shirt.

"Do you want me to call 9-1-1?" Lilah offered.

The woman's head snapped up. "I already called it and ordered an ambulance."

Lilah pursed her lips, wondering when someone was going to ask her how *she* was. After all, she *was* the one who had been rear-ended.

In the distance, she heard sirens, and as she looked south toward the center of Grantham, she caught the flashing lights of a police car. And another police car. The first car slammed on the brakes in front of Lilah's rental. The other blocked the entrance to the strip mall.

Some shoppers at the strip mall came out to aid the moaning woman. "Did you hit her?" a man, wearing a PSE&G uniform, asked Lilah.

Lilah tried to keep her cool. "No, they hit me."

"Are you on medication? I'm a nurse." A female shopper in crepe-soled shoes rushed to the woman, who now rocked back and forth.

"My heart. My heart," she keened.

More sirens approached from the other direction—this time the ambulance. It pulled into the strip mall parking lot, blocking the exit. The EMTs jumped out and immediately started questioning the woman on the ground. Soon, more stranded lunchgoers gathered around. Then, a green Mazda pulled up behind the first police car. Out jumped a twenty-year-old coed who looked remarkably like the woman on the ground, minus thirty pounds and the dark red hair dye. "Mama," she shouted and rushed to the moaning woman. Lilah, standing there like an outsider, took in all the commotion. The only other person not involved in the action was the driver of the truck. He had withdrawn several feet from his wife, though still within shouting distance.

Lilah could easily sympathize, if she weren't starting to feel sorry for herself. *I'm the victim here,* she wanted to scream, which of course she didn't. Instead, like the good citizen she was, she stood silently by, watching as the woman, talking again on the phone, was carried off on a stretcher.

Finally, two policemen came over and surveyed the damage. The older male officer, who obviously lifted weights in his spare time, looked up. "You were in the truck?" he asked. He wore a sensitive smile on his face.

"No, I was in the car that was rear-ended."

He blinked. "Are you all right? Should I call the EMTs?"

"No, I'm fine." Her neck was a little sore, but that was to be expected.

"So the woman was your passenger?" He nodded toward the ambulance that had just pulled out into oncoming traffic. Lilah waited for another accident to occur, which miraculously didn't.

"No, she was the passenger in the truck that hit me. Her husband, at least I presume it's her husband, was driving." Lilah pointed to the silent little man in the heavy blue trousers with a thick belt and short-sleeved shirt tucked into his pants. He looked like a good breeze could knock him over. He was nodding, his chin tucked into his concave chest, as the young woman from the green Mazda talked to him. His daughter, she figured.

"So why don't you tell me what happened?" the policeman asked nicely.

And Lilah ran through the whole scenario. He nodded at all the correct moments. Lilah felt in the comforting presence of Mr. Rogers, if Mr. Rogers had worn a walkie-talkie on the epaulette of his cardigan and looked like he could bench-press twice his weight.

His younger partner, his ferocious eyebrows furrowed into a corrugated line, looked on sternly. "We'll need your license and registration," he demanded. "And your insurance card."

Lilah blinked, a little taken aback by his aggressive approach, but decided to cooperate without question. One thing she had learned dealing with law enforcement personnel worldwide was to stand firm but act politely. She'd even kept her cool in dealing with warlords, when it came down to it. What was one obnoxious Grantham cop?

"My license's in my bag on the front seat of the car, which is a rental, by the way. The insurance and registration information is with the rental packet in the car, too."

"A rental," the policeman exclaimed with disdain.

Lilah schooled herself to keep from rolling her eyes.

"Yes, a rental," Lilah replied as if she had been asked for a weather report. "I am here for the Grantham University Reunions, and I rented a car to pick my father up at the airport. He's flying in this afternoon." She looked down at her watch. "Speaking of which, is this going to take much longer? My dad's due in in less than an hour."

The Mr. Rogers cop offered her another smile. "We'll try to hurry it along as much as possible. Let's go over to your car, and you can get the information for me. Then you can sit there and take it easy. We still have to talk to the other driver, and we need to put our report into the computer."

Lilah swallowed. What choice did she have? None. She breathed in slowly, then walked back to the car and retrieved the necessary documentation. Then she sat.

And sat some more.

She pushed up the sleeve of her suit jacket and glanced at the time—again. This was no good. She was going to need someone else to go to the airport.

She dug in her shoulder bag on the front passenger seat for her cell phone and dialed Mimi's number. After a few rings it went to voice mail. *Great!* They had planned to meet for dinner with her dad, so who knew where she was now. Still, it wasn't like her not to pick up her phone.

Now what? She sat back. Maybe she could leave her dad a message to call her when he got in? If necessary, she could ask him to take the train directly to Grantham Junction, then take a taxi into town. But she hated the idea of having him go through all that hassle.

The sun streamed in through the front windshield, and she could feel her face start to glow. She closed her eyes, and let herself bake. She should really take off her jacket, she thought, as she felt a bead of perspiration trickle down the middle of her chest and catch in the underwire of her bra. It was the only one she'd brought this week-end, and she needed to look presentable for her award. Her eyes still closed, she contorted to free one arm.

There was a knock on the window.

She stopped midsleeve and opened her eyes, expecting one of the policemen, hoping it was Mr. Rogers and not Rambo.

It was Justin.

She looked at the door to wind the window down, then realized it had an electric roll-down feature. She'd need to start the car to put it down, and she wasn't sure she should do that given that she was supposed to just be sitting here. Probably Mr. Rogers wouldn't mind, but Rambo? Her mind was turning uncharacteristically to mush.

She threw up her hands. "I can't open lower the window without starting the car," she mouthed silently.

Justin circumvented that problem by simply opening the door. "I leave you alone for a few minutes and look what happens?" he joked.

Lilah didn't laugh. On the contrary, she did the last thing in the world she wanted to do.

She burst into tears.

CHAPTER THIRTEEN

"LET ME COME AROUND the other side to get out of the way of the traffic," he said calmly, nodding at the oncoming stream of vehicles.

He circled the front of the car, opened the passenger door and slipped in the seat next to her. Without asking permission—without saying a word—he reached across and took her hand that lay limply in her lap. He pressed it gently as they sat in silence—he studying her, she squeezing her eyes and sniffing loudly to hold back any more tears.

"I told myself I wouldn't cry. I never cry." She wiped the back of her hand across her nose, then shook her head. "It's so stupid, really. I mean, I don't know why I'm so upset. I deal with stress all the time. Any given day I don't know if I'm going to be able to pay my monthly rent or if Sisters for Sisters is going to suddenly collapse because the race that's supposed to take place in Chicago in March gets snowed out. Then in Congo there're marauding militias, or the endless red tape and needless bureaucracy. It normally doesn't bother me."

She stared at him. "So tell me. If I can do all that, why does a stupid fender bender get me all upset? I mean, it's just a few pieces of metal—not even mine for that matter. So big deal. That's what insurance's for, right?"

He nodded.

"And even if I can't get my father in time and I can't

get Mimi on the phone to pick him up instead, I know I can always contact him when he lands and explain, right?" She nodded as if agreeing with herself. "Right?"

"Right, most definitely right. He'll just want to know you're not hurt. You're not hurt, are you?"

She shook her head and sniffed loudly.

Justin squeezed her hand again before letting go. Her vulnerability caught him off guard—touched something deep within. He was used to dealing with the hurt feelings and bruised egos of five-year-olds. He knew when to be patient. When to be understanding. Or when tough love was the better remedy.

But when it came to handling a grown-up—check that, a woman…the woman who had been for more than ten years the woman of his dreams, the same woman who now needed his help—he was less sure. Because he didn't want to screw things up. He so much wanted to do the right thing because he sensed that whatever he chose to do could be really, really important.

Don't blow it, he lectured himself.

Then he took a deep breath. "I'm not necessarily the wisest person." Heaven knows, his father had told him that daily as he was growing up. "But did it ever occur to you that you're upset precisely because you *have* to handle all of that—all the big, important stuff under which most people crumble? And maybe, just maybe, this fender bender came along at a moment when too many things *had* accumulated, on top of little things like, I don't know, jet lag and the stress of travel, things that leave most people comatose for a few days maybe?" He reached over and rubbed her slumped back with a gentle circular motion.

She looked up from her hands and slanted her gaze at him. "Not wise? I don't know about that. Is this a new phenomenon, or were you always just hiding it beneath all that charisma and sex appeal?" She peered at him.

Now he *knew* he was going to blow it.

"Okay, so the superwoman has finally crashed to earth," she mocked herself. "So, tell me, if it's okay for me to fall apart after a fender bender, is it also all right for me to be upset that I won't be there on time to pick up my father? It looks like the police still have to do their paperwork, and that's *after* they talk to the guy who hit me, who I am sure is now making up some scurrilous story—"

"Scurrilous?" Justin asked.

"Yes, scurrilous." She sniffed. "It means fake."

"Yes, I know what it means. It's just that I can't say that I've ever heard it used in conversation."

She frowned. "Now, on top of everything, you're making fun of me, aren't you?"

Justin shook his head. "Of course not. I would never make fun of you. It's just that I had forgotten how you had this very…very…rich vocabulary."

"It comes from being an only child and growing up on an island. I read a lot of books. It was that or sail or take up knitting, and since I never had highly developed small—let alone large—motor skills, I picked reading. I merely had to turn pages. It seemed safer."

He bit back a smile and the sudden impulse to take her in his arms. Instead, he enjoyed the warm glow that permeated his being and which had nothing to do with the sun beating through the car windows—though it was incredibly hot in the car.

Lilah cocked her head and stared at him.

Justin held his breath.

She wet her lips.

For Justin, the air molecules in the car seemed to stand

still. The only noise was the whizzing of traffic outside and the occasional honk of a car horn. Not to mention the violent thumping of his own heart.

Finally, she broke eye contact to glance down at her watch.

Justin kept looking at her, feeling a little light-headed, but aware that air was beginning to return to his lungs.

Lilah nervously shook her hand with the watch, sighed and then stared blankly around the dashboard, out the side window, at her feet—anywhere but at Justin, it seemed. "To make matters worse, I'm not having any luck getting ahold of Mimi to go to the airport instead of me. And even if I could, I'm so out of it that I can't remember off the top of my head which airline my dad was taking. So in the end, there's really no point in trying to track her down because I'd have to dig through my bags for the relevant information to give her." She rubbed her forehead in frustration. "I'm rambling. Sorry."

"Tell you what. Let me pick him up. You can call him when he lands to alert him. I'll even hold up one of those signs, all very professional," he joked. He bent his head to get her attention and help her out of her funk.

"Oh, I don't know…"

He placed a fingertip under her lowered chin and tipped her head up. "I'm happy to do it. Really." He could feel her pulse fluttering through her skin.

She swallowed. "If it's not too much trouble?" She swallowed again.

"No trouble at all," he assured her. "In fact, if I hadn't stopped off to buy some groceries at the Shop Rite, I never would have seen your car pulled over. I would have felt horrible not knowing that you were stranded out here. So, please—" he leaned closer "—let me help. It's the least I can do under the circumstances."

She tightened her lips around her teeth and finally nodded.

As she did so, he could feel the pressure on his finger under her chin. He could feel a lot more, as well. He swallowed. "So, if you're sure you can handle all this?" He nodded toward the police car parked ahead.

She nodded.

Again the pressure. He shifted uncomfortably in his seat.

"I'm sure it will be fine. I mean, I took out all the insurance. The car looks perfectly drivable—a few scratches and dings—but I figure I just take it back to the rental office as soon as I'm through here. And that will be it."

"Absolutely," he added with a decisive nod.

"You're right. I'll be okay." She nodded back.

He stared at her, unblinking for a good ten seconds, then satisfied that she was calm enough to drive, he reluctantly removed his finger from under her chin. Maybe he should be more worried about his own emotional state?

He reached around to the car door. "So you'll call your dad?"

"I will. But hold on. I'll get you the details, otherwise how will you know what terminal to go to?"

"You forget. I have the flight information on my handy-dandy phone."

"That's right. I did forget all about that." She reached out and placed her hand on his sleeve. "I wanted... What I mean to say..." She pursed her lips. "I realize that I haven't thanked you." She waved vaguely around the car. "For everything really. I wasn't myself just now, maybe not since I've arrived."

So, the old Lilah really is still there, Justin's inner voice sounded in jubilation.

"And I know I haven't said it. But, I always remember you as being helpful. So natural with people."

His pulse started thumping along at an accelerated clip.

She grasped his sleeve more firmly. "This is terrible."

"It is?" *It is?*

"I mean, this is the worst time and all to decide to say this. I mean, you're in a rush and all, doing me a favor."

He shook his head. "There's plenty of time." *Time? What's time?*

Lilah pursed her lips and winced as if in pain.

Not a good sign, Justin worried.

"You see, it's like this. I'm attracted to you—the old you, the party-boy you." Lilah looked at him with desperation.

Justin tried not to say the wrong thing. "And that's bad?"

She shook her head. "No, that's good. But I'm also attracted to you—the new you, that is, the current you. The caring teacher. The guy who loves kids."

"Well, not some days. I could tell you—"

"Don't interrupt, okay?"

"If you say so."

"I say so. Where was I?" She cocked her head in thought.

"The new, improved me—if that's all right to say?"

"Yes, that's right. The new, enlightened though vulnerable you."

"And that combination's good, right?" He wanted to get it straight.

She shook her head violently. "No, that's bad. Very bad. Because if I were to have sex with the *old* you, it would be meaningless and maybe even revenge sex for all the obvious reasons. But if I go to bed with the *new* you it would involve this emotional component that could potentially make the whole thing significant, even lasting."

He frowned. "Now I'm completely baffled. Could you just go back to the sex part? My brain kind of stopped with that one word."

"Arghh!" Lilah threw up her hands. "Don't you get it? Things are too unsettled. *I'm* too mixed up with my life, my goals, to get involved, *really* involved, with anyone right now."

"Hold it. Are you telling me that you're just not that into me, or whatever the appropriate breakup line is in women's magazines?"

"Do I look like the type of woman who reads women's magazines, let alone has time?" Lilah shook her head. "I can't deal with this. My lack of certainty about where I am. My impressions of you today versus my memories of you before. Besides, you really do need to go get my father."

Justin forced himself to wait a beat or two before responding. "I don't like to leave this discussion hanging— and it's not over, not by a long shot. But for now, let's just say I recognize my cue." He pushed down on the handle and cracked open the door. The noise from the cars speeding by assaulted them. He lowered one leg to the pavement and got out. But before he closed the door, he lowered his head and stared at her a moment. "You've got my cell phone number if you need to reach me?"

She nodded.

He grasped the car door. "One thing before I go."

"What?"

He held himself still. "You know, while you're sitting

here trying to figure out what you think of the new me and the old me, you might also try asking yourself where the old you has gone."

CHAPTER FOURTEEN

MIMI STUMBLED INTO the kitchen and instinctively made a beeline for the coffeemaker, a gleaming stainless-steel automatic espresso machine. She pushed back her bangs and tucked away a lock of hair—some mysterious foreign substance was sticking together a few strands—and placed a coffee cup on the tray and pressed the button. She closed her eyes and breathed in deeply, anticipating the rumble of grinding gears and the narcotic aroma of freshly ground beans.

A mechanical whirring came to life—then stopped prematurely.

Mimi opened her eyes and focused on the machine. A red light was illuminated. "Crap." She grabbed the edge of the counter and stared at the dials.

"It helps if you add water." A smarty-pants voice sounded behind her.

Mimi swiveled to face the source of sarcasm. She raised one eyebrow. Seated at the kitchen island were her half brother and his little sidekick. It looked like they were munching away on sandwiches or something flat that fitted on small plates. "If you're such an expert, how come you didn't already fill it yourself?"

Press put down a grilled cheese sandwich and hopped off the stool he'd been sitting on. He stopped next to her and lifted out an empty plastic box from the back of the coffeemaker. "Some of us don't need to fill the water up because we've been up for hours and no longer feel the urge to caffeinate." He dramatically arched one brow.

Mimi stared at him and realized that he had the same mannerisms as she, not to mention the same dark eyebrows. Disconcerted, she raised her arm and squinted at the ancient Rolex that had belonged to her late mother. She held the watch as close as possible since she hadn't yet put in her contact lenses. "Three in the afternoon?" she screamed.

"That's what comes from polishing off a whole bottle of gin."

"I didn't polish off a whole bottle of gin. I seem to recall Lilah doing a little drinking, too," Mimi argued petulantly.

"Yeah, but after we'd taken her to campus and returned home, you seemed deep into a bottle of Frangelico." He walked to the sink.

"Frangelico? Are you kidding me? My lips would never touch such sickeningly sweet stuff." She shivered in distaste.

"I beg to differ." As the water filled up the container for the coffee machine, he pointed to the sink.

She padded over in her bare feet and looked into the giant stainless-steel trough. A pig could have bathed in it—two pigs even, she thought. Unfortunately, it wasn't a pig—or two—in it now, rather, a telltale brown bottle with an ornate calligraphic label. No wonder she tasted sawdust and felt poison darts piercing her sinuses.

She tilted back her head and decided to brazen it out. "Just because there's an empty bottle, doesn't mean I left it there," she protested, looking down her nose at him, which, frankly, wasn't so easy given that he now towered over her, a healthy boy-man's body reaching somewhere in the six-foot-two range.

"You didn't. You left it on the patio next to the pool. Noreen picked up after you. She didn't want someone tripping over it and having it break, leaving shards of glass everywhere." He didn't seem the least bit intimidated by her haughtiness. Instead, he moseyed back to the coffeemaker, his stretched-out boating shoes scuffing along the floor, and stuck the beaker of water in its appropriate place. Then he pushed the button and the coffeemaker sprang to life.

Mimi would have skipped with glee if she were at all capable—which she wasn't. Instead, she tossed her hair—a mistake, since it sent her mind reeling. "It's so nice that Noreen feels the urge to pick up after me. I mean, she was never *my* nanny."

Press passed her the filled coffee mug. "Why are you so mean to Noreen? She never did anything to hurt you."

"It's complicated." She took a large gulp. The hot liquid scalded her tongue.

He shrugged. "What isn't? You're not the only one whose mother was dumped in this family."

But yours didn't commit suicide, Mimi thought but didn't voice out loud. Instead, she turned to her usual attack mode. "So I'm supposed to feel sorry for you? Is that what you're getting at? Well, I've got news for you. Lilah's women in Congo? The ones who risk rape and dismemberment? Those are the people I feel sorry for, not rich preppy boys whose biggest worry is whether their BMWs have gas or not." She was coming on overly strong, but something about being back in Grantham and the family home rekindled all the stuff that she didn't want to deal with.

"Hey, there's no need to get all bitchy with me," Press shot back. "Anyway, I thought I was the one family member you tolerated?"

She sighed. "You are. Sorry, I'm not being fair." She took another gulp of coffee. "That still doesn't mean that I have to act like Miss Congeniality, mind you. That would be too much of a stretch." She waved the empty coffee cup in front of his nose—even stopped to show Matt—before marching over to the dishwasher and putting it in. "Voilà! Please to notice. Noreen doesn't have to clean up after me."

"I'm sure that makes the poor women in Congo feel better, too," Press snapped back. He shared more than his dark eyebrows with his half-sister.

From out of the corner of her eye she could see a hand waving. "I think your buddy Matt needs something," she said to her brother without bothering to turn. She always was good with names—drunk, sober or hungover.

Press shook his head and turned toward his friend. "What's up? You still hungry?"

Matt dropped his hand. "No, I'm fine, really. I couldn't stuff another thing in." He patted his concave stomach.

Oh, to have the metabolism of a teenage boy, Mimi thought ruefully.

Matt leaned toward Press. "Remember—you know—what we talked about earlier?" He ended his words with a nod, another nod, and then a chin waggle.

Press opened his mouth and then a second later pointed his thumb up. "Oh, yeah, that."

Mimi fluttered her hand toward the direction of the pool house and took a few steps. "You know, maybe this is my cue to do something along the lines of having a shower?"

"Hold up," Press called out. "I need you for something."

She stopped. "Perhaps my wisdom?" she asked sarcastically. Yet something inside her actually meant what she said. Not that she was about to admit that she wanted—or needed—to be of help to her family. But Press was right. He *was* the only member of the family she tolerated, more than tolerated. *Love* was maybe putting too strong a slant on it, but *like* was definitely true.

"Actually, it's a favor—for Matt." Press glanced back at his friend. "Go on. Ask her."

Mimi blinked brightly. "Ask me what?"

Matt stood, shuffling in one place and fidgeting with his empty plate. "If it's not too much trouble… About the women in Congo and Lilah's work—"

"I'm always happy to talk about Lilah's work," she replied and walked over closer. A just cause. Work. These were topics she was comfortable with.

Matt gulped and then looked up and focused directly on her. "I'm majoring in politics with a particular interest in international affairs, especially Africa."

"Then Lilah is the perfect person to talk to," she responded.

"In fact, I was interested in more than talking to her. What I mean is, I was wondering if she ever took on summer interns?"

"I'm not sure. She runs a pretty lean budget."

Matt shook his head quickly. "I wouldn't expect to be paid. I mean, I worked in the Admissions Office at Yale all during the school year, so I have enough money to live on. It's just, I was wondering if maybe…if it's not too much trouble, you could mention to her that I'd like to talk about the possibility of an internship—or really, if that's out of the question, just talk in general," he ended hastily.

Mimi digested his words and smiled at his nervous enthusiasm. She hesitated, realizing she was not naturally generous and deciding she would make amends. She raised her arms. "Sure, why not? I know she's passionate about what she does, and, believe me, she could definitely use an extra set of hands."

Mimi could see that Matt was so excited that he was practically jumping up and down on his toes. "Listen, I'm supposed to meet Lilah and her dad for dinner tonight. I don't see any reason why you couldn't, say, join us for dessert."

"Talking to her over dessert would be incredible." Then he stopped. "Crap. The timing's not going to work out. I'm supposed to work with Press tonight." Matt scowled.

Press waved his hand. "No problem. I'll cover for you."

Matt lifted his chin. "You're sure? You can have my paycheck for the night, of course."

"Don't even go there. I promise you'll pick up the slack tomorrow and Sunday. Besides, how much work can it be hauling beer kegs in and out?"

"At Reunions?" Mimi asked with a jaundiced look. "Well, that's your problem, I guess. Meanwhile, let me call Lilah." Mimi automatically reached for her phone in the back pocket of her jeans. Only then did she realize she was still wearing the flannel bottoms and T-shirt that she'd slept in. She shook her head. "My phone's in the pool house. I'll have to call her later. But in any case, I'm sure it will be fine. Listen, here's my number. You can text me now, and that way I'll have your contact information. And while you're at it, shoot me a résumé, too." She rattled off the numbers—not bothering to stop even when she heard the back door opening behind her.

CHAPTER FIFTEEN

A SUBPOENA.

Lilah frowned at the rectangular form. The handwriting filling in the boxes on the duplicate copy was barely discernable. "I don't get it. What's this all about?"

"You need to show up to court," the young policeman said brusquely, pointing to the heavyweight piece of paper in her hand.

"But I was the one who was rear-ended. How come I have to appear?" Lilah protested. So much for the calm demeanor. It had been a long day.

The cop frowned, glanced at his partner who was still in the police car, then turned back to Lilah. "Hold on. I'll go check."

Lilah rubbed her forehead. This could not be happening. She was the innocent party. So why did she have to appear before a judge? She eyed the cop on his way over to Lilah's car. He was pigeon-toed, she noticed, a pigeon-toed tough guy. Not a pretty combination.

The cop placed his hand on his hip—near his gun, Lilah couldn't help noticing—and leaned over her open door. "Since the woman in the other vehicle called for an ambulance before we got here, you have to come to court."

Which didn't make any sense at all. Lilah shook her head. "I've never heard of such a ridiculous thing. I don't even live in Grantham. I've got a business to run, commitments. The case is cut-and-dried. They hit me and now I'm supposed to show up on…on…" She glanced down at the ticket and tried to make out the writing. "On June…June 29? But that's almost three weeks away. I'm scheduled to be in Congo two days before that. I've got my flight already booked."

"You'll just have to make other plans, then."

"I'm supposed to tell women in a war zone that they'll have to wait while I go to traffic court for an offense I didn't even commit?" Her voice cracked.

"We all have to make sacrifices. Are you questioning my authority?" The policeman leaned in closer.

Lilah's focus flickered on his gun before she stared at him. "Not at all, Officer," she said in as pleasant a voice as possible. "Just the absurdity of the situation."

She saw him frown at her words. "I guess it's like Camus said. At any street corner—or piece of Route 206, in this instance—the feeling of absurdity can strike any man, or woman, in the face," she attempted to explain with a smile.

If anything, he frowned more.

Lilah had a very bad feeling about her court date.

"WHY AM I NOT SURPRISED to find you two boys here?" Noreen announced her entrance into the kitchen with a cheerful hello. "There's also a mango cheesecake in the refrigerator that I made last night. I know it's your favorite, Press." She whisked her way to the center island where she deposited her BlackBerry and a hefty set of keys next to the ever-present fruit bowl.

"I won't say no," Press replied and eagerly hustled to the refrigerator. "I don't care if you're not hungry. You've got to taste this, Matt. It's amazing."

Noreen beamed. "Use the larger dessert plates—the

Italian ones. I don't want you to shortchange yourselves."
Then she pivoted neatly on her cross trainers and beheld
Mimi. "There's more than enough if you want some,
too. I'm so delighted that you decided to stay with us for
a few days, even with all this construction. Right now
they're working on the new guest bedroom, and the dust
and noise is almost intolerable." On cue, a power saw
whirred into action and a staple gun beat out a steady
tattoo.

Mimi growled deep within her throat. "I'm staying
here because this is *my* house, too."

"Of course." Noreen bit her bottom lip. "If I may be
candid...?"

Mimi nodded but still managed to frown.

"It's just that I know you haven't always felt entirely comfortable staying here, but I'm hoping that will
change." She whipped off her tight-fitting warm-up
jacket, revealing a turquoise tank top with built-in bra,
and started fanning herself. "I don't know if it's peri-
menopause or just the aftereffects of the workout, but I
am sweating up a storm." She rolled her *r*'s lightly.

Noreen's version of sweating appeared to be a dewy
glow, Mimi thought. No unattractive wet circles under
the armpits for her. And what was particularly annoying, seeing as Noreen appeared to be coming from the
gym—*The gym! Who had time to go to the gym?*—was
that she looked as neat as a pin. The scrunchie anchor-
ing her ponytail still gripped each hair precisely in place,
setting off the diamond studs in her ears to perfection.
Two carats, at least.

"You work out?" Mimi asked, not really caring but
still retaining the vestiges of good manners that her
mother had emphasized so much.

"Yeah. I take Zumba classes three times a week."

Mimi didn't have the faintest idea what she was talking about.

Noreen got up. "Let me just get some water."

To Mimi's irritation, she didn't grab some plastic bottle of designer water from the fridge, but instead cupped her hands under the sink and drank right from the faucet.

"Don't forget to put your dishes in the sink when you're done." Noreen looked over at Press and Matt. The two were gobbling down two humongous pieces of cheesecake.

"This is amazing, Mrs. Lodge," Matt said between bites.

"It's Press's favorite. He fell in love with it when the family took a trip to Australia. I did an internet search and found a couple of recipes, which I combined to make this one. I think it came out nicely." She eyed Press.

He swallowed and nodded. "As good as the one we had at the teahouse outside Kakadu," he said, referring to the national park in the Northern Territory that was pure Crocodile Dundee country.

Mimi sniffed. This was the first she'd heard about any family trip to Australia. Not that her schedule—or her inclination—would have allowed her to join in.

Noreen seemed to sense her discomfort. "I'm sorry you couldn't come with us. It was our honeymoon, and over Conrad's objections, I insisted that it had to be a family affair. You unfortunately couldn't make the wedding, and I assumed the honeymoon was out of the question, too. In retrospect, I'm sorry if I jumped to the wrong conclusion."

Mimi remembered that she'd thrown away the engraved invitation on sight. "I was in Iraq at the time, as I recall. I didn't have time for fun and games."

Press looked up. "You don't need to be so damn snotty about it."

"Language, Press." Noreen gave him a schoolteacher's glare.

"Sorry. So darn snotty," he corrected.

"And lose the attitude or you can kiss that cake goodbye," Noreen chastised, wiping her wet hands on the sides of her black leggings.

The woman lacked love handles and any sign of cellulite, as far as Mimi could tell. She didn't even have those turkey-waddle upper arms that Mimi was starting to detect in herself. That was all pretty awe inspiring, not to mention the fact that she was the first person she had ever heard reprimand her half brother, or "Prince Press," as she sometimes thought of him.

Noreen faced Mimi again. "Your absence was noticed, but, between you and me, there were *more* than enough toasts to go around. Besides, you know the old Irish saying?"

"Which one is that?"

"That the Irish don't want anyone to wish them well. They want everyone to wish their enemies ill instead." She laughed. "Besides, what you were doing is so much more important. I can't imagine the courage it takes to be a combat reporter."

Mimi blinked. Maybe it was time she actually got to know Noreen?

"Actually, speaking of courage, I think it would be a fabulous idea to get together with your friend Lilah again. I want to hear so much more about what she does and discuss some ideas I have."

So much for her brush with glory, Mimi thought. Still, she was grown-up enough not to pout. "You can join the line. Matt here is first. But, you know, if you need to talk about Africa, th—"

The noise of multiple staple guns grew suddenly louder, preventing any reasonable conversation.

Noreen leaned toward her. She put her hand to her ear in frustration.

"What I was trying to say," Mimi shouted, "is there's always me."

By the time she'd hurled out the last word, the construction noise had stopped.

Followed almost immediately by the sound of footsteps drawing to a halt behind her.

"Strange. When have I heard those self-centered words before?" a critical male voice inquired.

Mimi's jaw dropped open. She turned slowly, and raised her chin defiantly. "Fancy meeting you here," she said without the slightest hint of joy.

"Are you implying I shouldn't be here?" said the distinguished-looking man. With a full head of slicked-back salt-and-pepper hair and a pinstripe suit to match, he balanced his leather briefcase on one of the stools by the island. "When last I checked, the property tax bill was made out to me," he replied, compressing his nostrils against his aquiline nose.

Press grabbed Matt's empty plate and rose. "Time we headed out. Tony will be waiting for us."

Mimi narrowed her eyes. "Coward," she grumbled softly as the two scampered out the door. Then she looked at the man she'd spent the better part of twenty years trying to avoid—those twenty following the first ten of absolute childhood adoration.

She studied him, refusing to give an inch. Did he look older than she remembered him? A little thickening around the waist? His eyes more deep-set and not quite so clear? A few broken capillaries in the skin on his cheeks?

She wanted him to be weak. Vengeful as she was, she might have even hoped to see signs of some debilitating condition. And she yearned to be able to say, "Oh, how the mighty have fallen." But except for the expected signs of middle age, he looked as fit and imposing as always. Which was unfair, totally unfair.

She stood, shoulders back. "Just because you pay the bills, doesn't mean you've ever lived here, Father," Mimi said and stormed out of the kitchen.

CHAPTER SIXTEEN

THE BALL BOUNCED THROUGH the legs of the shortstop and trickled out to left field where the player picked up the ball and threw it clean over the head of the first baseman. The laughing batter, a woman from Lilah's class at Grantham whom she remembered as a total stoner but who had earlier informed her that she was now a thoracic surgeon in Cincinnati, scampered to second base. There was much clapping and cheering from the stands and sidelines.

A beer was thrust into Lilah's hand. "The winning strategy appears to be to hit the ball on the ground," her father, Walt, quipped. He squished next to Lilah on the bottom row of the bleachers and took a sip from his own plastic cup.

The tradition of the current year's graduating class playing the tenth reunion class was long-standing at Grantham. Many crocodile tears and much cheap beer were annually spilled over the outcome, and the manager of the winning team claimed the right to wear the trophy—a goofy lion's tail made of unknown fibers.

"What? None for me?" asked the woman to her father's right.

"Why, Daphne, you never drink beer," Walt said with a surprised tone.

"Don't be ridiculous! I always drink beer at baseball games," she retorted, adjusting her hand-knit cardigan sweater. A single horn-shaped button held the moss-green top together in the front.

"But you never go to baseball games," Walt countered.

"A technicality," she said with the authority of a first-grade teacher, which is precisely what she'd been before becoming principal of the elementary school on Orcas Island. She stared at her husband, batting her lashes with hauteur, and waited. As a complete and welcome surprise to Lilah, her mother had finagled the time to join her father on the trip.

He laughed. "Okay, no need to spell it out. I'll go get you a beer. Meanwhile, guard this one with your life," he said to Lilah. "I don't trust her." He winked and pointed to his wife.

"I could use a beer, too, so why don't you let me?" Justin offered, springing up from the raised seating behind Lilah.

She could feel his knees brush up against her shirt as he rose. She looked down at the sneaker that he placed next to her as he sprang down gracefully onto the grass. She opened her mouth, and realizing she was about to sigh, she snapped it shut and sucked in the sides of her cheeks.

"Why don't you both go on the mission?" Daphne suggested. "Consider it part of your male hunter-gatherer role," she said with a laugh.

Justin smiled imploringly at Lilah's mother. "Would you like some chips or pretzels, too?" Then he zeroed in on Lilah. "Anything else?" The corner of his mouth twitched.

Lilah shook her head. She didn't really want to voice out loud what she wanted.

Daphne patted her rounded stomach. "That's okay. I'm saving myself for the pig roast." The two men took off and Daphne slid closer to her only child. "Walt knows it's all a ploy so that I can sit next to you, but he also knows better than to complain."

"He's always had a way with strangers," Lilah observed, admiring Justin as he easily chatted to the gathering of soon-to-be graduates and the alums. Almost reluctantly she shifted her gaze to her father, his gray hair curling over the collar of his barn jacket, his face deeply lined and tanned from hours on the water. He was busy regaling her surgeon classmate with some story.

Daphne chuckled. "It's true. The man is a natural-born charmer. Is it any wonder he took up the charter boat business?"

Lilah did a double take until she realized that her mother had mistakenly thought her comment referred to her father. "I can't imagine him doing anything else," she responded.

It was true. Lilah's father had been an engineer for Boeing, devising the complicated computer models for designing airplanes. Then one Friday evening when Lilah was eight, he walked in the house after flying his Cessna from Seattle to the island and announced, "That's it! I've had it. No more corporate life for me."

Daphne, who'd been fixing dinner in the kitchen of their cottage overlooking the water, had looked up from the sink and said, "I've always said that life's too short to keep doing something you don't love. But tell me. What do you plan to do instead? Read mystery stories all day?" She hadn't shown the least bit of worry in her face or her voice as she continued to peel potatoes.

Lilah had many memories of her mother peeling potatoes.

Her husband had crossed the room and put his arm around her shoulder, a gesture that didn't require him to raise his arm that high. Her mother barely reached five feet two, while her dad was a strapping six feet. He dropped a kiss on the top of her head and together they looked out the window over the sink. "We're lucky to live here, aren't we?" It was late spring and the sun was beginning to set. Light dappled the water with iridescent splotches. Beyond the blanket of fir trees that covered the rocky soil down to the shoreline, Mount Baker stood supreme in the distance. There was a moment or two when no one talked and her mother had moved to put the pot up to boil.

And that had been the start of her father's business taking tourists on whale-watching tours. From one boat he'd expanded to four, hiring biology grad students and naturalists to work for him in the summer months when the demand was high. But even as the business grew, Walt found occasion to go out on a boat twice a week. Like her mother said, he was a people person—who right now was making all-new friends as he filled the large plastic cups.

Daphne reached for the beer, took a sip and made a face. "Now I know why I never come to baseball games. Here." She passed the cup back, glanced over her shoulder to check on Walt again, and then hunched close to her daughter. "Quick, while your father is out of earshot, are you sure you're all right? When Justin picked us up at the airport, saying that you'd been waylaid when your car was rear-ended, I have to tell you I was more than a little concerned." Her eyes roamed Lilah for signs of injury.

Lilah shook her head and focused on Mimi stepping into the batter's box. That didn't prevent her from watching Justin out of the corner of her eye. He bent down as a woman stood on tiptoe to kiss him on the cheek. Lilah felt a sudden pang of jealousy. She turned quickly to her mother. "I'm fine. Really," she said, to reassure herself as much as in response to Daphne's question. "It was just a minor accident, more paperwork than anything. And the car rental agency was very understanding." Without even thinking about it, Lilah rubbed the back of her neck.

"Are you sure you don't have whiplash? Sometimes these things can come on you after the fact. Maybe that's the reason you declined to play in the game, which looks like such fun, dear."

The pitcher threw a slow arching ball, and Mimi went after it, shifting her weight forward with true athletic grace. There was a loud crack as the metal bat made contact.

Their team manager led the cheers. He was a member of the State Department's policy committee for Latin America who was sporting a T-shirt that read Diplomats Never Kiss and Tell. At the same time, he looked down at his lineup card. "Hey, Justin, where are you?" he shouted as he continued to clap away. The man had clearly mastered multitasking.

Lilah tried not to obviously stare as Justin hustled over to him. She was becoming obsessive—which was positively ridiculous. So instead, she followed the flight of the ball that Mimi had walloped but good. She held up her hands, ready to clap. "Mom, I'm not going to say it again. I'm fine. The only reason I'm not playing is because we had too many people and with my lack of hand-eye coordination, I thought for the good of the team I'd simply serve as a substitute. Remember Dad's attempts to teach me fly-fishing?"

Her mother patted her on the leg. "It's hard to forget."

The right fielder took off—the lion's tail attached to his cap—and made a final dive with his outstretched glove. Time stopped for what seemed an eternity. All heads turned, mouths opened. Mimi glanced over her shoulder as she rounded third.

"Well, it looks like only one of our brave warriors is returning," Daphne announced.

But Lilah's focus was on the game. The outfielder slid on the grass. The ball tipped the edge of his over-size mitt, hung precariously in, then out. He squeezed the glove together.

And it slipped in.

His young teammates jumped from the benches and ran out to congratulate him, sloshing beer as they raised him from the grass and doused him ceremoniously.

The opposing team members shook their heads and decried the cruelty of fate.

Deflated, Lilah turned back to her mother. "What did you say?"

"I said that—"

"Justin apologized, but he's up to bat soon," her father interrupted as he trotted over to join them. "Maybe he will avenge the honor of you and your classmates?"

"We can only hope," she replied with a smile. Honor was the last thing on Lilah's mind where Justin was concerned. And frankly, she could do without her classmates at the moment.

A dejected Mimi headed toward the bench. "Hi, Mrs. Evans. What a surprise. I'm glad you could make it. I didn't think you could get away." Mimi bent over to give her a kiss on the cheek. She rocked back on her heels. "And, Mr. Evans, you look great. That hit you got in the first inning is the only thing keeping us in the game." She gave him a hug.

He juggled the plastic cups. "Yes, your manager was kind enough to let me be in the starting lineup. If I didn't have a bad shoulder, I'd have stayed in the game. I can't tell you how irritating it is." He held out a beer to his wife. "As you requested."

"Why don't you give it to Mimi? I think she needs it more than I do."

"Thanks. Just what the doctor ordered." Mimi took a large gulp.

Lilah couldn't help thinking how cute her parents were and how lucky she was. "And, Mom, what Mimi said about you making this surprise visit? I thought you were up to your eyeballs in end-of-the-year commitments and graduation stuff for your school right now. And I just wanted to say again how much it means to me that you came."

"You can thank your classmate, really." Her mother cast a pleased glance at Justin. He was standing in the on-deck circle, talking with another classmate—Hunt Phox, a local Granthamite who was next up to bat. Hunt had rowed lightweight crew with Justin.

"Once he explained over the phone just how important the award was, and how much I would regret not being here, I knew he was right," Daphne went on. "It was also his idea to make it a surprise. You know, he can be very persuasive—not to mention charming." Daphne looked at her daughter with a certain twinkle in her eye that Lilah didn't normally associate with her no-nonsense mother.

"And did I tell you how much fun it was to sit in that little backseat of his car? Your father had wanted me to sit on his lap, but I insisted," her mother mused, a smile twitching at a corner of her mouth. "I felt deliciously young and silly wedged in sideways like a pretzel." She stared at Lilah. "He's quite a find, your young man." Then she raised her eyebrows to include Mimi in the discussion.

"Not too shabby," Mimi said with a smile on her lips.

"He's not 'my young man,' Mom," Lilah clarified, scratching her ear. She glanced away, avoiding her mother's gaze. "So where did you guys end up staying? I know that Mimi had wanted you to stay at her dad's house, like you did at our graduation, but there're renovations going on."

"I can't tell you how much that teed me off," Mimi complained.

Her mother patted the place next to her on the bench. "Here, have a seat and don't fret about it, Mimi. I wanted to see you, not your father's house anyway."

Lilah was so proud of her mom. She might be overly earnest sometimes, but her heart was always in the right place. "You know, by the time I got around to inquiring about arrangements, the alumni association said the accomodations had already been taken care of. Did they find you some hotel miles and miles away?"

"Didn't you know? Justin had arranged with the alumni association for us to stay at his parents' house on Edinburgh Avenue. We thought it was a bit unusual, but Justin insisted that his parents frequently put up visiting scholars in the extra bedrooms now that he and his sister have moved out. It's their way of extending hospitality to deserving members of the university community."

"It's perfect, just a few blocks from campus, just beyond the social clubs," Lilah's father chimed in. "That's why we called to tell you not to bother to pick us up. We were able to walk here, which was so nice after being cooped up in the airplane for so long."

Mimi sipped her beer thoughtfully. "The ever-remarkable Mr. Justin Bigelow. Will wonders never cease?" She gave a teasing smile over her shoulder to Lilah, who made a big show of looking toward the action.

Hunt Phox slammed a single over the second baseman's head and moved the runner into scoring position. He stopped at first and bowed ceremoniously as everyone around Lilah clapped. Mimi added a wolf whistle.

Naturally the opposition booed loudly. "Lucky hit, gramps," one supporter called out near the keg.

"It's the new prescription," Hunt shouted back, pointing to his wire-rim glasses. "Works like a charm."

"You rock, Hunt," Mimi shouted out, her hands cupped around her mouth. "So, Daphne, did you meet his family? Justin's, I mean. I vaguely remember his dad—this absentminded professor type. But he did teach this popular lecture course about epic Greek and Roman literature. We nicknamed it 'Gods and Bods.' All the jocks took it because you were guaranteed at least a B. And then there was his mother who I sometimes saw wandering around campus with a butterfly net and a sketch pad."

"A nature lover?" Walt asked. "Then she should pay us a visit on Orcas."

"No, we haven't met the mother, just his father," Daphne provided the necessary information. "They're actually on sabbatical this semester, but Stanfield made a quick trip back—something to do with the trustees. He seems nice enough." She sniffed at the end of the sentence.

Lilah glanced at her sideways. It was the sniff, not the words that caught her attention.

"Didn't Justin have a sister, too? Do you remember her?" Mimi leaned forward to look around Daphne at Lilah. When Lilah didn't respond, she tapped her on the leg. "She was a few years ahead of us. Kind of weird, homeschooled, I think. A real brain. Valedictorian, too."

Lilah shook her head. "I'm not sure. There were a lot of brains who went to Grantham. They scared the he—" she saw her mother raise an eyebrow "—the heck out of me," she corrected herself.

Daphne nodded toward Justin, who had just stepped into the batter's box. "Well, I feel totally confident with our current batter."

"C'mon, Justin," her father called out. "Two runs and we beat these upstarts."

Justin glanced over and flashed a broad smile.

Lilah could feel herself blushing even though she knew he hadn't really directed it at her, or had he?

Justin dug in with the toes of his front shoe. As he did, his hips swayed in his well-worn jeans.

A catcall could be heard from the stands. And it was decidedly high-pitched and feminine.

The pitcher wound up.

Justin left the pitch alone as it barely skimmed the dirt. "Scared to throw one over the plate, huh?" he heckled the pitcher.

Mimi put two fingers against her teeth and whistled loudly.

Walt watched her with admiration. "You know, I always wanted to be able to do that," he admitted.

"The benefits of an underbite," she replied. "By the way, Lilah?"

She only glanced over after the pitcher threw another ball. This one was so high that Justin caught it with his arm extended and threw it back himself.

"Somewhere in between, next time," he shouted.

Lilah glanced at Mimi. "What?" she asked, her head turned away from the action.

"I hope it's not an imposition, but I'd invited Press's friend Matt to join us for dessert, forgetting totally about the pig roast going on now. But I don't see why he can't meet you here instead," Mimi said. "The kid's really interested in your work in Congo, and I think he could be useful to you. He's studied international relations, so he's got the theory under his belt. And think how you're perennially short-handed in the main office in the capital. You know kids that age. They're so tech savvy, he could probably update all your computer software, get it working faster and make data more easily available to help speed up diagnoses. Who knows? You might even find a use for him in the field."

Matt. Lilah cringed at the memory of her sleepy behavior in his presence last night. "We *could* use someone to help with evaluating the cell phone pilot project," she thought out loud. "Okay, tell him to come. Though I can't promise him anything remotely resembling a paycheck—"

"No problem. From what I understand, he worked all through his first year at Yale— A student, majoring in Political Science. Like I said, no dummy. Very genuine. He's just a bit shy about talking himself up."

"All right, already. I'm sold. If you vouch for him, that's good enough for me."

Mimi pulled out her phone and texted Matt. "Good. I'll tell him that we're not going to a restaurant as I'd originally thought, and he's to come by here in a little while instead."

"All young people should be encouraged to serve a greater good," Daphne went on with a knowing harrumph. "And talking to someone in your position will give him confidence, if nothing else. A mentor can make such a difference. I know from talking to Justin that without the influence of his mentor, a woman named Roberta Zimmerman—a real pedagogical dynamo at Bank Street School, let me tell you—he never would have gotten to where he is today."

"What is it with you and Justin anyway?" Lilah asked. "You've only just met."

"True, but you can tell a lot about someone from first impressions."

"And your mother's first impressions are legendary," her father said. He clapped after Justin hit a fly ball foul down the first baseline. "Straighten it out, and you're golden," he called out.

There were shouts and whistles. Lilah shifted her attention to the field. The pitcher readied with his mitt in front of his face, shielding the ball in his other hand. Then he separated his hands and lowered his pitching arm to lob the ball underarm.

Lilah held her breath.

"What I was getting at was the fact that he's dyslexic," her mother said.

There was a crack of the bat.

Lilah turned to look at her. "What?"

And that's when the foul tip caught her in the side of the head.

CHAPTER SEVENTEEN

NOREEN FINISHED DISCUSSING the problems in the guest bathroom with her contractor—the rainwater showerhead was not centered correctly and the drain was definitely not the one she had chosen…she'd asked for square holes, not round—before wishing him a good weekend putting his boat in the water on the Jersey Shore. The man lived to go deep-sea fishing. She didn't begrudge him that. She just wished he employed a better plumber.

She waved goodbye then returned by the kitchen to the small room off the conservatory in the left wing of the house. She knew she'd find her husband there in his newly finished study. The old library was in the process of becoming a state-of-the-art entertainment room. Not that she had anything against reading. She was, after all, a member of two book clubs, one just for books in French.

No, the reason she had relegated Conrad's study to the back of the house was that he used it for smoking his wretched cigars. True, the penetrating smell had a certain appeal, conjuring up the privileged old world of exclusive men's clubs—nothing her late father, the struggling family doctor, would have been allowed to join, that's for bloody well sure. "Consider your daughter's health," she had admonished Conrad soon after she showed him the ultrasound photo of their daughter in utero. "I will not have her lungs poisoned or elevate her risk for heart disease."

He had agreed not to smoke anywhere near the baby.

"And I would also like my daughter to continue to have a father as she grows up into a fine young woman," she had added.

"My other children have never shown any desire to have me watch them grow up," he had scoffed.

Noreen could feel the tinge of sadness beneath the sarcasm, but that was a whole other conversation. Instead, she'd said, "Did you ever think that maybe I would like you to keep me company as we both watch her grow up?"

Conrad had immediately softened. Noreen remembered a particularly tender night of lovemaking and a black pearl necklace on her place at the table at the end of the week. The first had touched her heart. The second had appealed to her vanity, something she reluctantly acknowledged.

Still, he hadn't stopped smoking. Hence, the mega insulated, jumbo filtering system that served his new study.

And that's where she found him now, puffing thoughtfully, a tumbler of vodka in his right fist, the latest Harlan Coben novel on his lap. He had already changed clothes, his bespoke suit for work replaced by khaki trousers and a Brooks Brothers white polo shirt. On his feet, Noreen couldn't help noticing that he wore well-worn boat shoes with no socks, just like his son. Around his waist, only slightly less trim at sixty than when he was Press's age, he wore a needlepoint belt with the crest of Grantham emblazoned in a running pattern. She had needlepointed it for him for his birthday last year, and he had been quite taken with it. She would have made one for her stepson, as well, but she knew it was something Press wouldn't be caught dead in. Needlepoint belts just didn't seem to go with the tattoo of a little-known dinosaur fossil that he had on his forearm.

Conrad looked up when she came in and smiled appreciatively. She had showered and changed into impeccably fitting designer jeans and a crisp white shirt, the cuffs expertly rolled up and the tail tucked into her trim waist. It had been a real struggle to regain her figure after Brigid's birth, but one she had refused to give up on. Her large yellow-diamond engagement ring, four carats, Tiffany setting, gleamed on her left hand. A single gold bangle rubbed comfortably with her Patek Philippe watch on her wrist.

They had been married for eight years already, and she knew without question that his joy at seeing her was still genuine. Just as she knew that she found his healthy, but somewhat jowly, face and shock of white-gray hair still as attractive as ever.

"And how are the renovations going? Still burning up my hard-earned money?" he asked, not totally facetiously.

"Not as quickly as I would like, and not without issues. I won't bore you with the shower mix-up in the guest bath."

"For which I am eternally grateful." He smiled and closed his book, shifting it to the side table. Then he patted the arm of his leather club chair, a signal for her to join him.

She readily slipped on the rounded arm of the chair and scooted around to face him. Their eyes were almost level. "It's just the process can get frustrating, especially since I'm in the house much of the day. Sometimes I wonder why I obsess about it so much. In any case, the contractor is one of the few 'green' builders in

Grantham, and since I think it's important to practice what you preach, I'm not about to let him go."

How the builder reconciled building "green" with burning gallons and gallons of fuel every weekend on his boat was a contradiction she had never quite figured out. But then Noreen had discovered long ago that almost everyone was a mass of contradictions.

"Well, tonight you can put all that aside," Conrad said. He picked up one of Noreen's hands and brought it to his lips, offering a tender kiss.

"Tonight?" she asked. Her brain went to mush as he nibbled on her fingertips.

He brought her hand to his chest and covered it with his own. "Reunions? The gathering at Lion Inn? Some of my classmates were members there. Hadn't I mentioned it?"

"You may have said something vaguely about it, but I don't think so. Otherwise I would have put it on my calendar." Like most mothers, Noreen lived and died by her calendar. "Unfortunately, tonight's out of the question. Don't you remember this morning? Brigid and her friend are going to the new Pixar film, and then afterward she's invited her here for a sleepover."

"Can't Cook watch them for you?"

Noreen got up off the chair, letting his hand slip away, and walked over to the French doors. "No, Cook has the weekend off." She undid the latch and opened the doors wide. The high-powered air cleansing system was handling the odor of the Nicaraguan tobacco all right, but she needed the separation. It was typical of Conrad that he assumed her schedule would mesh seamlessly with his at a moment's notice.

"I don't know why you don't get a nanny like all of our friends," Conrad said.

"We've been through this before," Noreen said, trying to keep the irritation out of her voice. Conrad enjoyed picking fights over nothing, she knew, not because he was argumentative by nature, but because he was spoiled. Anything that distracted those around him from giving him their absolute fullest attention he found annoying.

Still, despite all that, he adored her. As—despite the objections of her friend Vivian—she did him. Moreover, she refused to go along with Vivian's armchair psychology that Conrad represented a father figure for the father she had lost at a transitional stage in her own life. As far as she was concerned, love was another of those things that was a mass of contradictions.

So with a patience borne of love, she went through the litany of rejoinders that she brought up whenever he broached the subject of child care. "I enjoy raising our daughter myself." That was the selfish answer. "I feel it's important." The moralistic response. "When she grows up and sees a psychiatrist, I want to be the subject of her complaints, not a series of strangers whose names she can't even remember." An homage of sorts to Woody Allen.

Of course there was always the other obvious reason—the possibility that her husband would repeat his pattern and take up with the next nanny to come along. She knew that others thought this the reason for her reluctance to have help. She had once heard Mimi say it to Press when she thought Noreen was out of earshot. *They can believe what they like,* Noreen thought. Unlike everyone else, she actually gave Conrad credit for being able to love her and remain faithful.

"I wanted to keep Brigid all to myself, especially when she was so small and defenseless. So, you see, I was and am just being selfish, dear," she said, wrapping up her argument.

"No, you're not. You're terribly loving, selfless even. I don't deserve you." And as if to reaffirm his affection, Conrad made the ultimate sacrifice and put out his cigar.

Noreen circled back to his chair and kneeled in front of him. "You know, now that she's no longer a baby, you might find it enjoyable to stay in and play with Brigid and her school chum. I'm planning on making homemade pizzas and then playing Candy Land." She took his hand in hers.

"I'm not sure if I'm the best role model. I always cheat at board games."

She cocked her head. "Maybe your daughter could be *your* role model and show you a gentler side to life?"

"I think it's rather late, don't you?"

"It's never too late." Or at least she hoped. "You know, one of these days I'm going to ask you to contribute to your...our daughter's upbringing."

"Didn't I pay for that expensive nursery school? I never knew that Quakers could be so mercenary."

Noreen shook her head. "It was a terrific environment that instilled Brigid with a sense of cooperation and confidence." She had often wished she could send her husband there, as well. "I'm not talking about money, and you know it."

He leaned back and eyed her slowly. "My job is demanding. My daily commute extends the hours even further." Conrad was a founding partner in a private equity firm on Wall Street.

"No one's denying that."

He was silent for a thoughtful moment. "Is this conversation some roundabout way of telling me you're planning on leaving me?"

"Not at all. I'm merely saying that I consider myself extremely lucky to be able to raise our child without having to worry about how to pay for the bread on the table. Yet—"

"Ah, the all-important qualifier." He grinned knowingly.

Despite the smile, Noreen noticed he squinted a little nervously. She charged on. "Yet, as important as I think it is to be here for Brigid, I also believe I should show her—and show myself—that her mother is capable of accomplishing things outside our home. There are only so many PTA functions I can volunteer for or nonprofit boards I can sit on. All *they* want is *your* name and money anyway."

"Last I heard, both were still worth something," he said with a degree of pride.

"Of course they are," she agreed. "But you know what I'm getting at. How many pillows can I needlepoint? Pretty soon you won't be able to see our bed beneath all the cushions."

"There are other beds in the house," he offered.

She gave him a look of exasperation.

"You want to visit your mother in Belfast?"

Noreen shook her head. "No, she was just here for Christmas and New Year's. And now she plans on coming over this summer again."

Conrad raised his eyebrows at that last bit of news, but he held his tongue. Nonetheless, he leaned over to reach for his drink. "Perhaps you want to go to work, then?" he asked after a healthy sip.

"To tell you the God's honest truth, I'm not sure exactly what I want," Noreen replied. "I'm still mulling things over, but, yes, I have some ideas. And before you say anything—money's not the issue. I've never defined myself by a paycheck." *Unlike you,* she could have added but didn't. "It's more that I feel the need to contribute to society."

"But you do, you know," Conrad said with all sincerity. "You take care of Brigid and me in ways I can't thank you enough for. You make us both very happy."

Noreen smiled in appreciation. "I'm glad. And that *is* rewarding. But not enough. Don't you understand? Several years ago when I got inquiries from Allied Irish Banks in Dublin and UNESCO in Paris—following up on internships that I'd had with them in university—I didn't feel it was fair to you or Brigid. It was one thing to do consulting from Grantham, but given the travel these positions would have entailed, I turned them down. After all, my home is here." She paused. "But now she's older. And I'm older. Not to mention, you're older, too." The remnants of her Irish lilt made the end of the sentence sound almost like a question.

But then Noreen got serious. "As I said, I'm still considering my options, but I believe it's time to adjust my priorities. I owe it to myself and my late father." She paused to compose herself for a moment, then cleared her throat. "But I must tell you—whatever I decide on, it will entail a greater commitment from you in terms of Brigid. I'm not talking about being a househusband, just providing greater flexibility in terms of being here."

Conrad finished off the rest of his vodka. The ice cubes rattled in the empty glass as he put the cut-crystal tumbler on the coaster. "I'm sorry you won't be able to get out tonight, but I hope you don't mind if I pop over to campus, catch up with some of my old mates?" He simply ended the discussion by changing the subject.

Noreen could tell he was miffed. He wasn't used to having her assert her needs over his. Still, that did not mean she was about to give up. She loved him. But she also needed to be true to herself. She rose. "Just don't be too late, darling. It's your turn to take Brigid to soccer first thing tomorrow morning."

CHAPTER EIGHTEEN

"I CAN'T BELIEVE I CLIPPED you in the head with the ball," Justin repeated after the game was over. He and Lilah and her parents were seated at a picnic table. After a quick bite, Mimi had taken off to collect Matt so that he could talk to Lilah. All afternoon, a whole pig had been roasting away on a spit in the picnic area adjoining the baseball field. Now the players, their families and friends, were clustered around outdoor tables, eating far too much meat, potato salad, baked beans and the token green salad.

Justin's remorse was still going strong long after hitting her with the foul tip. Right after, he had rushed over and clucked over her like a mother hen until Walt had ordered him back in the batter's box to atone for his actions.

"It's not so bad. You didn't get much wood on it—or should I say, metal—so it wasn't moving that quickly," Lilah said, gingerly touching her jaw. "Anyway, the ice worked its magic. To tell you the truth, the impact seemed to counteract exactly the whiplash from the car accident."

"I thought you said your neck didn't hurt?" he said, frowning.

"It didn't—really. That was just a joke." Kind of. "Whatever else, this incident only confirms what I always suspected—that I have a hard head—"

"Stubborn as the day is long," her mother confirmed. This pronouncement came after she had also carefully inspected Lilah's head and declared her fit as a fiddle.

"See, both physical and maternal corroboration," Lilah said, trying to make him feel better.

He narrowed his eyes and studied her closely. Then his phone sounded. He quickly checked the caller ID, frowned and let it go through to voice mail. "Are you sure you're okay?" he asked, slipping his phone into his jeans' pocket.

"Don't worry about Lilah, Justin," her father reassured him. "The important thing was you hit the game-winning home run and now you guys have The Tail." Barbecue sauce dripped down his chin.

Daphne reached over and wiped it off. "How can you be so heartless?"

Lilah waved aside her mother's look of outrage. "It's all right, Mom. I know I'm still loved. I think it's more that Dad is just getting into the whole Grantham tradition thing."

"They're more yours than his," her mother countered.

"Are they? I mean, it's not like I'm all rah-rah about my old alma mater, and I'm certainly not one of those alums who can never seem to leave the place." Lilah caught herself. She put her hand to her mouth. "Oh, I'm sorry. I wasn't talking about you, Justin. Really."

She looked around to see if Mimi had returned yet.

"No, maybe you're right," Justin answered. "Sometimes I think it was too easy to come back and settle here. I look around the community—it's pretty, it's intellectually interesting because of the university and it's safe. But maybe almost too safe, personally, I mean."

"Justin, you came from Grantham. Your family's here.

It seems perfectly natural to settle here," Walt interjected. "In any case, you're doing what you love."

"And, tell me, why should you apologize for living in a place that's safe, beautiful and provides intellectual stimulation?" Daphne asked. "Most people would give their eye teeth to live in a place like this."

"I know. But trust me, it's not all sweetness and light—especially on the work front." He shook his head. "But never mind that. Anyway, compared to Lilah, what I do seems so trivial."

"Nonsense. Everything's not a competition—despite what you boys think. The important thing is to do something you love. Look at Walt. He quit working in Seattle because he realized his heart was on the island," Daphne said. "And luckily for us, he could take a buyout from Boeing."

"How many people realistically can do something they love and live in a place that's home?" Lilah protested.

Walt shrugged and nodded.

Justin cocked his head. "So where's your home?" he asked Lilah. "In a village in Congo?"

Lilah frowned. "I'm not sure. A part of me will always consider Orcas Island home. It's where I grew up, after all, and where I still love to visit."

"It grabs you in the gut, doesn't it, honey? You could almost never leave," her father said, his gaze focused on a faraway place.

"*You* could almost never leave, Walt." His wife nudged him in the ribs. "Justin's question was to Lilah, not you."

"So?" Justin prompted her again. "Anywhere else?"

Lilah wasn't sure what he was fishing for, so she did what came naturally. She was honest. "I guess since I still have my place in Brooklyn and use that as my home base, I think of New York as home."

"Oh, please, no one could think of that damp basement apartment as home! And it barely has a window," her mother argued.

"We all have to start out somewhere. And you should be happy that now there're bars on the windows," Lilah countered.

"Window," Daphne corrected.

"Okay, maybe not my apartment so much, but you gotta admit New York is amazing." Lilah looked at her mother for affirmation.

"I don't deny that, if you like city living, that is," Daphne responded.

"Please, enough with the devil's advocate." Lilah opened her arms wide in protest—and inadvertently pushed her paper plate over the edge of the table.

Justin, seated opposite her, somehow managed to scoop it up in midair. His large fist bent the sides of the paper plate over like a taco, saving the contents.

"Wow! Lightning reflexes. Thanks." She reached over to retrieve her plate. Her fingers brushed the back of his hand.

"Got it?" he asked, looking her straight in the eye.

Her throat tightened. She forced a gulp and nodded, then carefully set her plate on the table again.

Her mother was watching carefully.

"What did you ask me again?" She gripped her soggy paper plate with two fists.

"Home?" Justin straightened up.

She was still feeling the lingering touch of his hand like an imprint. "I guess, I guess…" She willed herself to think straight. "I guess for me home isn't so much a specific place in terms of geography, but the feeling I get because of the people that are there. If I'm in Congo, it's because Esther's there." She smiled at the memory of the celebratory dance and feast her friend had organized for her, the same day she'd gotten the phone call from Mimi about the alumni award. "Just like if I'm in Washington State, it's because Mom and Dad are there. I still think of us as the Three Musketeers," she said, smiling at her parents.

"All for one and one for all," her father said triumphantly.

Lilah reflected for a second. "And now, here, even Grantham is home—because...well—" she looked around at the three people with her at the picnic table and realized that suddenly the Three Musketeers had embraced a fourth member as easy as pie, as her dad would have said. Well, maybe easy for her mom and dad...

Lilah swallowed. "Because of you all here." She purposely left the "you" vague, but looked at her mother at her side, her father across the way—and then Justin.

"Hey, there, fellow victorious tenth reuniongoers. Look what the cat dragged in." Mimi broke the silence as she barged in with Matt trailing behind her. She waved hello and pushed Matt forward. "C'mon, don't be shy. You already know Lilah, and she's eager to talk to you. And these are her parents, Mr. and Mrs. Evans."

And like the polite young man he was, Matt made his dutiful introductions and offered firm handshakes. Then he turned to Justin. "I'm Matt Brown. I don't believe we've met."

"Justin." Justin held out his hand. "Won't you join us?" He got up, swinging one leg over the bench, and motioned for Matt to take his place. "I've finished eating anyway."

Lilah reached out. A foot of air separated them. "You don't need to leave. There's plenty of room. We can all squeeze in." Her eyes never left his.

"That's okay. The call I got earlier?" He pulled out his phone. "I should really call back before it gets too late. But don't worry. I'll be back. I have to fulfill my duties after all as the perfect host." He nodded.

"There's a man who takes his work seriously," Mimi noted mischievously as she watched him wander off to a quiet spot under a tree. She slipped in at the end of the table next to Walt.

Lilah stared at Justin as he waited with his phone to his ear, waving at a few people who called out to him. Then she saw his lips move, and he turned away from the festivities. She was curious and, she realized, more than slightly jealous—without basis, she told herself. But, still, who calls someone on a Friday night about business? And if it were personal, then who? And what did she look like?

Lilah was pondering the possibilities when a voice approached from behind. "Hey, can anyone join this gathering or is it a private confab?" a male voice asked. She looked around. "Hunt. Please, join us. We can always make room for you. Do you know everybody? My parents?" They exchanged hellos and the usual information. "And of course you already know Mimi, but I don't know if you've met Matt," she said

"No need to go any further," Hunt said as he half sat, half straddled the end of the bench next to Daphne. "Matt's dad and I used to run a company together before he started a nonprofit and I entered medical school."

"I'm still trying to figure out my first career let alone start a second one," Lilah responded not completely in jest, even though everyone laughed.

Her mother turned from Hunt on her right to Lilah on her left. "Don't worry, dear. All of life is a series of passages."

"Not to state the obvious, but for someone who's still trying to figure her life out, you seemed to have done pretty well," Hunt said with an easy charm. "Your award's completely deserved. My congratulations." The son of a well-to-do Grantham family, he had inherited generations of good breeding in addition to wealth—both of which he took with a grain of salt and a rare sense of humility.

"Thank you."

"And you must be very proud," Hunt said to her parents, who beamed. "But not to change the subject…"

"Oh, please do," Mimi said. She reached across the picnic table and snatched a carrot stick from Lilah's plate.

"Hey! That's my food," Lilah scolded.

"Complaints, complaints. Besides—" Mimi held the carrot stick vertically "—a girl can never get enough…" She eyed the taut shaft provocatively before taking a bite.

Lilah narrowed her eyes. "Let's keep this conversation PG-rated, okay?" she murmured.

Mimi rolled her eyes. "Oh, please, it's not as if Matt hasn't seen or done it all already."

Matt seemed to take a sudden interest in his cuticles.

Lilah leaned forward on her elbows. "I wasn't talking about Matt," she snarled softly, nodding her head in her parents' direction.

Hunt laughed. "I'm glad to see my former partner from Miss Dunham's Dancing School still refuses to behave properly. But the real question is, why have you chosen to foist your corrupting influence on this upright young man here, Mimi?"

"He's about to tell Lilah all about his life's dreams and his ambitions to save the world from famine, war and pestilence," Mimi explained.

Matt blanched even more.

"Tell you what." Lilah looked across the table at him and smiled, trying to reassure him after Mimi's sarcasm. "Why don't we start with your plans for the summer? We'll move on to famine, war and pestilence the next go-round."

And even though she was giving Matt her full attention, out of the corner of her eye, she managed to keep watch on Justin.

CHAPTER NINETEEN

ABOUT AN HOUR LATER, MATT WAS on the phone to Press. "Can you believe it? Lilah said this group in the field will be helping to evaluate the effectiveness of her pilot program to distribute cell phones to village women. They want to see if it's made a difference in terms of medical needs and emergencies and infant mortality."

"So you'd be going over with her, then?" Press balanced the phone between his shoulder and ear while he hoisted a full garbage bag out of the bin.

"No, that's the thing, see. The project's supposed to start in two weeks, but she has to appear in court on some stupid traffic accident that happened here."

"Huh?" Press wasn't really listening as he pulled the bag shut with the built-in ties and relined the pail with another. Matt might be hobnobbing with the alums, but he was busy working his butt off at Lion Inn. He dragged the bag full of used plates and bits of nachos and cheese dip and a lot of other things he'd rather not think about.

"So, you see, she'll have to join us later," Matt went on. "Anyhow, now I just have to convince my parents, but Hunt was there."

"Hunt?" Press headed through the kitchen and out the side door to the Dumpster.

"You know? My dad's old partner? Anyway, since he knows Lilah, he says he'll be an advocate in my corner. At which point, you wouldn't believe it, but Lilah went into gory detail about the possible dangers involved in travel to remote areas of the country. But the idea is that if there's even the remotest possibility of a threat, I'd stay in Kinshasa, helping at the headquarters there. And if I do go out with a traveling clinic, they always travel with bodyguards."

"And that's supposed to reassure your parents?" Press asked.

"Yeah, well, they're probably gonna freak out no matter what. Lilah said she'd talk to them and explain the logistics, and that the only way I could go is with their blessing." He talked a mile a minute.

"I said I understood that but that I wanted to handle it on my own first—to prove that I'm a responsible adult," Matt explained. "I mean, I'll tell them all about the safety precautions, and also explain how Lilah will arrange for all the documentation I need. And apparently I'll never be on my own. I'll fly over with the people from the medical organization, and then she'll join us when she's through here. Which is a bit much. You'd think I was some kind of baby. After all, I've been outside the country—with Dad and Katarina to Scotland after high school graduation."

"Yeah, that was lucky." He smelled his hands before reluctantly grabbing the phone off his shoulder.

"And get this. Lilah said she's prepared to pay for my airfare out of her budget. Is that great, or what?"

"Great." Press tried to sound enthusiastic. He waited in the driveway while the delivery truck from the liquor distributor backed in.

"So, I really need to talk this over with my folks. But then I promise that I'll be over as soon as possible." Matt's excitement traveled over the phone lines.

Press waved the truck back, then held up his hands

to stop it. He moved to the rear of it. "Don't worry," he replied into the phone. "I can handle things here. You're going to have your hands full anyway getting your dad to let you go to a war zone. I can't wait to hear how you manage that one. Knowing you, this will be the first he's heard about your plans."

"If I can get Katarina on my side, I know he'll go for it," Matt said.

"Divide and conquer." If he proposed something similar to his father, Press doubted his old man would care one whit. He'd be more concerned that he wasn't hanging around with high-flying investment types. Witness his lack of interest in the prestigious internship he'd won at the Museum of Natural History in New York. "Well, I suppose that means you won't be *that* far from the Grantham Club of Manhattan," he'd said between puffs on his cigar as Press stood at attention in his father's study. "Still, I don't know why you didn't consider an internship at the bank instead. It's so much more…"

"Acceptable? Like you would have done?" Press had finished for him.

Press narrowed his eyes, irritated even now after the fact.

The burly truck driver slammed shut the door of the cab and approached Press with a clipboard. "Hey, kid, you the one to sign for this delivery?"

Press nodded. "Listen, I gotta go," he said to Matt. "Things are starting to heat up here. But don't worry, for tomorrow night's shift I'm going to let you pick up most of the slack. You got it?" He ended the call and grabbed the clipboard. "Give it here. The natives are restless."

Together, he and the deliveryman wrestled the extra kegs down the short flight of side steps into the cooler that adjoined the downstairs taproom. When they finished, Press was sweating bullets.

"Yo, boy, more libations are in order," a loud voice called from the dark barroom area. "You call this a taproom, when all involved can see the tap is dry."

More laughter erupted. Despite the hearty guffaws and mega decibel chatter fueled by alcohol and bonhomie, Press identified the distinctive lockjaw accent. He took a deep breath and, tucking in the back of his Lion Inn polo shirt, headed out to the taproom.

"Coming." He hustled over to the deep rich mahogany bar and flipped up the hinged end to reach the other side. With a few long strides he stationed himself behind the taps. "Did someone say we're out already?" he inquired with a good-natured smile. "Let me just check it out." He added a wink as he reached for a clean plastic cup and pulled down the lever. He had just switched the kegs, so he figured it was more someone's inability to work the tap than a question of needing a new one.

"You doubt my word?" the same voice intoned. A large empty mug, the kind that the older alums still saved from their undergraduate days, was pushed into Press's face.

"Here, let me oblige." Press reached for the pewter mug.

And came face-to-face with his father.

Press wet his lips and didn't say anything as he abandoned the plastic cup and took the empty vessel. He placed it under the tap. Only a sputter of beer came out. "Must be a problem with the line. I'll have it fixed in no time," he said all eager-beaver-like.

Another middle-aged man, his face florid, and his orange-and-black reunion blazer looking the worse for wear, elbowed his way next to Press's father. "What's up, Conrad? Can't get any satisfaction from the young man, heh?" he joked. "That's the problem with the help these days. They just don't know how to do things right. I blame it all on the mamby-pamby educational system."

Conrad stared Press straight in the eye. "Would you agree?"

Press smiled broadly. "I'd look at his father."

"LILAH, SWEETHEART, I THINK your mother and I are going to have to call it an evening. It's been a long day of traveling." Her father rose from the picnic table and patted his stomach, noticeably fuller after two helpings of baked beans and the make-your-own sundaes. Then he placed his hand on his wife's shoulder. "Right, Mama?"

She beamed up at him. "No one can top your love of maraschino cherries, that's for sure, Walt," Daphne said. She patted his hand.

The sun was setting as the crowd began to disperse. A cranky baby hiccupped sobs, letting the world know how tired it was, and the children dragged on the arms of their parents.

"I understand." Lilah nodded. "And, really, I can't thank you enough for making the trek all the way out here."

"Our pleasure. Besides, we want to be bright-eyed and bushy-tailed for tomorrow—with The Parade in the morning and then the big award ceremony," her mother added.

"Do you think you'll actually get a medal that you can wear around your neck?" Walt asked.

"Somehow I pictured something resembling a bowling trophy. Something flashy that requires a small backhoe or a contingent of large men to carry around." Mimi stood next to the table, nursing the last of her beer. She had already driven Matt back home, and had returned to party away the night with Lilah and company.

Walt erupted in laughter and Daphne shook her head.

"You're incorrigible, dear." Daphne rose, moaning softly at the stiffness in her legs as she disentangled herself from the picnic bench. "Ach, my knees." She kissed Mimi on the cheek. "I'm glad you're around to keep Lilah from getting too serious."

Daphne turned to her daughter. She had a twinkle in her eyes, but there was a serious set to her mouth. "You will take care, won't you? Relax and enjoy yourself every once in a while."

"Mom, there's nothing to worry about. I'm fine. I'm an adult. I can take care of myself," Lilah countered.

"You'll always be my daughter and I'll always be your mother."

Lilah stuck her tongue against the inside of her cheek to keep from saying something. She pressed her hands on the table and hoisted herself up. Her mother wasn't the only one aching.

"Don't complain. You have a mother," Mimi leaned over and whispered.

"Justin, oh, Justin," Daphne called out. Justin was engrossed in a conversation with their team manager, who was just about to leave, too. He held a toddler over each shoulder. Both were limp from exhaustion and liberally splotched with food and orange soda.

Justin must have heard Daphne's cry because he looked around and held up his hand. He said a few more words to the manager before offering a quick goodbye. Proudly sporting The Tail cap, the manager saluted him. "It was better than closing a copper deal in Argentina."

Justin jogged back and joined the group. He rubbed his hands together with relish. "So are we all ready to hit Lion Inn? I have to hold up my reputation as a party animal even if it kills me—and all of you combined."

"Unfortunately, my mom and dad have decided to pack it in. It's been a long day, especially after the flight and all," Lilah explained.

"You'll be missed, but it's understandable. I'll just grab my car and give you a ride back to my parents' place."

"Don't even think about it," Daphne replied with a wave. "Walt and I like to take a stroll after dinner every evening anyway. We usually take a walk along the beach and watch the otters play."

"Helps with the digestion," Walt explained and looked around to make sure they had everything. He put Daphne's quilted shoulder bag in the crook of his arm like a seasoned husband, oblivious to the contrast of the flowery print to his rugged physique. He bent down to kiss his daughter good-night. "Take care of her, Justin," he added as he straightened up. He gave the order with a tongue-in-cheek inflection—or as much as a father of an only daughter can be casual about these matters.

"She's in good hands," Justin assured him.

Lilah wondered if he meant that literally. As she worried her bottom lip, she watched her parents walk away arm in arm, her still-handsome father looming over her diminutive but sturdy mother. Despite the size difference, their strides somehow matched.

"Aw, they look so cute," Mimi mugged. "Like Ren and Stimpy."

Lilah disagreed. "No, that's love, real love."

"Stop, before you make me blush." Mimi patted her cheek.

Lilah looked at her sideways. "You are physically incapable of blushing." Then she turned to Justin. "So, it's up to Mimi and me to see you preserve your reputation, then?"

Mimi held up her hand. "Hold on just a second...my phone's vibrating. I've been waiting to hear from my producer, so give me a minute." She stepped to the side.

Justin and Lilah stood there. First they were silent as they tried not to stare as Mimi furiously worked her phone.

Then Justin cleared his throat. "So you feel okay? Up to going out?"

"Oh, fine, fine." She twisted her neck all around. "No lasting stiffness." Then she felt her head. "And I don't feel anything where the ball dinged me."

"You sure?" He lifted his arm and touched her head as if to make certain.

She closed her eyes. The feel of his fingers rubbing over her scalp was hypnotic. "To tell you the truth, you do that much longer and I won't be sure of anything." She let her head fall back to rest on his hand.

"Okay." That was Mimi.

Lilah snapped her head up.

Justin dropped his hand to his side.

Mimi blurted, "It looks like I'm going to have to call it a night."

Lilah felt a moment of panic. That would mean she and Justin would be alone, which is what she wanted, but still...

"Problem at work?"

"No, problem at home. Noreen, of all people, needs me." Mimi put her hand to her chest in disbelief. "I mean, doesn't she realize I have a life of my own? Still, I guess when family—even mine—calls... So, I'll catch up with you tomorrow for The Parade, okay?"

"You better," Lilah warned her. "I have this recurring

nightmare that I'll be the only one wearing the class costume tomorrow," she confessed.

Mimi laughed and fished her car keys out of her pocket. "Aw, c'mon. It's absolutely mandatory that we all make total fools of ourselves. That's what's called class solidarity."

"And here I thought it was called insanity."

Mimi bumped hips with her and whispered loudly—way too loudly, in Lilah's opinion, "No, that's what's going to happen between you and Justin now that you don't have me as chaperone."

CHAPTER TWENTY

MIMI MADE HER WAY THROUGH the kitchen, passed through the butler's pantry to the formal dining room, and came to rest in the grand, two-story foyer of the family house. It wasn't every day that she got to wear dirty sneakers on an antique, mansion-size Oriental carpet, and she secretly enjoyed the idea of rubbing a little dirt into a family heirloom.

Then she realized that the maid would be held accountable for the cleanup, and she slipped off her running shoes and padded to the center of the hallway.

"Noreen? Are you there?" she called out.

"In the sitting room."

Mimi heard Noreen's voice from off to the left, and headed in that direction. If there were too many more renovations, she was going to need a road map next time she showed up.

Noreen was standing by a Chippendale couch, newly reupholstered. The claw feet looked tightly perched on the thick carpet. She held out her hand, inviting Mimi to sit.

Mimi sat on the edge of the couch—not the most relaxed position.

Noreen shifted a dainty Louis XIV armchair to face her. "I thought we could talk in here without disturbing Brigid and her little friend. They're having a sleepover and after make-your-own pizzas, they made bead bracelets for all the members of the family—here's yours by the way." She opened her hand.

Mimi reached for the pink-and-white concoction. "Gosh, I'm overwhelmed."

"You don't have to wear it."

"I'll definitely wear it." She slipped the elastic band on her wrist. "I'm touched. I'll have to say thank you."

"Maybe you could wait awhile? I've finally got them to calm down enough to watch a DVD of *Toy Story,* and I need a break from all the girlie one-on-one activity. Frankly, I'm dead to the world."

"Sure, whatever." Noreen always seemed like a whirlwind of perfect motherly energy, which Mimi had always found a little frightening. This was the first time she had ever seen her not jump at the opportunity to be the perfect hands-on mom.

"Maybe I could get you a drink? A brandy, maybe?" Mimi offered. "I've gotta confess—I'm not sure what the appropriate Mommy pick-me-upper is."

"A brandy sounds like heaven. Let me get one for you, too?" Noreen rose.

That was the thing, Mimi realized. Noreen even didn't stand up like normal people—she practically levitated. "Don't be ridiculous. You're the one who needs a break. And besides, everything else in the house might be different, but I still know where the booze is."

Mimi got up and went back to the dining room sideboard to organize the drinks. Something was definitely up, but she couldn't quite put her finger on it. Noreen didn't have that tearstained look of a woman scorned—a look she remembered her mother demonstrating on more than one occasion.

She headed back to the sitting room with renewed interest. Noreen was seated and turned her head with a swanlike grace upon Mimi's return. She accepted a brandy snifter. Mimi noticed the blue veins in her delicate wrists.

"Bottoms up," Mimi said, clinking glasses.

Noreen took a sip and gulped appreciatively. "Divine." Then she rested the glass on her knee. "I'm sorry to drag you away from the festivities, but I knew your father was out tonight at Lion Inn, so it was a perfect time to talk."

"Lion Inn? You saved me from bumping into him then," Mimi said. She settled back into the couch.

"It's regarding your father, you see, that I called you and asked you to come home to talk."

So Noreen might not be the aggrieved wife, but Mimi's instincts appeared to be spot-on. "Is this where you tell me that my father is dumping you and you don't know why? Because, you know, I've heard it all before."

"No, this is where I tell you that I have my doubts about staying with your father, but that I'm not ready to throw in the towel yet."

"What?" Mimi was incredulous for multiple reasons. She shook her head. "I mean, why?"

"You mean, why don't I want to leave him?"

Mimi nodded, and suddenly remembering the brandy, took a healthy gulp. The rich liqueur burned her throat.

"Because I love him. Is that so hard to fathom?"

"Frankly, yes, but then I might not be the most impartial person where my father's concerned."

Noreen studied her drink. "That's one of the issues that I believe Conrad needs to address if he is going to come to grips with his life—and make a difference in yours."

Mimi didn't know what to say. But then the doorbell rang, saving her from revealing something potentially embarrassing.

Noreen checked her watch and rose, not quite as ethe- really this time. "At last. I was expecting her a while ago, but she warned me that the trustees meeting could run long. If you'll excuse me."

Mimi tapped her snifter with her fingertips. Things were getting more complicated by the minute. She heard voices in the foyer and then steps coming her way. She craned her neck to get a better look.

Noreen stopped at the wide opening to the room. Next to her, a tall woman in a blue suit and a Chanel bag slung over her shoulder took over the room by simply stepping into it.

Mimi had witnessed the phenomenon before when she'd met certain heads of state or business tycoons. It was either the charisma of a natural leader or the unmit- igated gall of supreme narcissists. Sometimes the two went hand in hand.

"I don't know if you've met my old friend Vivian Pier- point?" Noreen asked, making the introductions.

"I'd have to turn in my reporter's credentials if I didn't recognize the CEO of eSales and a fellow Grantham alum, I believe." Mimi stood and exchanged firm hand- shakes.

"You believe correctly." Vivian spied her glass. "Is that brandy, by the way? I'd die for one." She turned to Noreen.

And Mimi got this weird vibe. *It couldn't be, could it?* She noticed that Vivian wore a boulder of an engagement ring, but stranger things had happened. "Let me get it for you," Mimi offered. "It seems like you two might have a lot to catch up on." She practically raced out of the room and poured a drink for Vivian. Then she looked at her own glass, gulped down the brandy that remained and poured another two fingers for herself. After this weekend, she was going to have to dry out her liver but good.

Undaunted, she took another sip and walked quickly back to the sitting room, waiting to see what new revelations would surface.

"What I wanted to talk to you about was Lilah," Noreen announced as Mimi took her seat again.

"Lilah? I thought we were going to talk about you guys?" She moved her drink between the two women who sat in matching chairs next to each other. Mimi expected Noreen to be swallowed up by Vivian, the business dynamo, but like a shape-shifter, Noreen seemed to have acquired some extra heft.

Noreen glanced over at Vivian, who raised her eyebrows before letting out a riotous laugh. "Well, that would really put it to Conrad."

"Don't pick on Conrad," Noreen warned her sternly.

Vivian was silent immediately.

Noreen turned and focused on Mimi. "Vivian and I are just friends—good friends from long ago."

"Oh," Mimi said, chastised. Truth be told, she was disappointed. She could just imagine the familial complications.

"No, it was about Lilah that I asked you to come over," Noreen repeated.

Mimi rolled her eyes. "What is it about Lilah? Everyone and his little brother wants to talk about Lilah."

"Don't be petulant. You sound like a child."

"And you sound like you're my mother."

"I'm not, but there are times when you need one." Noreen breathed in slowly and eyed her glass. "But those are issues that you need to deal with. For now, I need to talk to you as one adult to another."

Mimi nodded.

"I am interested in doing more with my life than what you see here. Contribute in a larger way."

"Honestly, there are only so many cookies she can bake," Vivian interjected.

"Not that there's anything wrong with being a strong supporter of the PTA. It's just that it's gotten to a point that it's not enough for me," Noreen explained. "And not only is that not good for me, it's not good for my daughter, and not good for my husband. So I need to do something. Something that uses my mind before I go crazy."

Mimi leaned forward. "And this has something to do with Lilah?" She tipped her head.

Noreen pursed her lips. "I can see what you're thinking. Some rich suburban mom wants to play philanthropist."

"Something like that," Mimi admitted. She took another sip of brandy.

"Then you sorely underestimate what Noreen's capable of," Vivian announced, her deep voice cutting Mimi's suspicious attitude to the quick. "She graduated number one in her class, you realize?"

"No, I had no idea. I just always thought of you as… as…"

"As a stepmother, and before that as a nanny," Noreen supplied. "That's all right. I'm proud to be married to your father. There's nothing wrong with that. And as for being a nanny, that was a decision that was right for me at the time. I was reeling from the shock of my father's death, and being away from the confines of an office and in a different country was the best thing for me. It was impossible to be morose around a child so full of life, and trust me, Press was a handful—in a good way. In any case, I don't believe I need to apologize for my decision. I happen to think taking care of children is an extremely valuable job in this world." When she spoke, her voice was noticeably an octave lower than the good-natured cheerleading tones she normally employed.

Mimi was quickly learning to reassess her view of Noreen as the spoiled trophy wife. "So what do you have in mind?" she asked.

"Good question. First off, I've had to evaluate what I have to offer. A quick and agile mind. A degree in finance. A keen interest in children, particularly young girls. Besides English, I'm fluent in French and Spanish."

"You're passable in Italian, too, if I remember correctly from our trip to Venice," Vivian said.

"Okay, Italian. But I wouldn't want to overstate my case."

Mimi swallowed. Noreen's intellectual résumé was going to quickly surpass hers, and she was too intensely competitive to feel comfortable about that.

"Plus I have access to people in high places," Noreen concluded.

"Very high places, and with expansive pockets," Vivian added. "We all know that Conrad will be more than happy to open up his checkbook if it means keeping you happy."

"I'm also counting on you, you know." Noreen addressed her friend. Then she leaned forward, crossing her arms. She tapped the toe of her Tory Burch ballet slipper on the rug. From upstairs, the soundtrack of the children's DVD lightly penetrated into the room.

"Ever since I heard about Lilah getting the award, I've been researching her organization," Noreen said with great deliberation. "The cell phone initiative is certainly a sound one, given her mission statement to elevate the health care of women and their children. I understand that new plans for microfinancing have also been suggested—"

"Where did you hear that? That's exciting," Vivian said.

"I have my sources," Noreen answered. "In any case, I think that the move into microfinancing is more problematic, especially in light of the possibilities for exploitation by nefarious groups on the ground. That kind of program requires constant monitoring."

"Corruption *is* a major issue in Congo." Mimi felt obliged to contribute.

"You're absolutely right," Noreen agreed. "You see, I want to become involved with Lilah's organization—as a financial officer. I don't look at this as some part-time star turn. I have personal experience living in Africa— I lived there as a child—and my degrees combine financial management with public health issues. I believe I can help set up a more viable financial underpinning to Sisters for Sisters. Yes, there'll still be the road races, and grant writing is a fact of life for a nonprofit. But what is essential for stability is the establishment of an endowment. And that's where I can contribute my expertise—with that and also in evaluating the management of existing programs to maximize resources. All of that together ties into focusing clearly on long-term strategic planning."

"In other words, you want to take charge," Mimi said. "I'm not sure how that is going to go over."

"Not at all. I want to help Lilah reach her potential. No matter what, she is still the driving force, the visionary. What I can bring, though, is a more professional business model to the organization. So? Do you think she might be interested, or is she so vested in her work that she will see me as an intruder?"

Mimi thought about it. "If you had asked me six months ago, I would have said she'd be reluctant to share her baby with anyone. Now, though, I almost get a sense that she *needs* to share the burden, that she looks dragged down by the responsibility. That…that…"

"That maybe she might like a life?" Noreen suggested.

"That maybe she might like to have time to share her life with someone else?" Vivian inquired judiciously.

Noreen looked at her. "You had someone in mind."

"Justin Bigelow."

"Justin?" Mimi looked surprised. "He's just a good-time boy. Great-looking, I agree, but for someone like Lilah—dedicated, serious…"

Vivian raised an eyebrow. "You'd be surprised. Besides, a little bit of party boy is something we could all probably use."

Mimi laughed. "Okay. Let's forget Justin for a while—as hard as that may be. On the subject of Lilah's nonprofit, and from the perspective of someone with no business expertise, what you suggest seems to make sense. But let me get one thing straight. You called me in to set up a meeting with Lilah?"

"No, I'm capable of picking up the phone or tracking her down myself. In fact, it's only right and proper that I speak to her myself, given what I'm asking. It's just that I wanted to get your read on Lilah's reaction before I approached her. I truly believe that given my background I can bring a real passion to what she's doing. And even though I might not have the longest résumé…"

"Don't underestimate your professional experience," Vivian interrupted. "Don't you still get calls from people at the World Bank?"

"That's just a bit of consulting here and there. Nothing as grandiose as you imply," Noreen dismissed.

Vivian coughed. "Please, the World Bank can call anyone it wants, and they called you."

Noreen shrugged, then turned to Mimi. "Expertise is one thing. The truly important thing is that I want to convey my real eagerness to Lilah directly."

"So, my work here is done?" Mimi rose.

Noreen held out her hand. "Actually, no. You see, if my plan works out, I will be mixing in travel with endowment initiatives and funding activities here in Grantham."

Mimi slowly lowered herself to the love seat again. "Travel?"

"Yes. I'd like to be hands-on. As soon as possible. The first thing would be to go to Congo and observe directly the effectiveness of Lilah's organization."

"Which means...?" Mimi waited.

"Which means that Brigid will not have a full-time mom. I have already broached the subject with Conrad."

Mimi snorted. "I bet he loved the idea of that. You don't need to tell me—he proposed getting a nanny."

"I know where you're going with that, Mimi. But for once, I think you're wrong. I don't expect your father to give up on our marriage so easily."

"She's right," Vivian said solemnly. "The guy's gaga about Noreen here."

"No, while I might agree to using babysitters, especially once school's out, I don't think a live-in nanny is the answer, nor totally necessary. Unlike some mothers, I don't believe in shipping children Brigid's age off to sleepaway camp. Besides, there are times when a child needs to be able to lie back in the grass and just look at the clouds and do nothing. Boredom can be very important.

"So, I have informed Conrad that I expect him to pitch

in and help with Brigid," Noreen went on. "He can use some of his vacation time if necessary, and telecommute when possible. There's no reason why he can't get her off to school in the morning and make her lunch, then go into the office a bit later. He has a driver anyway, so it's not as if he is tied to a train schedule. Frankly, the man could afford to retire, but I don't think that is going to happen anytime soon."

"He wouldn't know what to do," Vivian said. "Besides, can you imagine him home all the time? I know my mother is going crazy with my dad home all day now that he's retired. There're only so many Rotary Meetings to go to in a week." Vivian shook her head.

"So you're planning to lean on your friends a bit to help with all the chauffeuring, if I understand you correctly?" Mimi asked. "I mean, it's not like you don't have a cook and housekeeper to keep the house running and all. And they could pick up the slack as far as Brigid's concerned."

"You're right. I'm very lucky that I can afford full-time help. But I wouldn't think of asking the staff to do more than their job description. That would be exploitation."

All of a sudden Mimi had a weird thought. "You do know that I work full-time and live in Manhattan, and that my job is very demanding and requires me to take off at a moment's notice to all parts of the world?" She tried to preempt where she thought Noreen was going.

"I am well aware of that. But I also know that summer is the slow time for the television correspondence business. Rerun time. I also happen to know that you haven't taken a vacation in well over two years, except for this little jaunt to Grantham."

"And you know this because?" Mimi asked suspiciously.

"She has friends in high places, very high places, or haven't you heard?" Vivian said biting back a smile.

"Well, it's true." Noreen shrugged. "A woman in my Pilates class on Sunday is a fairly high-up executive at your network—no names here—and she's very informed about the business."

There were only so many women in top-level positions in television news, and Mimi had no trouble guessing to whom she was referring. She wasn't at all comfortable with this underground Pilates spy network. "So what you want me to do is take my vacation time to be a babysitter?" she shot back, annoyed.

"No, I'm asking you to spend some of your vacation gaining something you've never had."

"What? The opportunity to learn how to make beaded bracelets?" She raised her arm and shook her wrist. Actually, it was kind of cool, not that she was about to admit it right now.

"No, I'm offering you the chance to find out what it's like to be a valuable member of a family—to experience unqualified love and affection from a sibling. Can you top that?"

For once, Mimi didn't have a rejoinder.

CHAPTER TWENTY-ONE

JUSTIN AND LILAH SAT ON the window seat on the landing above the ground floor at Lion Inn. A bottle of wine stood between them, empty wineglasses in their hands.

"Care for some fresh air for a change?" Justin asked, nodding toward the window. Even though they were removed from the bombardment of sound and the sweltering crush of bodies on the first floor, Justin still had to raise his voice to be heard.

Lilah nodded, and he unhooked one of the leaded glass casement windows and led the way to the fire escape. Lilah followed, letting Justin help her clamber down to the narrow metal grid structure.

"You show a girl all the exciting places," she smirked as she settled down on the platform.

"A million-dollar view," he argued with a sweep of his arm.

It was true. Now under the stars, they gazed out over the rooftops of the campus and the town of Grantham two blocks beyond. Intermittent whoops and hollers from within interrupted the serenity of the night but couldn't entirely chase it away.

Justin crouched down as he balanced the glasses in one hand and the bottle of wine in the other. Lilah sat next to him, crossing her legs to fit in the narrow space. He handed her a glass and she held it as he poured. Then he poured himself one, settled the bottle behind him on the stone ledge of the mullioned window and turned to clink glasses. "To your award," he toasted.

"To our *West Side Story* moment here on the fire escape," she answered in return.

"Please don't tell me you want me to sing. I'm practically tone-deaf." He took a sip.

"What?" she asked in mock horror. "There's something the great and wonderful Justin Bigelow can't do?"

"You'd be surprised at the things I can't do."

"What do you mean?" Lilah rested her head against the stucco wall. "I mean, didn't you even go to the Olympics? Talk about rarified atmosphere."

"No, I quit after we won at the International Championships in Italy. I decided it was about time to get on with my life. I'd already taken two extra years after college to row full-time and eke out an existence as a part-time coach at the National Rowing Center here in Grantham. Enough was enough."

"And now you're some hotshot teacher according to Noreen and my mom. I mean, I'm not surprised you're terrific at your job—but I got to admit I was a little surprised. Especially since…ah…since…"

He could sense the hesitation in her words. "What you mean to say is you're surprised given that I have dyslexia, right?"

Lilah nodded.

"Your mom told you?"

She nodded again. "I never knew." Then she rushed to add, "Maybe she shouldn't have told me. I mean, before, when we knew each other in college, you never told me."

"Because I didn't know then, either."

"Didn't know?"

"I had an idea, but I didn't know for sure."

"But didn't your parents have you tested when you

were little? They're both highly educated. They must have been aware."

He laughed again. This time it wasn't as funny. "I think being educated does not necessarily correspond to awareness. Besides, I think it's fair to say that they were in denial, especially my father. You see, he—" Justin wanted to choose his words carefully "—he took my condition personally. He simply couldn't imagine that a son of his could have a learning disability. It had to be that I was lazy, that I didn't apply myself to my studies. It was much more reasonable to assume that I was rebelling against him, because when I took aptitude tests or in subjects not requiring heavy reading, I always did well."

"You call that reasonable?" Lilah sounded shocked.

He shrugged. "Well, if truth be told, he was right. I *was* rebelling against him. It was a role I slid into naturally since my older sister was the brilliant student who soaked up Latin and Greek when she was barely ten, so brilliant that my parents decided to homeschool her to allow her to advance at this hypersonic rate. Whereas I—"

"Instead demonstrated athletic superiority and social skills not usually associated with nerdy academic types," Lilah interrupted.

"Exactly."

"So when did you realize your— I'm not quite sure what dyslexia is really," she admitted.

"It's what's called a developmental reading disorder. Basically, my brain has difficulties processing graphic symbols, separating out the sounds in words and seeing the relationship between the sounds and combinations of letters."

She considered what he said then spoke. "So if I understand what you're saying, it has nothing to do with intelligence? In which case, I don't know why your father would be embarrassed about it."

Justin smiled, enjoying watching her gesticulate the way he remembered of old. Then he answered her question. "Who knows? It was his own ignorance, I suppose."

"So when did you figure out what the problem was?"

"That's the thing. I didn't, or maybe I just felt too embarrassed to seek help. Anyway, I developed these mechanisms for compensating. It worked pretty well, but even then I read slowly as a student, and still do today. That made it hard to take lit courses with a lot of heavy reading. I knew if I tried I'd just feel so stupid."

"But you weren't."

"Easy for you to say. You weren't the one who had to stay up all night just to keep up. You have to understand—a person can know they're not dumb but still feel that…well…they're stupid. Weird, I know, but true."

"I can believe you. The same way I can get on a scale or look in the mirror, and still think of myself weighing twenty more pounds like I did in college. It's not logical. It's all about self-perception."

"Exactly." Justin couldn't believe it. Without having to go on and on about what it was like, Lilah just knew. "You're incredible…you really are." And when he saw her flinch to deny his words, he immediately went on. "No, I mean it. So get over your own issues with self-perception."

"Believe me, self-perception isn't my only issue. But listing them ad nauseum would probably be a complete mood breaker."

"Hold on there. Me telling you about my dyslexia isn't a turnoff?"

She shook her head. "Not at all. It's like a key to this great, unsolved mystery. It explains so much about you in college." She touched his arm to emphasize her point.

And she didn't remove it—for a beat. Then two beats—two beats of silence except for breathing.

Until she nervously closed her fist. "But go on. You haven't finished the story. Explain to me more about how you got to where you are today."

"Okay, if you insist." He was dubious.

She nodded. "I'm sure."

He stared at the wine in his glass. This was the first time he had told anyone about his personal journey. "So college and compensating. Okay. The truth." He closed his eyes and thought, really thought. "I guess even though I didn't have a name for what I had, I figured out that the best thing was to gravitate to music and math. And then there were other outlets—sports, socializing." He opened his eyes and smiled at the stars glinting in the black of night. "I got pretty good at both and—what can I say—neither required me to read a thousand pages a week. Unlike what some people could do who I won't mention." He looked at her from under his brows.

Lilah bit back a smile. "So all those women were really a form of overcompensation?"

He shot back a crooked grin. "Okay, not completely. But they did help take my mind off of you." He waited for her reaction, wondering what she would say to that admission.

Instead, she took a long, thoughtful sip of her wine.

Damn. She wasn't going to make this easy.

"So when exactly did you get a diagnosis?" she asked, changing the obvious subject.

He could be patient, he told himself. "It was in Italy actually. Not to be overly dramatic, but it was this epiphany. The national rowing team was invited to visit this elementary school in Reggio Emilia—before the international competition held nearby. It was one of those goodwill outings—a photo op, really. You can imagine— these oversize jocks with little kids. Anyway, I was in this kindergarten, and the teacher, who happened to be an American on an exchange program to Italy, invited me to read a book to the class."

"In Italian?"

"I know—wild, huh? The weird thing was that even though I had never studied Italian, just Latin—I couldn't be the son of a classicist and not study Latin—I realized I could read it with very little difficulty. With a terrible accent, of course—but that only made the kids giggle and enjoy it all the more. Afterward, I mentioned how surprised I was to the teacher, saying that I had trouble reading out loud in English. I mean, even as a kid I found things like Dr. Seuss books totally confusing. I just didn't get them. Anyway, she looked at me and explained that Italian is totally phonetic—you pronounce everything exactly the way it is written. And for that reason dyslexia is just about unknown in Italy. In fact, to diagnose it, they have to perform completely different tests."

"So, you mean this total stranger diagnosed you?"

"No, this incredibly gifted teacher explained all the symptoms of what I had dealt with all my life. Suddenly, I felt this huge weight lift from my shoulders. As soon as I came back to the States, I went to a specialist, who confirmed the diagnosis. But even before I'd come back, I made a decision that if there was something I wanted— no *needed* to do—it was to try to make sure that no other child would feel the lack of self-esteem that had burdened me as a kid. And I realized that the key to this goal was early intervention and more broadly, early education. So, gone were my ambitions to go to the Olympics and support myself on a dead-end job. For the first time, I had a purpose in life—a passion."

"Talk about a turnaround. They should give the alumni award to you."

Justin laughed. "Not if you ask my principal. He hates my approach to teaching. He just wants me to follow the state's emphasis on teaching to the tests—even for five-year-olds."

"But I'm sure you'll win," Lilah encouraged him quickly. "Noreen told me how much the parents love you and how well the students do in your classes."

"That may be true, but my principal's brother works in the governor's office, and through him he's found a mouthpiece...you get the picture. And we all know New Jersey politics don't play fair."

"Which means?" She let her words float in the air, which was starting to cool. She rubbed her arms.

Justin saw it immediately. "You're getting cold. We should go in." He moved to gather up the bottle.

She stopped him by resting her hand on his forearm. "Is that what you want?"

"It's *more* a question of what *you* want." He waited.

And then she spoke. "You."

One syllable. A ton of meaning. Expressing just what he wanted. But still... He looked into her face, obscured by darkness except for shadows defined by the light coming from within the window. "You mean what you said about Stephen? That he's no longer an issue?"

She nodded. "He's no longer anything." Then she put the tip of her tongue to her top teeth. "One thing though?"

"About Stephen?" He was worried still.

"No, forget Stephen. I have. It's the phone call you had to make at the pig roast?"

"Phone call?" Her question came out of left field, and he wasn't ready for it.

"Don't you remember? You excused yourself when Mimi and Matt came over?"

"Oh, yeah, that."

"You called a woman didn't you?"

"That's right—Roberta." He smiled. She was jealous.

"She's...someone you're close to."

"You could say that." He couldn't help teasing her.

"She's..."

"Roberta is someone very important to me." That was the truth. "She's older, a good bit older." Also true.

He watched her digest that information as she wet her lips. They glistened in the backlighting.

Finally, she lifted her chin and spoke forthrightly, bravely—just the way he always pictured her. "There's nothing wrong with older. Society unjustly considers an older woman diminished in sex appeal, but frankly, I think having all that experience and knowledge gained over time can make someone that much more attractive." She rubbed her hand back and forth on her thigh, then glanced to the side.

Justin couldn't keep a straight face any longer. He reached for Lilah's upper arms and made her look at him. "Roberta is my mentor. She was the teacher in Reggio Emilia who's taught me so many things—about myself, about teaching. She's a master teacher at Bank Street School in New York, and I studied under her when I got my Master's in elementary education and teaching certification. She also happens to have been happily married to a successful artist for more than thirty-five years and has a daughter who's an incredibly gifted violinist.

I keep in touch with her because I like and admire the whole family. And when I need advice about my work, she's the one I turn to."

"It's good to have someone like that. But if you called, does that mean you have problems?" Lilah asked, relief evident in her tone even though he could see she was trying to show interest in what he was saying.

He caught her gaze with his. "I don't want to talk about work right now."

She shook her head. "Neither do I. I just needed to clear that up. Because even if this is a one-night stand, I could never do anything that would betray someone else."

He inched closer, removed her wineglass from her hand and twisted to place it on the window ledge. Then he tilted his head. "I would never betray anyone, especially you."

She tilted her head the opposite way. "You have a way with words, Mr. Bigelow."

"So, are you telling me something's going to happen?" he murmured as his lips brushed hers.

She answered, offering up her mouth to his for a kiss that was fierce, as well as fearless.

And when the kiss finally ended, he rested his forehead on hers—an act that required him to contort his back in ways he would probably regret tomorrow—but then who cared about tomorrow at this moment? And he said, his voice rising in a smile as much as a question, "Your place or mine?"

She raised her chin and twined her hands around his neck. "Heck, this is Reunions. For nostalgia's sake, why don't we do it in my dorm room? See if two people at our age can still fit on a single bed?"

He smiled with joy. If angels were trumpeting his happiness then, they would blow the roof off the Lion Inn and more. "As I remember, those beds are extra-long."

CHAPTER TWENTY-TWO

LILAH FIDGETED WITH the passkey in the lock at the entry-way door. It was one of those magnetic strip things, and she flipped it back and forth, trying to read the arrowed directions by the light of the lamppost. In keeping with the Tudor Gothic architecture of the university campus, it was a wrought-iron affair—very picturesque, but not giving the best light when it came to reading fine print, especially without her glasses.

Justin shifted the garment bag to his shoulder. On the way to her dorm, he had driven by his apartment and run upstairs to get clothes and things for tomorrow. Lilah had left her new rental car parked in the campus lot.

"Here. Do you want me to try?" he asked. He brushed the back of her hand.

She looked back at him, knew she was blushing. "No, I can do this, I know. It's just that I'm never very good at these things, and having you touch me like that is wonderful and all, but it makes me even more nervous."

Justin smiled warmly. "I'm nervous, too." He stepped away, wiggling his fingers. "See? No touching. Does that make you feel better?"

"It does and it doesn't." She swiped the card in front of the optical reader again and could finally hear the lock on the entryway door click open. "Eureka."

Justin held the door open for her. "So, now we've got three flights of stairs to look forward to?"

"No, haven't you heard? They've put elevators in since our day." She eyed the garment bag slung over his shoulder. "I wish you'd let me see the monstrosity I'm going to have to wear in The Parade tomorrow."

"Not on your life. I don't want you having any excuse to back out."

They rode the elevator to the third floor and got out. She turned to the left and headed down the hallway. The top floor, which had been formed by opening up the ceiling to the roof, was a jumble of angles and planes—slanting rooflines and alcoves with tiny windows. "I guess you know the way," Lilah said, pointing down the long, narrow hallway.

"What you do mean?"

"You're kidding me? You didn't look in the packet with the registration information?"

He shook his head. "I just have a copy of the schedule."

Lilah stopped in front of a door. She looked to the right.

Justin glanced at the room number. "It's not?"

"You bet it is." She pulled out the key from the pocket of her pants and unlocked the door. "Da-dah!" She flicked on the light switch and swept her arm around in a grand gesture. "Your senior-year suite."

Justin stepped in reluctantly. "This is more than a little creepy." He went to the center of the room and did a three-sixty. Two small bedrooms flanked a central sitting room. A bank of lead-paned windows filled the outside wall, exposing the stone crenellations of a small terrace amid the treetops of the courtyard.

"At least it's not furnished the same," he said. The hardwood floors were bare, and a single desk chair was pushed into the built-in desk by the windows. Each bedroom contained a single bed and a dresser. Justin had displayed an eclectic assortment of Grantham University memorabilia when he'd lived there, but now the paneled walls were bare. "It's not quite the same without all my empty beer bottles," he said somewhat nostalgically.

"I think Stephen threw those out as soon as he could."

"No, that would have been the sofa that I'd rescued Dumpster diving." He wandered among the rooms, turning the lights on and off, the single overhead fixtures providing a dismal atmosphere. "Without all the usual student stuff, it looks bigger." He swung around to face her. "Still, I'm a little freaked out, I gotta admit," Justin confessed.

"I suppose we could burn some soothing incense to impart the correct aura."

"We'd probably set off the fire alarm." Justin shook his head. "I'm trying to remember which bedroom was mine."

She pointed with her thumb in a hitchhiker gesture. "You had the one on the left."

"You have a good memory."

"For certain things."

"And you put your stuff?" He craned his neck to look into that room.

"In there." Then she walked to the windows and turned her back to them. "So what do you think?"

"What do I think? Truthfully? I'm trying to decide if what we're about to do here is some warped form of getting even—even though we'd both probably deny it was true."

"But I told you, the past is so over." She stepped toward him and looked up. "When I think about it, I was so naive."

"You were never naive."

"Oh, please. I was probably the only virgin in our freshman class—there's not a lot to choose from when you live on Orcas Island, trust me." She held up her hand when he started to say something. "But it wasn't just sex. It was the whole experience of coming east to an Ivy League school. I was this middle-class kid who lived on an island, for Pete's sake. I never knew rich people or people who went to prep school or who 'summered' in places like Nantucket or Martha's Vineyard. The first time I met Mimi, she scared me witless."

"She still frightens me," Justin joked.

"No, you know what I mean," Lilah insisted ruefully. "Or maybe you don't?"

"Please, I hardly grew up in the lap of luxury."

"But you did grow up in Grantham, which is about as far from the real world as it gets. Safe and sweet with the statistical claim of having more Cooper Minis per person than any other community in the U.S."

"To think we beat out Park Slope, Brooklyn."

"Stop it. I'm serious."

"I know," he said with an understanding nod. He put his hands on her shoulders, kneading them to help her relax.

She frowned and gazed up. "That's part of my problem, isn't it? My seriousness? Especially back in college when my whole attitude—my whole view of the world—was so black-and-white." She shook her head in exasperation. "What I used to think of as commitment to a cause now seems like the sanctimonious posturing of a girl."

Justin pulled her close. "Why are you so hard on yourself? You were young. We all said and did stupid things. That goes with the territory. Besides, your passion was always the thing that I thought was so amazing."

From the comfort and warmth of his chest, she spoke. "You're kidding? Me? The geeky, chubby, unathletic girl is the one you found amazing?" She tilted her head upward.

"Like I said, don't underestimate yourself." He kissed her lightly on the lips.

It would be so easy just to fall into his arms. But Lilah had never taken the easy route in life. She pulled away from him, however reluctantly, and wandered to the windows again. "Easy to say when I seem to be harboring all this guilt."

He came up behind her. "Guilt? What could you possibly have to feel guilty about? You live simply, you do good work and you have everyone's admiration."

"Stop it. You'll make me sound like a saint. I'm far from it." She whirled around to face him. "Don't you get it? I'm not perfect," she shouted, thinking of her ambivalence about accepting the alumni award.

"Does it matter?"

"I don't want to be put on a pedestal. I want to be treated as a woman."

Justin took a step toward her, and as if she were a rag doll, placed her hands on his chest. "Do you feel that?"

She could feel the hammering of his heart and nodded.

"I feel that way because you're a woman. A special woman. Can we agree on that?"

"I guess even I can't deny the power of empirical evidence."

"I'll take that as a yes."

"It's a yes, most definitely a yes." She moved closer, letting the length of her body mold to his.

"That being the case, let me use a hackneyed line— which I apologize for upfront but frankly, I'm too talked out for fresh thinking—are you still in the mood for romance?"

Lilah squeezed her lips together. She felt tears welling in her eyes, but she wasn't sad. She reached up and pressed her hand atop his. "Sometimes the best things are hackneyed."

He let out a deep breath. "Thank goodness." He hesitated. "But you know, I have one request."

She slanted her head and waited.

"Do you mind if we don't...don't, you know..."

"Have sex? You don't want to have sex?" She was taken aback. After all that outpouring of emotion, the physical proof of his desire.

"No, no, no." He shook his head emphatically. "I definitely just want us to be together."

She felt a rush of relief. She hadn't blown it.

"It's just that I want this to be special, without the ghosts of old memories floating around. Here, in this room?" He waved his hand around. "Call me overly sensitive, but there're still too many old school vibes. So, would you mind terribly if we spent the night instead at my apartment?" He crinkled up his brow.

"A sensitive male? I'm supposed to object to a straight, sensitive male?" She almost laughed, but she thought it might bruise his ego. "No problem. Let me just collect a few things." She hurried into the bedroom to locate her toiletries and some clothes, then stopped and turned.

"One question?" she asked a smile on her face.

He raised his eyebrows.

"Is your bed extra-long?"

"Lilah, the last thing you'll need to worry about is the length of my bed."

CHAPTER TWENTY-THREE

HE WAS RIGHT ABOUT THE BED. And he wasn't.

Truthfully? Lilah didn't notice much about his apartment, except that it was upstairs in an old house. That it had wood floors—she knew this because she kicked her shoes off and was barefoot. That there was the sound of street noise—until he closed the double-hung window. And that the bedroom was in the back.

The bed was unmade, but the sheets smelled fresh. She hadn't the faintest idea what color they were, though, or how many pillows he had or, indeed, where her clothes fell as she stripped on one side of the bed and he did on the other.

He pulled back the top sheet. She knelt on the mattress. Her heart pumped so hard she practically felt it straining against her throat. Excited, anxious, she watched him remove several foil packets from the bedside table. More excitement...more anxiety.

From the other side of the bed, he slid on his knees across the sheets. Then he reached up and ran a finger along her chin, the length of her neck to her collarbone. He circled one breast, his fingernail adding a light scrape to her nipple.

Lilah felt an immediate contraction deep within. She closed her eyes. And didn't open them until he had guided her down and began exploring her body with an almost reverent delight and an inexorable slowness that verged on sweet torture. She gulped for breath. "I can't wait," she gasped. Her nerve endings were going haywire.

"All good things come to those who wait," he murmured and his lips began to follow the path of his fingers. "I want this to be right for you."

Her head sank back into a pillow. "Any more right and I'd die." She hiccuped when his mouth touched the juncture of her thighs. "There's one favor I have to ask." She gulped air.

He looked up. "Are you all right?"

She inhaled deeply. "More than all right. It's just... just...can we leave the whole patience thing for later?"

He scooted up her body and placed his hands on either side of her head. "Anything to oblige the lady."

Their lovemaking was quick, ferocious, each taking freely, each giving back more.

And when it was over, Lilah lay exhausted in Justin's arms, her heart hammering in her chest—the only muscle in her body capable of movement.

She was sure she'd be up all night.

She fell asleep instantly.

IN THE MIDDLE OF THE NIGHT, Lilah rolled over in bed. She awakened to the sound of running water. *Maybe from the sink in the bathroom?* she wondered. She looked across for Justin, patting the sheets next to her. He wasn't there. And she had a moment of panic.

But then she saw him. Padding back barefoot, comfortably naked. In his hand he held a water glass. He slid under the top sheet. "I was trying to be quiet. I'm sorry I woke you."

"I'm not," she smiled, enjoying the warmth that radiated from his body.

"Water?" He held the glass to her.

"Thanks." She nodded and took it, then handed it back when she was finished.

He took a large gulp before setting it down on the table.

Somehow the act of sharing a water glass seemed every bit as intimate as their earlier lovemaking—maybe more so, given its casualness. And that intimacy made her realize that she couldn't lie anymore.

"Justin?" She pressed her lips together.

He turned back and waited.

"There's something I need to confess."

"Please don't tell me you're secretly married to some dashing aid worker in Africa?"

She shook her head and tried to smile. But this conversation was too serious to avoid by giving way to levity. It was also hard, really hard.

She cleared her throat. "You know how I told you that I had reservations about coming back?"

"We've been all through that, I thought?"

"Yes, I'm sure it seems like I'm beating a dead horse, but, but... There's something else." She looked to the ceiling and noticed for the first time the old-fashioned pendant light in the middle of an ornate rosette. She shook her head. There was no point delaying. "The other reason—probably the bigger reason if I have to admit it—and after what...what we shared, I am obliged to admit." She paused, then rushed on. "The award? The one you nominated me for?"

He nodded and shifted to sit up against the headboard, the sheet covering him from the waist down.

Lilah rested on her elbow and propped her head up with her hand. "I don't deserve it. I mean, okay, I started this nonprofit organization and it has helped Congolese women. I know because I've seen the proof. And I still believe in it—more than ever maybe, given the atrocities still going on there. But the thing is…" She hesitated as she attempted to put her feelings into words. "As much as I believe in it, the truth of the matter is I just can't get as excited about it as I used to. These days I'm just going through the motions—it feels like I'm not fully committed to it anymore, even though I want to be. I really do."

She sniffed. "So I sit around thinking—when I'm not trying to juggle the finances to keep things afloat and cut through multiple layers of red tape to make things happen…when I'm not doing all that that someone else could do a much better job than I. I mean, I almost feel criminal, especially now that Sisters for Sisters is generating all this interest and people come to me with their ideas."

She rubbed her forehead. "I guess I just feel overwhelmed. Like I want to run away from the whole thing. But I can't. I'm caught. So then I feel guilty and depressed that I'm not holding up my end. That I'm letting other people down who really need me. And even if I do somehow manage to do the right thing, that it'll never be enough given the enormity of the problem." She paused. "Does any of that make sense?"

He frowned in thought before offering her a tight-lipped smile. "Completely." He slid his arm around her shoulders and pulled her over to sit next to him.

She scooped up the sheet and tucked it under her arms to cover herself. Then she turned her head to face him. "Really? Because I'm not sure *I* understand it."

"How can I explain?" He set his jaw and narrowed his eyes. Then he looked down at her upturned face. "You know that line of Humphrey Bogart's from *Casablanca?*"

She placed her hand against her chest. "Do I know his lines? You forget I was vice president of the film club? 'Play it, Sam?' 'Here's looking at you, kid'? Somehow, they don't seem to be germane to our discussion though."

"Germane? God, that's so you." Justin laughed. He held up his hand in peace when he saw her frown. "No, I'm not laughing at you. I'm just delighting in you. But listen." He shifted over so their thighs were touching.

Lilah thought the contact probably diminished her focus, but it felt too good to say anything.

"I'm talking about the last scene at the airport," Justin went on. "When he tells Ingrid Bergman that she has to be with her noble war hero husband? He says something like, 'It doesn't take much to see that the problems of three little people don't amount to a hill of beans in this crazy world.'"

She could picture the rich black-and-white images as he spoke. "Oh, my God, it was so tragic."

"But so wrong."

"Wrong? You're saying that one of the greatest romantic lines of all times is wrong?"

"Absolutely. He's totally got it ass backward. I mean, as far as I'm concerned, you have to start with the problems of *one* person, then build from there."

He reached around and cradled her shoulders in his arm. "Listen, I think you—and I—have reached turning points in our lives. The problem is, we're both committed to our careers even though we're also totally frustrated at the moment, which in your case translates into blaming yourself and feeling guilty. And in mine, makes me blame the world and want to punch someone."

"So what do we do? Since punching's out of the question."

"Unfortunately, I think you're right about that one.

What I think we have to do is keep the faith, so to speak. Keep our options open, and not get all worked up because we don't have a ready solution at hand. Which all requires a very subtle mix of opportunism and patience. Patience is key."

Lilah shifted her weight so she could turn her shoulders and face him head-on. "This is the gospel according to Justin Bigelow?"

He made a face. "Are you making fun of me?"

"No, of course not." She paused and smiled. "Well, maybe just a little. But tell me." She stared at him, her chin slightly cocked. "When did you become so wise? Or were you always this way, but I was too blind to see it?"

Justin shrugged. "Boy, would I like to say I was always this way. But in hindsight, I think I probably demonstrated about as many introspective tendencies as most twenty-year-old males—in other words, close to none. No, as far as I can tell, any wisdom I've gained over the years comes from kindergarteners. I have grown to realize that nothing—and no one—is as honest, sometimes cruelly, and intuitively insightful as a five-year-old."

"Out of the mouths of babes, huh?"

He nodded.

"I think you're being overly humble." She pushed back the sheet and shifted so that she straddled his naked body. "Someone wise—no names—told me not so long ago not to underestimate myself. I think the same holds true for you." She rubbed her knuckles against the stubble on his cheeks. "Have I told you that I think you're incredible?"

"No, but, you know, the ways things have worked out—" he looked around the bed "—kind of gave me the feeling that you cared for me." He kissed her hand.

And this time, the lovemaking was imbued with a tenderness that spoke of a comfort with each other, an openness, and a feeling that nothing else existed beyond the confines of a queen-size bed and their imaginations. And when Lilah eventually fell asleep in Justin's arms, she felt subsumed by a peacefulness of mind and body and soul that she had never experienced before.

CHAPTER TWENTY-FOUR

IT WAS THREE IN THE MORNING, and Press was running on fumes. His back ached. The muscles in his arms throbbed. Hauling kegs was not an activity for the weak. Then there were his facial muscles. Was it possible to strain facial muscles with an excess of smiling? Probably, simply, from having to respond to the constant requests—most of them polite, but some pretty snotty. *Lesson learned,* he chalked up mentally as he bent over a toilet to clean it. Alcohol, forced bonhomie and a sense of entitlement were a lethal mixture.

This was the fourth time he'd cleaned out the basement men's room next to the pump room, and it was really starting to get to him. *How—and why—in the world could someone take off the ceramic basin of a sink and smash it on the floor?* he wondered.

"Hey, Press," Tony said, from the doorway. "The Grantham cops are upstairs and they want to talk to you," he announced. Then he regarded the busted sink and shook his head in disgust. "You guys have gotta be more careful. I tell you, after Reunions are over on Sunday, I'm closing the place down for a while."

Press dumped the scrubber he was holding into a bucket. "The cops?" He tried to figure out what the cops wanted with him. It was well-known around town that there was friction between the cops and the college kids. The police thought the university students were a bunch of spoiled rich kids who believed they could get away with anything. Which, granted, was kind of true. But maybe if the cops used a little more tact in their encounters, the students might respond more diplomatically.

So now for some unknown reason he had the cops on his back. But first he had Tony to deal with. "Hey, listen, it's not *my* fault that some alum went crazy." He nodded in the direction of the sink.

"Well, you and your buddy were on duty, right? How did you miss all this?" Tony stomped away, clearly ticked off.

"It's not like I'm the one who had all the fun tonight," Press muttered under his breath. He blew air noisily out of his mouth and trudged up the stairs to the lobby. The wood-paneled room with its faded Oriental carpet conveyed a stately collegiate atmosphere. But the smell of stale beer permeated the air. And in the corner of the room, stacks of large black garbage bags bulged with plastic cups and remnants of the platters of finger food. *Animal House* was probably a more accurate description.

Two cops stood close together by the entrance, their hands on their hips and their caps on straight—all business. They had their backs to Press as he approached them.

"Can I help you, officers?" he asked politely.

The two men turned around. One kept his hands on his hips. His feet were placed apart as if ready to go on the attack.

Press focused on him, uneasy with the aggressiveness, but then something else caught his eye. A small gap had formed between the cops when they'd turned around, and Press was able to see someone else standing behind them. Someone tall, middle-aged, and looking decidedly the worse for wear.

His father.

The one word that entered his mind was unmentionable in company such as this.

The policeman to his left smiled all folksy like. "Mr. Lodge here was trying to drive home when we stopped his car," he explained with a down-home slowness to his words.

The good cop, Press ascertained immediately.

"Naturally, seeing as it was Mr. Lodge, we didn't want to cause any trouble," the cop continued. He scratched his temple by his buzz cut.

"Naturally," Press repeated. He tried to keep his tone neutral, but inside, he was angry. "I suppose it wouldn't look good to have a former mayor of Grantham get in any trouble?"

When Press was still young, his father had had an uncharacteristic stirring of civic spirit and had decided to run for mayor. It was about the same time his then not-quite-young-anymore wife—and Press's mother—had been eager to assume a more prominent role in Grantham society. A Republican hadn't won a local election in town for more than twenty years, but then a Lodge had never run for office before. It went without saying that Conrad won.

Nineteen months later he was having an affair with the new nanny—Noreen.

Four months later, he declined to run for office again.

That may all have been ancient history, but Grantham's finest had been well schooled never to forget just who was important in town.

Press offered a curt nod of recognition to his father. Conrad overstraightened his back with the studied carefulness of someone who'd drunk far too much alcohol.

Press focused on "the good cop." "I take it he said that I could drive him home, Officer?"

"Mr. Lodge did say there was a college student working here who could take him, but...ah...you should know that you won't be able to use his car. He had a bit of a fender bender—took out the bumper and a front headlight after a telephone pole got a little too close."

"Funny about those telephone poles," Press responded.

His father seemed unaffected by the news of the accident. "I'm sure this young man will be happy to help out," Conrad announced, his patrician lockjaw accent laid on thick.

So the hired help doesn't even get a name, let alone an acknowledgment as being his son, Press thought.

Tony entered the room and dropped a couple of garbage bags onto the growing pile.

Press turned to him. "Listen, Tony, I'm going to have run a quick errand." He nodded toward the gathering at the front door.

"Yeah, well, you do that. But then you better hightail it back here to help clean up."

Press could have easily stormed out then and there. Here he was the one doing the work—for Matt, for Tony, and helping his pathetic dad—and at the same time having to suck up to the cops. He set his jaw. "Fine. I'll be back as soon as possible. Let me just get my car."

"Hold on. Not so fast." The young cop stepped up close.

Too close, as far as Press was concerned.

He sniffed loudly. "Is that alcohol I smell?"

"I haven't been drinking. I've been cleaning up after everybody else who has. That's why my clothes smell," Press protested. He couldn't hide his irritation.

The young cop rolled his shoulders. "Would you be

willing to take a Breathalyzer test?" he asked pugna-
ciously.

Press counted to ten to get his temper under control.
"I'm happy to take the test—now, here, wherever."

"The kit's in the patrol car. This way." The cop indicated with a shake of his head. He led with his chin.

Press noticed his father, who'd propped himself up by
leaning against the heavy wooden side table. *He can't
even stand up, and I'm the one who has to take the test,*
Press thought with disgust.

"Do whatever you need to, Officer," Conrad said with
a tip of his head. "Meanwhile, if you don't mind." He indicated a chair next to the table.

"Of course, sir."

Which only irritated Press further. Still, like a good
soldier, he trotted out with the second patrolman while
Mr. Mayberry RFD stayed to amiably keep his father
company.

They stopped next to the squad car that was parked
in the club's driveway. In a matter of minutes, Press
breathed into the tube and waited as the reading came
back that he had an alcohol level of 0.0.

"I guess you're okay—for now." The young cop
snapped out his warning.

Press didn't bite. "If I'm going to drive Mr. Lodge
home, then you'll need to move your car." He didn't
bother to wait for a response, but turned and headed
back to the club's small parking lot. He fished the car
keys out of his pants' pocket as he passed the line of recycling cans next to the Dumpster.

He eyed the mounds of empty wine bottles, evidence
of just how good a time everyone had had that night.
Everyone but him. Disgusted, Press pulled back his foot
and kicked a can, kicked it hard, really hard. The plas-

tic bin tipped over. The empty bottles clunked to the asphalt and spread across the driveway. The clatter echoed through the stillness of the wee hours.

He heard footsteps come running. Press turned. And saw the young cop take in the mess, then reach for his side. "Whoa!" Press immediately held up his hands. "I'm going to pick it all up, no problems, okay?"

The patrolman reached around behind him. And pulled out a long, thick pad. Then he started writing.

Press blinked. *What the*... "Listen, I said I'd pick everything up," he sputtered in disbelief. And to prove his point, he bent down and righted the plastic container. That's when he noticed that the top edge was cracked where it had banged against the pavement.

The policeman lifted his head, eyed the can a beat later and with a smirk started to write some more.

"Name? I'll need some ID."

Press stared at him, baffled. "Sure, sure." He reached for his wallet in his back pocket and handed him his driver's license.

The cop shone his flashlight on the card. He hesitated for a moment. "Lodge? Conrad Lodge III?" he asked.

Press shrugged.

The cop finished taking down the information and ripped off a sheet from the pad. He handed it to Press along with the license.

He could barely make out the faint writing under the spotlight anchored to the side of the building. "Creating a public nuisance? Destroying public property? I don't get it. All I did was kick a garbage can." Press looked up, holding the ticket out.

"You'll receive a summons to appear in court in the mail," the policeman said, his eyes narrowed. "The court date's in two week's time—it's on the bottom of the ticket."

"And my father?"

"I wouldn't go running to daddy, if I were you." The cop raised his chin, the beak of his cap tilted upward. The harsh light fell on his badge and the straining buttons of his uniform.

Press shifted his shoulders. "I suppose you ticketed him for DUI, too?"

The cop opened his mouth but didn't offer a comment. Instead, he adjusted his cap and turned to get his partner.

Press watched him go. "Fantastic. My dad gets away with drunk driving while I'm arrested for nothing," he mumbled under his breath. His only hope was that the cop was worried about his job, having issued a ticket to the Great Man's son.

Speaking of the Great Man. Time to rescue the One and Only. Justin strode toward the parking lot. Well, Mr. I've-Got-A-Major-Stick-Up-My-You-Know-What policeman could rest easy. Press wasn't about to let the old man know what had happened to him. He'd probably get *more* grief.

He started up the Beemer, and in the sanctuary of a locked car with the windows rolled up, he could finally say what he'd been thinking the whole time. "Family is more f-ing trouble than it's worth." Then he said a whole lot more one-syllable words not fit for family consumption.

CHAPTER TWENTY-FIVE

LILAH WOKE ON SATURDAY with a sense of dislocation—
and a nagging buzz in her ear. Lying on her stomach,
she lifted her head and focused with one eye. Next to
her were broad shoulders and the back of a head with
the sexiest bed-head hair she'd ever seen.

Oh, ri-ight, she thought with a pleased smile. It was
all coming back to her.

Unfortunately, so was the insistent tinny noise.

The shoulders next to her shifted, and she could hear
a grunt. "Who would call this early?" Justin asked. He
blindly fumbled for his cell phone on the side table.
When he didn't locate it, he lifted his torso and scanned
the floor.

His pants. They lay in a heap just beyond fingertip
reach. He stretched and hooked the waistband. Then he
trolled them back to the bed like a fisherman reeling in
the day's catch.

The buzzing continued as he fumbled in his pocket
and located his phone. Eyes almost closed, he pulled it
out. Nothing.

And then the buzzing stopped.

He squinted at his phone and pressed a few buttons.
Then he glanced across the bed. "You're still here?" he
asked with a felinelike smile. He threw his phone to the
foot of the bed and rolled over, snuggling up against her.

"Yeah, you just can't get rid of me." She nuzzled

her chin against the hollow of his neck. His skin had a divine, almost sweet smell. "Who was that?" she asked lazily.

He shook his head and she could feel his chin move back and forth over the top of her head. "Nobody. It wasn't my phone. Come to think of it, it wasn't even my ring tone. Probably just some random street noise."

He shifted and pulled her up so that their heads were level. "There. That's better."

"Wait a minute. That must have been my phone." Lilah started to squirm away.

He pulled her back. "Can't it wait?"

She wiggled out of his grip and sat up on the side of the bed. "It's just that very few people have this number, and it could be an emergency."

"And you claim you're worried that you've lost your passion for your work? I don't think so," he said, spreading his arms out.

He looked very tempting, but she still got up and hunted around the room, unaware that she was naked until she saw a pile of her clothes on the floor. "Oh, right." She picked up her shirt and held it across her chest, a display of modesty that was really crazy considering what they'd done and that he had an uninterrupted view of her behind.

She tripped over her sneakers and walked through the open bedroom door to the living room. "Ah, ha," she called out, then scampered back and scrambled into bed. She sat cross-legged and checked her voice mail, pulling the top sheet up to her neck. She relaxed immediately when she heard the message, and then pressed Reply.

"Mom, did you ring earlier?" she asked. "I'm sorry I didn't pick up but I was in the shower." She noticed Justin raise his eyebrows at her white lie. She shrugged.

"Yes, Lilah, I just wanted to let you know that Justin's father is driving us to The Parade. Stanfield is going to march, too, and since he has a faculty parking sticker, we'll be able to park on campus. Isn't that wonderful?"

"Wonderful." What else could she say?

"And when you see Justin, could you tell him how delighted we are that he thought to get us your class outfits to wear, too?"

She glanced over at Justin. "Justin got you class outfits?"

He shimmied up next to her and tugged on the sheet.

She batted his hand away.

"Yes, they're just wonderful!" her mother exclaimed. "We feel absolutely in the Grantham University spirit. Can you believe it from a pair of aging hippies? Stanfield didn't buy his class blazer, but we forced him to don an orange tie as a way to show off his school colors. So we'll meet up with you at the start of The Parade." There was some noise in the background. "Just a minute."

Lilah nodded in singsong fashion as she waited while her mother spoke to someone in the room with her.

Justin slipped under the edge of the sheet.

Lilah stilled.

"Lilah? Lilah? Are you there?" Her mother came back on the phone.

"Yes, Mother." Lilah squeaked when Justin rested his hand atop one of her exposed thighs and began a slow two-finger march upward. "You're killing me," she whispered.

"Stanfield says to meet where your class is supposed to congregate. There'll be some sort of sign or flag apparently."

"No problem. See you then."

Justin cupped his fingers between Lilah's legs.

She rang off without waiting to hear any more. "That was my mother," she said, closing her eyes as he rubbed gently.

He surfaced. "I gathered." He kept rubbing until he hit a particularly sensitive spot.

"She wanted to let you know that your father is taking them to The Parade." She breathed in deeply as a ticklish warmth traveled to her core.

"That's nice. It leaves more time for us." He angled her head to kiss her at the same time.

But she pulled back and covered her mouth. "I didn't brush my teeth last night."

"You think I really care?" He kissed her, dipping his tongue into her mouth, a subtle exploration that mimicked the resumed motion of his fingers.

The kiss ended but Lilah remained with her mouth open. "Oh, wow." She went to put her hands behind his head when she realized she still had her phone in one hand.

She arched her back to stretch for a side table.

"Perfect positioning." He nuzzled between her breasts.

She looked over her shoulder and somehow located the table on her side of the bed. She fumbled the phone down, and the jostling lit up the screen.

She bolted upright. "Oh, geez. It's nine-thirty. The Parade begins at ten. I hate to be late. In fact, I'm never late."

"Don't worry. It never begins on time. Get a group of Ivy League graduates together, people more used to leading than following, and they find it next to impossible to line up behind each other." He pulled her back. "Besides, a little morning frolic will only help to get us in the Old School spirit."

"You think?" Still, she didn't object. Far from it.

And while neither said I love you, their lovemaking was more than a culmination of animal urges, even human ones. It was more a communication that was… well…just perfect.

"You were right about this thing not kicking off on time." Lilah held on to Justin's arm for dear life. They'd arrived at the campus parking lot south of the ice-skating rink at around ten after ten. The Parade marshals were still working hard to get the classes together. She craned her head, looking for the pennant that proclaimed their class year. The oldest classes were nominally stationed up front, with the remaining classes descending in order—a loose term—all the way down to the seniors who would graduate in a few days.

Absolute bedlam was an understatement.

More than just the graduates marched. There were their families—older, younger, siblings, spouses and pets. Then there were the marching bands, a few tacky floats and some golf carts decked out in orange and black crepe paper to carry the older alums who were unable to walk the distance around campus.

Finally, she spotted their class banner and pointed it out to Justin. They pushed their way through the noisy throng. People from her class who she didn't even remember recognized her and stopped to congratulate her.

Lilah leaned her head to Justin to speak under her breath. "Wow. Now I know what it's like to be the belle of the ball."

Justin squeezed her hand. "And you're the belle-est of them all." He raised his arm and waved. "I see them over there," he said to Lilah, smiling, and parted the waves of people with his wide shoulders.

"Hey, kiddo. Don't you look cute!" Her father leaned over to give her a peck on the cheek.

Lilah was convinced that he would be able tell that she and Justin had had sex, but his expression seemed sunny and uncomplicated when he straightened up. *Thank goodness.* Relieved, she gave her parents the once-up-and-down, then flapped her arms to the side and looked down at her getup.

"I never thought I'd be caught dead looking like a ninja, but I guess the rule is never say never," she joked. Each Reunion class adopted its own uniform as a sign of solidarity. For her year the outfit consisted of loose orange pants and a matching martial arts jacket tied with a black belt.

"Excuse me, you had a very active imagination as a little girl, and you used to play dress-up and devise all kinds of imaginary scenarios," her mother corrected. "I distinctly remember how fond you were of this particular pirate's costume. You used to go around exclaiming, 'Shiver me timbers,' when anyone talked to you." She looked at her husband, and they chuckled at the recollection.

"So you like to dress up?" Justin whispered into her ear.

"Hello, hello, hello," Mimi swooped in. On her, a bright orange ninja outfit actually looked menacing. She surveyed the general scene before turning back to the group. "So I presume everyone was waiting for me to arrive? I'll have you know that I have an excuse—a very good one, mind you. I came with my dad, Noreen and little Brigid, who insisted I braid her hair and attach little orange and black ribbons to the ends. Do you know how slippery little ribbons are? And then there was the production of getting out the door—making sure to go to the bathroom first, kiss every doll goodbye—you name it. And did you know that kids who are eight and under eighty pounds have to have a car seat? I remember how my mom just threw me in the trunk of the station wagon."

"Yes, children can be a handful sometimes," Stanfield responded.

Lilah noticed Justin clench his jaw. She slipped a hand behind him and rubbed the small of his back. She could feel the tension in his muscles. Then she shot an interested smile at Mimi. "So now you're an expert on children?"

Mimi rolled her eyes. "Hardly—more like forced into being aware of the under-three-feet set for the first time. It's all very puzzling, but I'm not complaining as much as I would have thought." She frowned at this self-realization.

She held up her wrist. "Did I show you the bracelet Brigid made me?" At the same moment, her eyes drifted to Lilah and the position of her arm.

Lilah saw Mimi give her a look, then raise her eyebrows when Justin leaned closer.

"So that's the way it is, huh?" Mimi asked Lilah.

"You can draw your own conclusions," Lilah gave her a nonanswer. She noticed her parents and Stanfield were busy chatting about vitamin D of all things.

"Earth to Lilah," Mimi called out.

Lilah looked at her askance. Meanwhile Justin leaned back to greet another long-lost classmate.

"This is Mimi here, sugarplum." Mimi sidled up close. "At the risk of using a vocabulary I would never be caught dead using on camera—may I say that you two are adorable together?"

Lilah pondered how much to divulge, especially in

public, even if her parents seemed oblivious to the situation. There were times—most of the time—when Mimi was not exactly tactful. She tapped Justin on the sleeve for assistance, but Stanfield got in first.

"Walt and Daphne were wondering how many seniors at Grantham High School are accepted as undergraduates each year," Justin's father asked him. "I don't get involved in these matters, and I thought perhaps you could provide some perspective?" He sniffed, narrowing the nostrils of his aquiline nose.

"I can only comment on my entering year," Justin answered. He shifted his stance to better engage in conversation with Lilah's parents, thereby turning his back to Lilah. As he did so, he brushed her hand with his pinkie.

Mimi quickly noticed all. "So? Now that your escort is otherwise occupied, we have a moment to ourselves." She waited.

Lilah stepped closer. "Could you keep your voice down, please?"

"Sure, sure, whatever." Mimi lowered her voice a notch or two.

Lilah breathed in. "Okay…it's like this. Last night, when we went to Lion Inn? By ourselves?"

Mimi nodded rapidly.

"We managed to find a quiet spot to talk."

"There was a quiet spot at Lion Inn during a Reunions party? I can't believe it."

Lilah opened her eyes wide. "Do you want to hear this or not?"

Mimi rubbed her hands together. "Definitely."

"One thing led to another. And to make a long story short, I spent the night at his place."

Mimi whistled. "So you got lucky."

Lilah frowned. "I really wouldn't characterize it that way."

"What do you mean?" Mimi homed in on her. "How else could you characterize successfully nailing the heartthrob fantasy of the Class of 2002? Good on you, girl—that's all I can say." Mimi bobbed her head emphatically.

"But that's not what it's about," Lilah protested. That term, *nailing?* It was so not what had happened. "You know, I like to think we've all moved beyond the kind of scoring we did back in college," she replied.

"Maybe in some ways. But Justin Bigelow?" Mimi covered her mouth. "I mean, this is so cool. You and Justin. Can you imagine what Stephen would have to say about it?"

Lilah sighed. Mimi was making it sound like some soulless hookup, a totally immature way to get back at her ex-fiancé. "Maybe at one point that might have been the case, but now...now—"

"Trust me, it's always the case. Revenge is totally sweet," Mimi crowed.

Lilah thought Mimi's words probably said a lot more about herself. When would her friend move beyond the childhood family betrayals?

Lilah felt a tap on her shoulder.

"Hello there," a woman's voice sounded behind her, the faint lilt unmistakable.

Lilah turned. "Noreen."

"Delighted I could find you in all this mayhem. And, Mimi, we only just parted."

Mimi didn't seem to bristle.

And then Lilah saw the others look her way, not *her* way, exactly—more Noreen's. And with good reason. It wasn't every day that one stood toe-to-toe with a ravishing redhead wearing a blazer with small black lions embroidered all over, not to mention the black miniskirt with a matching pair of platform designer gladiator sandals. Even her father's jaw appeared to be scraping not too far off the ground.

If it took a long time to dress her daughter, Lilah could only imagine the hours it took to produce this kind of preppie dominatrix look. Though, given the way Noreen seemed devoid of any makeup and that there was a noticeable blotch of something that looked remarkably like chunky peanut butter on her skirt, she reevaluated her perception of Noreen as a slave to fashion.

"Noreen, let me introduce you to my parents and Justin's father, Stanfield Bigelow," she offered, looking around to draw them closer. They all inched forward. Justin, on the other hand, appeared to have been grabbed by the manager of the softball team and was involved in a heated discussion. Lilah focused on their little group and supplied everyone's name.

Stanfield and Walt pretended they weren't the least bit enamored.

Daphne thrust out her hand. "I've got to tell you. I love your shoes."

God bless her mother, Lilah mused.

"So you're marching, too, I see?" Daphne went on.

"With my husband's class." Noreen pointed toward the banner for the class of '72 farther ahead in the pack of people. "I'm not a Grantham alum, but I realize the importance of tradition in knitting society together, which is just a fancy way of saying I tolerate Conrad's eccentricities," Noreen said conspiratorially.

Daphne nodded. "So, you're Conrad Lodge's…" She hesitated.

"Third wife," Noreen supplied for her. "And hopefully

his last. I tell him that any more, and he'd need a score-card to keep track. Don't you agree, Mimi?"

Mimi was busy looking around, her eyes darting close to the ground. "Forget scorecards. Where's Brigid? You didn't—?"

"Leave her with her father for a change? Yes, I did. I decided he needed the experience of providing parental supervision."

"You trust him?" Mimi's mouth formed a large O.

"There are times as a parent when you just have to take a leap of faith," Noreen replied.

Mimi's eyes widened. "Well, you certainly have more faith than I do." She searched the crowd again before turning back. "You know, why don't I just amble over and make sure he doesn't let her get lost when this thing gets going? To suddenly feel all alone and afraid is the scariest thing when you're a child."

Lilah glanced at Noreen, then at her mother. Clearly they were all thinking the same thing.

"You're probably right. Why don't you go check the situation out, then?" Noreen suggested.

They watched Mimi charge through the mass of people.

"You're a kind woman, even if Mimi doesn't give you credit for it," Lilah noted, turning back to Noreen.

"It's not always about the credit, is it?"

Justin stepped over to join them. "Where's Mimi off to? Right when The Parade is about to start, too."

"She's off to rescue her sister from their father," Lilah answered, only half in jest.

"I know the feeling," he mused and slanted his eyes in the direction of Stanfield.

Lilah slipped her arm inside his. "Hey, stick by me. I'll protect you."

"My hero," he crooned and gripped his chest dramatically.

Lilah bit back a smile.

Noreen stuck out a manicured hand. "Noreen Lodge. And you must be Justin Bigelow. I guess Vivian was right."

Lilah was pleased to see that Justin didn't overtly salivate. Then she latched onto Noreen's words. "What's that about Vivian?"

The Parade began gradually moving. Scooters with the octogenarians led the way.

"Oh, nothing." Noreen shook her head. She stepped closer, raising her voice to be heard over the sound of a Louisiana-style jazz band. It had swung into action with a rousing rendition of "Won't You Come Home Bill Bailey." "To tell you the truth, I purposely left my daughter with Conrad because there was something I needed to discuss with you, and I thought, why wait? After all, we're captive members in this whole thing for at least an hour."

"It's a private matter?" Lilah asked. She was confused and not totally sure if she was prepared to hear about the complicated machinations of the Lodge clan.

"Personal *and* professional, I suppose you could say."

Lilah looked at Justin. "Do you mind? It might be better if this was a two-way conversation?"

He made a mock cry of despair. Then he planted a quick kiss on the top of her head when she growled. "Oh, all right. Don't get all worked up. Just remember. I'll be thinking of all the ways you can repay me afterward for entertaining our parents the entire time." He squeezed her hand to his chest before letting go and joining the others.

Lilah flashed a smile at his retreating figure, taking

in his loose gait and the easy sway of his shoulders—
and the way others from their class naturally seemed to
gravitate to him.

"He has this sort of golden glow about him, doesn't
he?" Noreen observed.

Lilah glanced over and saw her watching Justin, too.

Then the striking redhead cleared her throat. "But
enough about fantasy." She focused on Lilah. In her own
way, she seemed oblivious to the stares she also generated.

There was that word again—*fantasy*. Okay, so being
back in Grantham with all these classmates reliving
their glory days, and meeting Justin again and sharing…
well…sharing whatever…wasn't part of her normal routine. But what was routine about her life? Wasn't it more
that what had happened over the past couple of days was
not so much living a fantasy as following a fortuitous
path in life? Her life?

Noreen continued, interrupting Lilah's inner debate.
"I want to talk about reality—a very real reality."

CHAPTER TWENTY-SIX

PRESS LOUNGED ON MATT'S BED and listened as his friend recounted the conversation he'd had with his parents the previous night about working for Lilah in Congo.

And he thinks he has problems? Press couldn't help thinking. But he checked himself from laying his woes on Matt. This wasn't about one-upmanship on stuff that had recently gone down, even though a not-so-little voice in his head screamed, *Me. What about me?*, making for a whopper of a headache.

So he rubbed his forehead and listened, glancing around the room while he kept an ear to the conversation. Matt's bedroom in his family's small but historic cottage had a slanted ceiling that always reminded Press of some Parisian garret. Only instead of looking out on Notre Dame Cathedral, the small dormer windows afforded a view of the pine trees on the heavily wooded property deep in the country.

And finally, when Matt finished his rambling recap—a sure sign that he was upset—Press searched for something positive to say to his friend. "Listen, it doesn't sound like it's all bad. Didn't you say they thought it was a great opportunity? I mean, it gives you something to work with." He picked up a pillow from the bed and started to toss it in the air. It was some needlepoint-y thing. It looked kind of like a medieval tapestry with this stag in profile—not at all Matt's style. But his friend had once explained how it was a present from a friend of his stepmom's, and Katarina—his stepmom—had apparently thought it was "magnificent," to use her word. And since Matt thought Katarina practically walked on water, who was he to argue?

We should all have such stepmoms, Press thought.

"Yeah, they were excited, but their 'criticisms' as you put it, seem pretty insurmountable to me," Matt shot back. "Like, how am I going to convince them that traveling to a potentially dangerous place isn't all that dangerous?" He nervously swiveled his desk chair back and forth.

"I thought you were going to tag along with some people from that doctors organization?"

"I told them that, but they seem to think that's not good enough. They think that because I'm not officially part of their organization, they wouldn't feel directly responsible for me."

"So basically what you need is a chaperone, right?" The pillow hit the ceiling and ricocheted across the floor. Press got up to rescue it.

Matt shook his head in disgust. "It's like they think I'm some kind of baby. It's not like I haven't gone away to college on my own. And, geez, when I was still living with my mom, *I* was the one who had to take care of her and do everything until she died."

Press didn't say anything. He walked over to Matt and tossed the pillow at his chest. And because Matt was Matt, it bounced off and he only grabbed it as it tumbled down his legs.

"So, say their objections are unreasonable."

"I just did."

"So maybe you don't agree, but maybe also you

shouldn't object? Maybe you should try to think of some-one suitable to accompany you?" Press suggested.

"Know any nannies who want to go to Congo for the summer, no expenses paid?" Matt asked sarcastically.

"Not offhand. But I do know someone who knows more than a thing or two about nannies."

Matt pricked up his ears.

"My old man."

THE PARADE WENDED ITS way at a snail's pace through campus, finally passing the newest residential college, which had been built to mimic the older academic Gothic buildings. Then the marchers began to trudge uphill by the smaller gymnasium before filing through a wide arch that heralded the arrival at the oldest part of the campus. Up ahead loomed the main administration building. With a brace of sculptured lions flanking the entrance, the stately stone edifice had once housed the Continental Congress during some of the bleaker moments of the Revolutionary War.

"I hear what you're saying," Lilah said finally as they reached the green. All through the march upward and onward, Noreen had presented her proposal to Lilah. And Lilah had listened, only occasionally asking questions. At first she'd been surprised, even irritated that some-one would want to horn in on what was more than just her livelihood. But then she found herself intrigued, even impressed, and guiltily, maybe even a little relieved. Still, that didn't mean she was about to commit to anything.

"And I must say, you've clearly given it a lot of thought," Lilah continued. "It's just that—"

Her phone started to ring.

"Could you excuse me a minute?" She reached into the side pants pocket of the ridiculous outfit and glanced at the screen on her cell phone. She recognized Matt's number. "Hey, what's up?" she asked. She had taken a real shine to the earnest young man from Yale. In a way, he reminded her of her own dorky self at that age.

"I spoke to my parents," he said.

"And?" She listened as he explained the situation. "Right, I understand their concerns," she responded. "But you can assure them, I would never put you in harm's way. You know, maybe it would be a good idea if I talked to them directly—to explain in more detail what we'd be doing. I know that I can definitely use the extra hand in the operational headquarters because I'll be stuck here for a while. And did I tell you about the computer help I'll need?"

"No problem. Word, PowerPoint, Excel, MATLAB. I know all sorts of programming that could be useful for organizing and analyzing information."

"That's great, even if you've already lost me." Lilah chuckled. "But more important, I think it'll be good for Sisters for Sisters to get a fresh pair of eyes on the organization, and your education and enthusiasm are nothing but fresh."

"I just hope I can live up to your expectations," Matt said. "And as for speaking to my parents, I think it's definitely necessary. Even though they both were impressed with what you do, they're worried the work is too dangerous. I'm not a little kid and I'm not planning on doing anything stupid, but they don't seem to understand that."

Lilah smiled. He actually sounded pretty young. It was a difficult age—walking a tightrope between adulthood and adolescence. "No, they're just being good parents," Lilah reassured him. She looked around, as if searching for a solution to the problem.

Noreen, who had discreetly tried to appear as if she wasn't listening, lowered her chin. "Problem?" she asked.

Lilah nodded.

"Anything I can do?"

And then it hit Lilah. Maybe, just maybe... She held up her hand, index finger extended, to hold Noreen's attention for a moment. But first she addressed Matt. "Listen, I think I have an idea that could do the trick. But I need to hammer out the details. Could you give me a little while to get back to you?"

"Sure. You bet." Matt sounded hopeful. "However long you want."

She smiled at his eagerness. "Don't worry. I won't keep you hanging for too long. I promise to get back to you today." Then she said goodbye and hung up.

Lilah slipped her phone back in her pocket and quickly glanced over her shoulder. Her parents had been adopted by a multigenerational family who were a startling vision in orange and black. And she caught a glimpse of Justin trailing next to his father. He had a slightly pained look despite the smile on his face. He seemed to sense her attention, and lifted his chin. The smile widened. She grinned back, almost stumbling on the irregular flagstones of the campus walkway as the procession passed through the college's wrought-iron gates to Main Street.

She righted herself and turned back to Noreen, who had no trouble navigating the path with her extreme footwear. "I think your proposal has a lot of merit. And from what you've just told me about your childhood experience in Africa, your schooling and international financial experience, you certainly have a business background that far exceeds mine."

"I don't mean to overstate my employment experience, though," Noreen qualified.

"No, I get it. It sounds like you have the necessary professional exposure and have kept up your contacts in important organizations. Truthfully, the prospect of gaining your insight into establishing an endowment, as well as financial planning—not to mention Vivian's promise of support—is all pretty incredible. But probably most important, I think your enthusiasm, your fervor for Sisters for Sisters is genuine. And it comes from something rooted deep within you."

Noreen stumbled.

So she wasn't immune, Lilah thought. Then she went on. "And you're right, the project *has* reached a threshold. It's gained enough attention that more—a lot more—people are taking an interest. I mean, I know we're small potatoes compared to other organizations, but I don't think I'm being too full of myself to say we have made an impact on the lives of some women and their children."

"I wouldn't be interested in joining your organization if I didn't think you had. Nor would Vivian have expressed interest if she didn't believe in it, too—she's very picky where she chooses to donate her money," Noreen interjected. "And let me make it clear, I firmly believe that it is *your* organization. It's not as if I want to take it over—only participate as effectively as I can to maximize and potentially expand on all the good things you've already done."

Lilah paused to say the next bit carefully. She rubbed her hand over her mouth. "To tell you the truth, your interest in the organization couldn't have come at a better time. Between you and me, I've been feeling burned-out—guilty that I don't seem to have the same drive that I had early on. But still, I'm not ready to walk away from the project. Not by a long shot. How can I?" She stared at Noreen as she kept pace with the crowd.

"I'm not asking you to," Noreen assured her. "I'm offering to shoulder some of the burden."

It was one thing to mentor Matt for the summer, but quite another to take on a full-time partner. Lilah pondered her decision when the pace of the march came to a standstill. Up front, a band started playing the Grantham fight song. Voices young and old joined in to sing the lyrics. On the sidewalk in front of the shops, crowds gathered, waving banners and cheering. The smell of caramelized sugar permeated the air from a cotton candy vendor who was set up in front of the town's movie theater. A light breeze carried the scent, making the mild day that much more enticing.

The song reached the chorus, and as one, the alums raised and lowered an arm as they belted out, "Huzzah for Grantham U. Huzzah for Grantham U."

Lilah found herself involuntarily raising and lowering her right arm in time to the music. "If we go ahead with this, we'll need to draft an agreement with a lawyer, of course." She raised her voice over the din.

"Of course," Noreen shouted back. Ever in tune with the proper protocol, she, too, went through the hand motions like it was some light aerobic exercise.

Lilah thought some more as the old school spirit soared in slightly off-key fashion. Then she spun around, and cupping her hands around her mouth, shouted to her mother that she would join her in a few minutes.

Daphne nodded, but kept on with her enthusiastic hand motions, and being a natural overachiever, she raised and lowered both arms.

Lilah chuckled under her breath, then turned back to Noreen. She reached out and tugged her out of the street and away from the marchers. They ended up next to a low wall that bordered the university library. "Okay, it's like this. I agree."

"You agree so soon?" Noreen seemed stunned.

A first, Lilah figured. "Yes, but on one condition." She still had to raise her voice to be heard. "That it'll be on a trial basis, for your sake as well as mine. I think it's only fair that you really get a sense of what this all could mean to you. First, have you ever been to Congo?"

Noreen shook her head.

Lilah leaned in close. "Then you need to go there in person. That way you can see if, indeed, this is a cause you can put your heart and soul into—that you can commit to it despite the inevitable hassles and disappointments that I guarantee *will* come up—regularly. That way you can decide if it's worth the investment—financially and emotionally."

"That seems reasonable."

All of a sudden the music stopped and cheering erupted. Noreen waited for The Parade to start going again before she finished. "As I was trying to say earlier, I may not be prepared for everything from the start, but I like to think that I am up to the challenges."

"You might well be. I have no doubt. But what about your family?" Lilah pointed over her shoulder toward the marchers. "You have a little girl? And even though you'll probably spend most of your time here in the States—in fact, Grantham is probably as good as any place since most of the meetings and communications are online—there'll be times when you'll have to travel. Are you prepared to leave your daughter, even for a short while?"

Noreen pursed her lips. "I haven't talked directly to Brigid about it since I didn't want to get her involved until I knew one way or the other how you felt. But I know she knows how much I love her, and I know she'll be proud of the work I'll do. The hard part will be convincing her she can't come along."

"And who would take care of her while you're away?"

"I've already spoken to Conrad and Mimi about helping to pick up the slack. I think it might be time and actually good for both of them."

"Mimi? Really?" Lilah blinked. "So that's why she had to rush home last night?"

"Yes, I wanted to discuss it with her up front," Noreen confirmed.

"And she's okay with it? And your husband?"

"I'm not sure *okay* is the best word. Both of them were immediately imagining all these horrendous scenarios of what could go wrong, but they'll get over it. I promised I would leave detailed instructions, not to mention backup systems in the form of friends, a list of babysitters and even my mom. And while Congo certainly isn't around the corner, I presume I'll still have satellite phone communication. Besides, I'll let you in on a secret. Sometimes I think it's good for people not to be in constant touch. That way they're forced to rise to the occasion and realize they can muddle through all on their own. I know it did me the world of good when I arrived here all by myself."

Noreen had thought it all out, that was for sure, Lilah realized. She was smart. She was tough and caring at the same time. *And* she was realistic.

What had Justin said last night? *Was it only last night?* She swallowed. Yes, it was only last night when he talked about being open to good things happening.

She lifted her head and saw Justin wave over the heads of her classmates and their families, indicating where they were for her to catch up. She waved back in return.

"I guess we need to get a move on," she said, turning to Noreen. "But before we do, let me ask you one more question. What do you think about coming on board with Sisters for Sisters sooner rather than later? Actually traveling to Congo in the next couple of weeks?"

Noreen cocked her head. "I'm listening."

"Then let me fill you in on the phone call I just had with Matt."

CHAPTER TWENTY-SEVEN

"WHAT'S THAT YOU SAID, Father?" Justin asked, turning back to face Stanfield. He had been looking where Lilah had stepped out of The Parade with Noreen. "Sorry, I didn't hear."

"Yes, I can see that your attention is elsewhere," Stanfield said.

Justin wasn't sure if his father was being critical, but he probably was—knowing his father. But for once Justin let it go. And why? Because of the love of a good woman. Originally, he'd hoped for a carefree weekend involving a trip down memory lane, and what he had got was so much more—he was sure of it. Now he just had to convince Lilah.

So, with only half an ear, he listened to his father talk about his research—and with the other half and the lazy smile on his face, he contemplated how good life could be. All right, he'd only just renewed his friendship with Lilah. And, okay, it was all happening pretty quickly. *But sometimes you just know,* he told himself.

Justin had never been in love before. Oh, he'd had a secret crush on the *idea* of Lilah Evans, but that was different than the real deal. And after last night, really starting with their conversation last evening, he felt they'd connected in a way that was so close—so right.

If he could just buy a little more time. Convince her how great it would be to run her nonprofit from

Grantham, for instance. He wouldn't insist on a permanent move. Even *he* knew that suggestion was premature. But maybe, if she was in the U.S. anyway, organizing fundraising runs or talking to other people, did it really matter where she was staying? Couldn't she do all that over the phone or via email? And if she needed to go into New York City, wasn't it an easy hour train ride?

Speaking of New York City, he couldn't wait to introduce Lilah to Roberta. He had this feeling they'd hit it off right away.

He adopted a certain bounce to his step and for a change Justin actually felt magnanimous toward his father. He might even listen to the old man—especially because Justin thought he heard mention of his mother.

"Mother?" Justin repeated.

"Yes, I know I should tell her, but I just don't have the heart." His father seemed genuinely downcast.

"Are you ill, Father?"

"No, no, nothing like that. It's your sister."

"Penelope's ill?" To Justin, Penelope had always seemed like one of those impervious people—impervious to germs or bodily mishaps like broken arms or stubbed toes. He sometimes wondered if she were also impervious to affection, both giving and receiving.

"No, thank goodness. Though for her, this is perhaps worse," Stanfield said philosophically.

"I'm sorry. I'm not following you." Maybe he'd been wrong about Penelope's lack of human attraction? Maybe someone she'd grown close to was unwell?

"She didn't get tenure."

A sick friend? What was he thinking? Not getting tenure meant that Penelope was effectively fired from her faculty job. They might give her a year's grace period to let her look for another post, but the meteoric rise of her career had come to a crushing halt.

"She called me at the American Academy in Rome, where we've been staying while on sabbatical. Apparently the decision came down in early spring and she'd tried to fight it, but was unsuccessful. That's why I'm concerned about your mother. I haven't told her, and she's still in Italy, blissfully unaware of the development. Naturally, she'll be devastated."

"I imagine that Penelope's the one who's devastated," Justin observed. And he meant it. To say that they had never been close was an understatement, but she was still his sister.

"You're right, of course. It never occurred to her that this could possibly happen. True, her book on Catullus has yet to come out, but then she's such a perfectionist, she didn't want to rush it," his father said matter-of-factly. "In fact, the whole Reunions and meeting with the trustee turned out to be a handy excuse for me to come back here. I couldn't let her be alone in this moment of failure." He looked at his son. "She flies in on Tuesday, you see."

Justin tried not to think about all the failures he had experienced growing up. Never once had his father offered a shoulder to cry on. "Bigelow men don't cry," he could imagine him saying.

Stanfield stopped. Their fellow marchers streamed around them. He bent his head low. "She's not strong like you, you see," he said with a certain quaver in his voice.

Justin coughed out a laugh. "Not strong? Penelope could bite through steel if she thought it would help her academic career. Knowing her, she probably has."

"But she's never failed before, don't you see? You of all people must understand?"

"Excuse me?" he said, offended. "I'm supposed to empathize because I'm such a failure myself?"

"I never considered you a failure," his father replied quickly.

"Well, it sure felt like it when I was growing up. And the fact that I'm a kindergarten teacher doesn't appear to cut it compared to a chaired professorship at a prestigious university."

"On the contrary, do you know how many people stop me at the supermarket or in the dry cleaners to tell me what a difference you've made in their children's and grandchildren's lives? And several of our junior faculty have told me what a remarkable teacher you are."

Justin couldn't believe what he was hearing. "You've never said anything."

"And as to your...your issues growing up—"

"They weren't issues, Father. I suffered from undiagnosed dyslexia," Justin stated firmly.

"Yes, well, mistakes were made."

Justin noted his father's refusal to accept any responsibility in the matter, which didn't come as a surprise. What was surprising was that his father was talking to him at all. He supposed he should be grateful for these baby steps of progress.

"I will admit that our relationship has never been an easy one," his father continued. "The bond between father and son is complex, going back to the Greeks."

Justin looked to the heavens. *Great. Our dysfunctional relationship viewed through the lens of Greek tragedy,* he thought.

"The way you were big and athletic. I always found it a bit intimidating, you know. And you certainly never seemed to take any notice of what I had to say." Stanfield laughed. Then he cleared his throat. "Yes, you may have experienced failure as a boy, but it toughened you up. Made you into a mature man, a man that any father would be proud of." He nodded his chin curtly.

Justin frowned. "Thank you." He really didn't know what else to say.

"There's one other thing, though." Enough people had moved by that they were caught in the middle of alums from three classes below.

"Yes?" Justin asked.

"I was wondering if you would be the one to talk to your mother. You have a way with people, and somehow coming from you, she might take the news about Penelope better." Stanfield's black-and-orange rep tie fluttered in the breeze.

Justin noticed there was a small spot on the silk.

And he also noticed that for the first time in a long time he wasn't angry with his father. It was like Archimedes shouting, "Eureka!" in the bathtub. His father would have been pleased with the classical reference, he thought with a twisted grin.

And why wasn't he angry? Because now he knew—his father was weak. The reason he hadn't been able to deal with Justin's dyslexia wasn't intellectual snobbism or even disappointment that he had a son who would never live up to his high academic expectations. No, the reason his father had been incapable of offering love and support was because he was scared.

No, Justin wasn't angry. He was sorry. Sorry for the inevitable anxiety and disappointment that life must bring to his father on a regular basis.

"Sure, Father," he said in the end, "I'd be happy to talk to Mother."

CHAPTER TWENTY-EIGHT

THE UNIVERSITY'S BASKETBALL arena was the location for the awards ceremony that followed The Parade. Even with temporary carpeting covering the hardwood floor and the array of tables festooned with white linen and china, the large, high-ceilinged space still looked like an indoor sports center.

Lilah was expecting rubber chicken, and she wasn't disappointed.

But everything else at the ceremony was pleasantly... well...wonderful. It was so great to see her parents and how happy they were. They were seated at the head table with President Forsgate, Vivian Pierpoint, Mimi, Stanfield Bigelow—a seating arrangement that Lilah found somewhat mysterious—and Justin. Of course, Justin.

She hadn't needed to change the order of the place cards to make sure he was next to her. Vivian had taken care of that she noticed as they approached the table.

"I want to hog Stanfield all to myself, so I switched Justin's card with mine," she had said conspiratorially to Lilah. "Somehow I didn't think you'd mind." She waggled her eyebrows.

"No problem," Lilah had responded, thanking the gods on high.

What could be better than listening to your mother give Mimi advice on raising young children—and Mimi actually listening? Or your father and President Forsgate finding out they have mutual friends in the aerospace industry? But the best of the best was having Justin here with her.

"Have I told you how terrific you look?" he said, leaning into her shoulder.

"I bet you tell that to every girl in a ninja outfit." She smiled.

He smacked his forehead with the back of his hand. "Oops! You found me out."

She kicked him playfully under the table and looked up and nodded as a waiter came by asking if she wanted coffee with dessert. This being Grantham, there was a heavy orange theme to the menu, and dessert was a pumpkin mousse. Just like the luncheon the other day, she passed it on, this time to her father.

"Always thinking of others," Walt said, taking the plate. He winked at her before digging in.

Then the president stood and took his place at the raised podium. "Hello, everyone. It's time for the festivities to begin, but please don't stop eating."

Walt did, though, a measure of his love for his daughter. He placed his hand atop Daphne's and beamed in pride as President Forsgate ran smoothly through his opening remarks.

"As you all know, Lilah Evans, class of 2002, is our Distinguished Alumni Award winner this year." There was a thunderous round of applause from the gathering.

"Lilah truly embodies Grantham's motto of service for the greater good. In fact, her example has already inspired another member of our community." The president raised his arm and pointed to Vivian.

"In honor of her senior paper advisor, Vivian Pierpoint has endowed the Stanfield Bigelow Award to be given yearly to an outstanding senior to carry out an international project that will benefit everyone. Vivian and Stanfield are here today. If you could rise."

Vivian rose and looked totally comfortable taking a bow. She needed to encourage Justin's father to rise, however. "You, too, Professor. President Forsgate knew that you especially would appreciate the goal of the prize."

Stanfield looked totally flabbergasted. "Maybe the man understands what Grantham is about after all," he begrudgingly admitted.

"Congratulations, Father." Justin turned to him. "You are a gifted teacher. I didn't come by my skills in a vacuum, you know. Now it's time to take a bow." He helped him up by the elbow.

"That was very magnanimous," Lilah said softly to Justin.

"No, it's the truth." He looked at Lilah and breathed in. "None of us are perfect, even our parents."

"I don't care what you say. I know better." She reached for his hand and squeezed it. And then she saw the president lift a plaque and heard him invite her to join him on the podium.

This time it was Justin who squeezed her hand.

Lilah marched up the stairs to the podium, taking in all the clapping and excited cheers.

"This is overwhelming," she said to the president.

He passed her the plaque, and they stood together while the cameras clicked and flashed. Finally, when the applause had died down, he reached under the lectern and spoke into the microphone once more. "Before I turn over the podium, I have been given strictest instructions to inform everyone that the annual Tenth-Reunion-Graduating Class softball game took place yesterday, and lo and behold, the class of 2002 won."

There were a few catcalls and foot stampings.

"And as you all know, as part of the tradition the winning team gets to keep the Tail for the year. In honor of their 2002 classmate, the team has decided to give Lilah Evans the honor of being the Tail bearer."

President Forsgate raised his hands and displayed the tail for all to see. More cheers erupted, and they grew louder when Lilah gamely allowed him to place it on her head.

Then it was her turn to speak. "I never thought I'd be given an award dressed like this. Thank you." She glanced over at the president and straightened the cap. He acknowledged thanks with a tip of his head. Then she turned to the crowd and began speaking.

"Thank you, all of you, for coming and giving me this honor. Of course, I'd like to thank my parents, who are here today." She indicated with her hand. "And my good friend and fellow classmate Mimi Lodge. Without the TV coverage, Sisters for Sisters wouldn't be enjoying the success that it has today."

Mimi waved, then crossed her arms and leaned back in her chair.

Lilah gazed at Justin. "And I want to especially thank another classmate, Justin Bigelow, who spearheaded my nomination. Without his efforts, none of this would have been possible. We haven't been in touch since graduation, yet seeing him again has reminded me that the ties formed in college withstand time and distance. That even though people change—which sometimes is a good thing, believe me—the bonds are still strong. I was reluctant to come back because it had been so long and I had been out of touch with the university, but I realize now that wherever I am, I will always have a home in Grantham and be part of the Grantham family."

This last statement particularly resonated among the audience members since, naturally, it was exactly the sentiment behind the Reunions weekend.

"Finally—" and here, Lilah took off the Tail because she didn't want to diminish what she was about to say "—I can't go without mentioning the brave women of Congo—my sisters and, I hope, soon to be more of yours." She scanned the crowd for Noreen. Conrad had booked a table with some classmates, and when Lilah caught her eye, Noreen smiled warmly.

Lilah gripped the sides of the rostrum to steady herself. This next bit was not going to be easy. "And now in particular, I'd like to dedicate this award to my good friend, Esther. Let me tell you her story.

"Esther lives in a small village in eastern Congo. She is my age—thirty-two. The rebels, seeking support for their own malicious gain, killed her husband when he refused to join them. They didn't stop there though. They captured one of her sons and they forced him to be a child soldier. She has not seen him in over three years. On another occasion, a rebel group again came to her village, and this time raped her and her ten-year-old and eight-year-old daughters. Then they raped her remaining son. When that was not enough, they hacked off one of her legs and cooked it in a soup pot over the fire in her home. They even tried to make her son eat it. When he refused, they shot him in front of her."

There were gasps from the audience. She could see her mother cover her mouth. Even Vivian, so assured, looked taken aback.

"Yes, it is terrible, but somehow Esther survived. And just three months ago, she danced on a new prosthetic leg that Sisters for Sisters's traveling clinics helped her secure. And when I told her about this award—" Lilah lifted the award, then set it down "—she told me to return to my village of Grantham and accept the honor. And to tell everyone that she is rejoicing in her sister's— *my*—good fortune."

Lilah had to stop and take a breath. She wet her lips and looked out over the crowd of loyal alums. There was silence in the entire hall. Even the waiters stood still, coffee urns in their hands, clearly stunned by Esther's story.

"You may know the adage that people give not so much to causes as to people. So, Esther—" Lilah held up the plaque "—when I see you next, I am bringing you this award. A Grantham University education may have given me the wherewithall to go out and fulfill a dream. But you give me the humility to appreciate what true courage is. Thank you all again."

She lowered the plaque. And the silence continued. Until she went to step down from the podium, at which point the whole place erupted. It could have been a bas- ketball championship with everyone standing, clapping and cheering. President Forsgate insisted she take another bow. Overcome, Lilah bit her lip and tried to make her way back to the table through the phalanx of well-wish- ers and hand shakers.

Finally, she saw her parents, both in tears. They reached out to embrace her.

"My brave, wonderful dear," her normally unflappable mother said, hauling Lilah close to her sturdy chest.

Her father kissed her on the top of her head. He was too moved to speak.

Vivian reached across the table to shake her hand. "I hope more Grantham graduates will touch the lives of others the way you have."

"Well, thank you for your generosity," Lilah said.

Mimi didn't bother to stand on ceremony. When she saw that the crush of people was making it difficult to get around the table, she simply pulled out a chair, stood on it and used it as a stepping stone to walk across the table.

Lilah looked up at her and laughed. "Only you, kiddo."

"Well, if Mohammed won't come to the mountain, the mountain will come to Mohammed." She gave Lilah a fierce hug. "See, it was worth it, right?"

Lilah pulled back and nodded.

Then she frantically looked around for the one person who mattered most at the moment. Justin.

As more people thrust their hands at her, she twisted her head back and forth, spotting him and his father with President Forsgate. It was Stanfield Bigelow's day, too, she realized, recognition of the difference he had made in other's lives.

Smiling and nodding at people in the crowd, she fought her way against the tide and reached Justin's side. She yanked at his arm. "Hey, you. How about letting me get to your father to congratulate him on his honor."

Justin spun around. "Never mind my father. He's getting enough love from the president and all his former students. You're the one who deserves the attention." He pulled her up against his chest. "Answer me one thing. When you said that you found a home in Grantham, did you mean it?"

She nodded eagerly. "I meant it because of you, and... all right...maybe all the silly hoopla of Reunions. But mostly you." She paused, unsure whether or not to continue. "I do have one question."

He cocked his head.

"The Tail? Was that your idea?" she asked.

"Are you mad?"

"Mad? Why would I be mad to have to receive the biggest award of my life while forced to wear an orange ninja costume and a ratty coonskin cap?" And then she couldn't wait any longer. She went on tiptoes and tilted her head. She puckered her lips, but barely scraped his chin. "Ach! You're too tall!"

"Not for some things," he answered. He picked her up, whirled her around and kissed her silly.

And when he eventually put her down, the world was still spinning.

"How long have I got you?" he asked, resting his forehead on hers.

"I'm around for at least two weeks."

"Two weeks?"

"I'll probably have to go back to my place to pick up my mail and get some clean clothes, but basically I've got to stick around for that court hearing for the car accident, remember?"

He looked to the heavens—or more like the upper stands, this being a basketball auditorium. "Thank God for our judicial system."

"More like overzealous Grantham cops."

"Whatever. I'll take it."

She lifted her head. "And I'll take you."

CHAPTER TWENTY-NINE

LILAH AND JUSTIN STOOD on the platform of the Grantham Junction station as the express train pulled away bound for New York. It was Sunday evening around seven, and the parking lot was ghostly empty except for a few couples returning from Broadway matinees and a bevy of taxicab drivers lounging against their cars, hoping for fares.

"It seems like I'm always saying goodbye." Lilah waved, then let her hand drop. "Yesterday it was my parents going back to Washington. Today, Mimi for New York."

Justin put his arm over her shoulder. "Hey, Mimi is coming back in less than two weeks to help take care of Brigid while Noreen is with Matt in Congo. And until she arrived on Friday, you didn't even know your mother would be visiting. So, even though she had to get back to her school, don't you think it was an all-around good thing that she could come at all?"

Lilah stared up at him. "I always wondered what it would be like to know a glass-half-full person, and now I do."

Justin seemed stricken. "Is it irritating?"

Lilah shook her head. "No, immensely comforting." She stood on tiptoe and brushed his lips with hers. Then hand in hand they descended the stairs and ambled to Justin's car.

Earlier in the day, rather than squeeze everyone into Justin's car—despite her mother's pleas that it would be fun—they had used Lilah's rental car to drive to Newark Airport. Afterward, they'd coordinated dropping it off at the agency and driving back to the dorm, where she got her stuff.

"Look at it this way. You have me all to yourself—at least for the rest of the evening and tonight. Tomorrow reality sets in, and I need to go back to work," he said, unlocking her side of the car.

"I'll take whatever I can get." She grabbed his hand and kept him close. "So do you plan to wine and dine me?"

"On a teacher's salary? More like I was going to retrieve a six-pack of beer from my fridge and take it along to the little Mexican restaurant in the shopping center. And then, unfortunately, I need to do my lesson plans for the week because someone who will go nameless has dominated my time all weekend, preventing me from doing any work whatsoever."

She gave him a mock pout. "Already we're falling into a rut. Where did the first bloom of romance go?" Then she nuzzled his neck. "Don't worry. I think it sounds fabulous. Besides, I'm totally backed up on my email, and now that I have the passport information from Noreen and Matt I need to book their tickets and put in for visas for Congo." She ended with a kiss on his jaw. Then she looked up. "Hey, were you paying attention to anything I said?"

Justin shook his head. "Sorry. I heard you mention Congo and I suddenly had this idea. You want to come visit my kindergarten class?"

"Sure, I'd love to."

"How about tomorrow? I have this idea for doing a

whole unit on Africa for the week. You can come in and tell them about the kids in the villages—what they wear and how they live. You've got some photos on your computer, right? Then we can have an activity table where they build a village."

She nodded, though he hardly looked at her.

"And there're all the animals. Fantastic. Perfect for art and a jungle animal science project—where we can also do some word recognition. Not to mention make pictures and write letters to your kids over there, describing their houses and stuff. And of course I'll have to read them parts of Kipling's *The Jungle Book*. And for math—" he seemed to focus on some indistinguishable point "—we can do something to figure out how far away it is." Absentmindedly he reached down and opened her car door. "I have a giant floor map, and we can plot the airplane route or something." He spoke quickly, moving his head up and down.

Lilah stood there with her arms crossed and just looked at him.

It took Justin a few moments to wind down before he noticed Lilah. "I did it again, didn't I? Completely went off in my own little world."

Lilah grabbed his upper arm. He had on an old Grantham Lightweight Crew sweatshirt, and she couldn't help remembering how he looked in college—the same trim and lanky body, but his curly hair had been longer and unruly, and he'd had a perpetual two-day-old beard. He was the same, but not the same. Whichever way, she felt very lucky.

"It's a wonderful little world, and I'd be happy to come to class tomorrow—honored, in fact. I just hope I know how to interact with five-year-olds."

"Don't worry. It's a lot easier than adults—just non-stop."

"Then I better get to bed early tonight, especially if we have to drive into Brooklyn after school tomorrow to get my stuff," she said. She sank down into the passenger seat, by now used to the squeak it emitted. "You remember the plan, right?"

Justin circled the car and folded his body into the driver's seat. "Not to worry. I didn't forget about going to Brooklyn. It'll work out perfectly. That way we can see my mother."

Lilah coughed. "I thought she was in Italy."

"Not that mother—my academic mother—Roberta. She's dying to meet you."

Lilah set her jaw. "Now I'm really beginning to feel the pressure. First your class, next Roberta."

"Don't worry. It'll be a piece of cake," Justin insisted, starting up the engine and putting the car in gear. But before he backed out, he gave her a quick but glorious kiss.

She was left levitating a few inches above her cracked seat.

Then he looked over his shoulder, backed out and shifted to first. He slanted her a sly grin. "We can go to bed early tonight. But do you really think you're going to get a lot of sleep?"

THE NEXT DAY SHE WAS exhausted but exhilarated.

Lilah sat on a pint-size chair, her visitor's badge dangling in front of her, while she helped Noreen's daughter, Brigid, and two other classmates make a hut out of Popsicle sticks, construction paper and library paste. The smell of the glue made her think back to when her mother still taught first grade. When she'd hug her at night before going to bed, she'd have that pleasing, sweet smell on her fingertips.

So far, the kids had figured out how to make the cylinder base, but they were deep in discussion about how to make the roof.

"We need a circle, not a square," Brigid announced, rejecting a dark piece of paper.

"Do you have a compass?" Lilah asked.

"What's that?" another girl with glasses asked.

"It's something you use to draw circles in math class," Lilah explained, trying to remember just how they worked. "It's got a pointy part that you stick in the middle of the paper and then you put a pencil in a holder that's attached to the other end and it goes around in a circle."

"We're not allowed to use pointy things in school," a little boy said. He managed to get the words out despite chewing on the end of the string that went through the hood of his sweatshirt.

"That's a problem, then." Lilah sat back and crossed her arms.

"Did I hear someone say there's a problem?" Justin came over and squatted among the children.

"We need circles to make the roof, but we don't have a campus," Brigid said with a frown.

"You don't have a compass?" Justin repeated without making a big deal about correcting her. "Well, let's think. How else can we make something round?" He put his chin on his hand. "Can you show me something else that's round?"

Immediately, his question generated all sorts of answers, and more students gathered around the table, naming different objects.

"So if we have something round—" Justin picked up

the coffee can of crayons "—how can we make something else round?"

"I know, I know." Brigid clapped. She grabbed the can and put it on a piece of paper, then traced around it with a crayon. It was a wobbly job, but then she held it up for everyone to see.

"It's a circle." "Let me." "I want to make one, too," they shouted.

"The question is—is that the right size circle for the hut?" Justin asked. "Why don't you draw circles of different sizes and see which works best?"

The table became a beehive of tracing and cutting.

But the little girl with glasses tugged on Justin's sleeve. "I want to use a compass, but we can't have pointy things."

"Hm-m-m. Maybe we can make a compass without a pointy thing?" He looked at Lilah. "Suggestions?"

"What about a rubber band and a crayon. One person holds one end…" she ventured.

Justin held up his hand. "Great idea, but not too much advice in advance. Let me just hunt down some rubber bands." He stood. "I know I have some in my desk, but at the front office they have those big ones that would be perfect. Could you watch the kids while I hustle down to get them?"

Lilah wasn't sure of anything, and she raised her eyebrows dubiously.

"C'mon, a Grantham University education ought to be good for something." He clapped to get the class's attention. "Listen up, everyone. I'm just going to get some rubber bands so we can all make compasses. I'll be right back. In the meantime, Ms. Evans will be in charge, but treat her nicely. She's new here."

He winked and headed out the door.

Brigid hugged her arm and looked at Lilah soulfully. "Don't worry. We were all new once. You get over it."

"JUSTIN, IS EVERYTHING all right?" Justin's principal, Frank Gunderson asked, while stationed at the open doorway of his office.

"Frank," Justin said, coming to a halt. He was about to filch some rubber bands from the assistant, who basically would give him anything if he asked nicely. "Everything's fine. Thanks."

Frank stepped toward him, a note of concern still crowding his expression. "You left the children alone?"

"Of course not. They're with our visitor—Lilah Evans, the founder of the international organization Sisters for Sisters and a recent award winner from the university. The class is getting a firsthand glimpse into life in Africa. It's been very educational." If he'd known Lilah's grade point average, Justin would have given that information, as well. He was sure it was stratospheric, and that was just the kind of factoid that his principal found so meaningful.

"Yes, I heard you had a visitor. I was reassured that you followed proper protocol, checking her in."

Justin didn't remind Frank that he always followed proper protocol.

"You sure she's capable of watching the children?" the principal asked. He was the type of person who sweated profusely on his forehead. Justin shouldn't have held it against him.

That was the least of what Justin held against him.

"If she can deal with Congolese rebels, I think she can handle the class for a few minutes. I just came in search of large rubber bands." Justin said the last in the direction of the assistant, who immediately jumped up and went to the locked supply cabinet.

Frank frowned, an indication that he didn't seem to appreciate Justin's sarcasm. "Well, you should get back quickly, but before you go I have something to say that shouldn't take long."

Justin waited.

"I've decided to take over day-to-day control of the curriculum. In particular yours."

"I don't understand?" And he really didn't. He could only take the principal's announcement as a direct assault on how he ran his classroom.

"You should have seen this coming, Justin. We've had this discussion before, or words to that effect. Take this thing of going off on some Africa tangent?" His frown deepened. "It deviates from the standardized kindergarten curriculum. The State exams are at the end of the week, and the other teachers are prepping their students."

Justin counted to ten before he responded. "I'm sure my students will do fine. All the work throughout the year has been excellent preparation. And we will certainly take time to discuss what will be happening during the tests. We will even run through some typical questions—just like we've done sporadically throughout the year. Besides, in terms of using a whole week for last-minute cramming? In my experience, that's not the way to go with kindergarteners. It just makes them uptight."

Frank breathed in noisily. Clearly, he didn't like being crossed. "We'll just have to see. In my case, my mind is made up. From now on, you will provide me with daily lesson plans two days ahead of time that I will review and revise as I see fit. Our school has a reputation for excelling on standardized testing, and as principal I consider it of paramount importance for the welfare of our students."

"Justin?" The assistant pressed a wad of rubber bands in his hand.

"Thanks," he said to her with a smile. "If you'll excuse me then, Frank, I'll get back to my class. And don't worry—you'll have the requisition order for the rubber bands by the end of the day."

Justin didn't bother to wait around. "The welfare of the students, my foot," he muttered angrily under his breath. He recognized a power play when he saw it. Even if his students performed on par with or better than the other kindergartens, Frank would come up with another excuse to take over his class.

There was no way he could remain under these conditions, but given that there were only two weeks left to the school year, it wasn't as if jobs were still around for the choosing—especially in this economy.

He'd wait and figure something out, take the summer to reevaluate and try to land a job in the fall. Anyway, he'd see Roberta tonight, and he would talk to her then. One thing was for sure, though—he wasn't going to say anything to Lilah. He didn't want to burst the blissful bubble the two of them seemed to be operating in now. It was too fragile, too new. He didn't want to jeopardize something that was almost…almost unreal.

"SO, SHE'S A DOLL." ROBERTA snapped a lid on a plastic container of leftover kugel from dinner. Lilah was on the top floor studio with Roberta's husband, Oscar, who had offered to show her the paintings he was currently working on. That meant that Roberta had Justin all to herself.

"Yeah, she's terrific—everything I remembered." Like one of the family, Justin was loading the dishwasher.

"But I thought you said a few days ago that she wasn't the same?"

He looked over while he held a dinner plate. "True, there was a bit of awkwardness when we met, but now that we've gotten past that—it's like going back in time, only more. Look. I get to live out my fantasy." He leaned over and put the plate in the bottom rack.

"And that's good?" She put the leftovers in the refrigerator.

"Excuse me—what man doesn't want to live out his fantasies?"

Roberta laughed as she filled the sink with hot water and dishwashing liquid to clean the pot from the brisket. "Tell me, then, if your dream world's intact, why do I sense there's something wrong with the real one?" She donned rubber gloves and plunged the casserole dish into the soapy water. "It's your principal, isn't it?"

"Yeah, earlier today—he's put the screws to me even more. I was going to talk to you about it if I had the chance."

"So here's your chance."

Justin looked around for any more dirty dishes and spotted a lone wineglass on the dining room table. The ground floor of the house was an open plan, with the living room area up front, the large dining room table, and then an island separating the new kitchen from the back of the brownstone. The tall white walls were covered with Oscar's monumental figurative paintings, and by the front bay window a music stand stood at the ready for when their violinist daughter returned for visits.

He retrieved the goblet and walked back, taking his time to think. "You know, maybe now's not the best time after all. I think I'll mull over the situation a little more."

Roberta rinsed off the pot and put it in the drying

rack. Then she drained out the water. "Well, you know," she said over her shoulder, "I'm always here for you when you're ready."

The sound of footsteps coming down the wooden staircase could be heard.

"See, now wouldn't have been enough time anyway," Justin said. He glanced to the opening from the hallway and waited.

Roberta looked up. "What? You two don't talk about these things?" She sounded perplexed. "It's not good to hide your emotions."

"Yes, yes, I know. It's just…just that I don't want anything to mar the fantasy right now, you know? It's all so new."

Roberta didn't say anything.

When she still didn't respond, Justin looked at her askance. "What? I know you're dying to say something."

Roberta cocked her head as her husband's voice could be heard discussing the portrait hanging in the stairway that he'd done more than twenty-five years ago of a gardener in the Tuileries in Paris. Then she directed her gaze at Justin. "You want to know what? Well, all I can say is I'm not the artist in the family—not by a long shot—but I have learned over the years how to be a good observer. And it seems even to me that the most creative things— painting, music, literature, even life—deep down, are based on reality. Unvarnished reality. Fantasies? They tend to disappear over the long haul."

CHAPTER THIRTY

THERE WAS NOTHING LIKE municipal court to dispel any sense of fantasy. Lilah had spent most of the past two weeks since Reunions in the safe cocoon of Justin's apartment, keeping up on business, but also getting the chance to read a book and go for a run, just for fun. She hadn't wanted anything to mar the perfection, and had even been a bit distracted when she'd gotten a call three days ago from Mimi, who'd arrived just before Noreen and Matt took off for Congo. Her friend had wanted to get together for dinner. If Mimi had been put out that she'd had to share her friend with Justin, she'd done a good job of keeping it under wraps.

When she'd offered a good-night hug after pizza, Mimi had whispered, "I'm so happy you're happy—really."

And Lilah had relaxed. Until today.

Grantham Borough Hall was located at the end of Main Street, a sixties stone box elevated to some grandeur by placing it up a shallow span of marble steps. In front was a public sculpture commemorating some Revolutionary War heroes, a massive bas-relief that romanticized and sanitized the action. Below, a tasteful border of perennials offered abeyance, and a wide lawn stretched to the road. Grantham residents might have to pay for water and garbage pickup, and their fire department was strictly volunteer, but for their local property taxes they got a picture-perfect municipal space.

Justin was able to accompany Lilah to the afternoon session on the Thursday because school was only a half day, in anticipation of graduation on Friday.

They passed through the metal detector outside the entrance to the courtroom, then went inside, circling around a false wall that partitioned off the rows of seating.

They grabbed two seats toward the front, and Lilah scanned the room. In front on a raised dais was the seating for the judge, recording secretary and various members of the police department. A low fence separated that area from several tables. Again, there was another policeman—Lilah recognized the younger eager-beaver cop in her case—as well as what appeared to be the prosecutor. He had a stack of files in front of him and a line of people waiting to speak to him.

The rows of seats were more than two-thirds full with stunned-looking people, most holding a summons. Some were chatting softly with well-dressed men sitting next to them. Municipal Court appeared to know no boundaries when it came to the type of people there: young, old, poor, well-to-do, white, black, Asian, moms and business-types. Lilah felt as if she was in an alien world, that even though she spoke the same language and nominally knew her rights, she didn't quite know the rules.

Then she saw the older man who hit her car standing in line to talk to the prosecutor. Next to him was a younger woman—the family resemblance was unmistakable—dressed in a business suit and carrying a briefcase.

"I wonder if I should have gotten a lawyer," she said over her shoulder to Justin.

"Why? You were the one who was rear-ended. For the

life of me, I can't even figure out why they wanted you to come," he said. He was content to stretch out his legs and close his eyes after an intense morning of teaching. Justin had explained that by the end of the school year, the kids were totally wired, ready for summer vacation to begin.

Lilah continued to note the crowd. Her attention came to rest on an unexpected face. She blinked, then nudged Justin. "Hey, isn't that Press Lodge sitting to the left, at the end of our row?" she whispered and nodded in Press's direction.

Justin glanced over his shoulder. "That's him."

Lilah leaned forward to stare at Mimi's half brother again. He had on a blue blazer, standard white shirt and tie. His jaw was set rigidly, his eyes darting around the front of the room.

"Try not to be so obvious, okay? It doesn't look like it's the kid's best day," Justin admonished her.

Lilah sat up straight. "You're right. I wonder what's wrong. And did you happen to see the two people sitting next to him? I swear they look familiar."

Justin was looking straight ahead and didn't respond.

Lilah nudged him again with her elbow.

He ducked his head down. "Oh, all right." He reached for the bottom ribbing of his crewneck sweater and pulled it over his head, leaving his wrinkled Oxford cloth shirt exposed. He twisted around to lay it over the back of his chair and sneaked a peek. Then he straightened around and said softly to Lilah, "Those are the owners of Hoagie Palace—Angie and Sal."

"You're kidding me." Lilah went to turn around again, but Justin rested his hand on her leg. In honor of going to court and not completely sure what it would entail, she'd dressed for the occasion in her dark blue pants suit.

"Okay, I get it," she said at the feel of his hand. "I just hope he isn't in any real trouble."

"I doubt it," Justin responded. "If he were, don't you think his father would have come, too?"

"I CAN'T THANK YOU ENOUGH for being here," Press said to Angie. Her husband, Sal, sat on Press's other side. "Coming here in the middle of the afternoon must have been a big inconvenience."

Angie patted his leg. "You're family. Family always comes first," she assured him. "And it's good you got the lawyer like Sal told you. You should never come to court without a lawyer." An old man, sinewy trim, in a well-cut blazer and orange-and-black rep tie sat on Sal's other side.

"Yeah, I got his name from some other members of Lion Inn. Apparently, Mr. Costen has a lot of experience defending Grantham students in cases around town." Press leaned forward to speak with the attorney. "I brought my checkbook with me to pay you," he said.

"No need until this is all over, Press." Bruce Costen gave him a friendly smile.

"And put that checkbook away," Angie scolded him in a friendly way. "We've already been through this. Sal and I will cover you, and then you'll pay us back later on. The city is very expensive, and I don't want you starving in New York this summer on your internship." Her New Jersey accent stretched out the *o* in New York and swallowed the *r*.

"Press, just to bring you up-to-date," Bruce politely interrupted. "I've already met with the prosecutor, given him your résumé and the list of community activities you've participated in. Very impressive, I must say. In my day at Grantham, we didn't do much besides go to class and have a good time." He winked at Sal. "But those were the old days, right?"

Sal nodded philosophically. He sat with his arms crossed, his upper arms bulging in his short-sleeved shirt. Sal didn't do much of the short-order cooking anymore, but he still had a stevedore's body from years of hauling boxes and crates of produce. "Press is a good boy. I still don't think he should plead guilty to the charges just because some punk cop wants to throw his weight around."

"It's a no-win situation, as I explained earlier," Bruce said. "It boils down to his account of the incident versus Press's version, and the court—no matter how unfair it may seem—invariably sides with the police. In any case, I've already worked out a community service deal with the prosecutor, and I'm pretty sure we should be able to waive a fine. This judge is pretty straight. Then, when Press has completed the hours, I'll move to get the whole thing expunged from your record. That way everyone will save face and Press shouldn't suffer any long-term circumstances."

Sal shook his head. "What a way to run a system."

"I'm a little concerned about the community hours if I'm in Manhattan this summer," Press confessed in a low voice.

"You should be able to fit it in on weekends," Bruce reassured him. "And I'll make sure the judge gives you enough time."

As if on cue, the bailiff announced, "Court is in session. Everyone rise for the Honorable Judge Helen Freyman."

There was a general shuffling of feet, some murmurs, and when everyone had sat down again, the judge ran through the procedures and rights. "Luckily, today, we don't have a completely full afternoon docket, so we should be able to get everyone done," the judge announced. She looked to the bailiff, and he called the first case.

Press stared down at his hands. When he'd glanced around the room, he was pretty sure he spotted Mimi's friend Lilah Evans. Great. That was all he needed—to have word get back to his old man. Maybe he could catch her before she left and explain how he wanted to keep this quiet.

Press knew he had screwed up, and he was determined to handle it himself. But when Angie had caught him down in the dumps last week when he'd come in for a hoagie, he hadn't been able to hold back. And being Angie, she'd immediately phoned Sal and they sat down and talked to him. "Yes, it's stupid, Press, but we'll get through this. It will be a good story to tell your grandchildren."

Like he was ever going to have children, let alone grandchildren. Not when he knew how messed up families really were.

And when he'd gotten the name of a lawyer, they'd let him deal with him directly—"It's your responsibility, son," Sal had said. "We're just here for you." In the same way they had insisted on paying the fee, a godsend truly since while Press might come from a well-to-do family, his allowance was miserly at best. "Having to stretch a dollar builds character," his father liked to say. This as he sat in his custom-made suit smoking one of his fancy cigars.

Whatever. Now he sat there and listened as the judge introduced each case, followed by the attorney for the defendant, and then the prosecutor having his say. It was like a well-rehearsed dance, and it would have been even more interesting if he wasn't as nervous as hell.

"I NEVER KNEW YOU COULD argue away a speeding ticket," Lilah said to Justin.

He glanced at her. "You get many speeding tickets?"

"Never."

"Then I don't think you have to worry."

"But why don't they tell you these things? If more people knew, don't you think they'd come to court to get the charges lowered and make sure they didn't get points on their license?"

Justin stared glassy-eyed at the front of the courtroom where the umpteenth traffic case was dispensed of. "I get the feeling more people know than you think," he said.

Press's case was called, and Lilah listened to the proceedings with rapt attention. "Oh, my God, that's the same idiot cop who's made me come to court," she whispered.

Justin looked at her askance. "What did you expect? Grantham is a small town and the police force only so big."

She moved closer. "Poor Press. I can't believe he was charged for kicking a can."

"It's not fair, but nobody ever said the law was fair."

Lilah was shocked. "But it's unjust. I can't believe it. How can you?"

He gave her a jaded look. "This is New Jersey... anything's possible. And students versus the cops in Grantham...well...we all know there's no love lost on either side. If his attorney recommended he plead guilty, he probably thought it was the most painless way to end the whole incident."

"But we're supposed to have a justice system that

other countries look up to. Painless shouldn't be the criterion for decision-making," she protested.

"Well, consider this. At least he can afford a lawyer. A lot of people in this room can't."

Another naive balloon had just burst. "It's eye-opening, that's all I can say." And why wasn't Justin more outraged, she wondered. He seemed to accept what was doled out as a given, accept the rationalizations inherent in the system. If she were Press, she would have pleaded not guilty and argued her case.

PRESS AND HIS LAWYER stood at the railing in front of the judge. Bruce had already explained the events and entered a plea of guilty.

When he finished, the judge looked perplexed. "I'm confused. Is the recycling bin destroyed?" She turned to the officer in question.

"It sustained a crack in the top," he replied formally. Press struggled to keep quiet.

"But it's still in use, then?" she asked again.

Bruce spoke softly to Press, who gave him the information. "Yes, Your Honor, it is."

The judge rested her chin on her hand. She had short curly hair, and beneath her robes she wore a bright pink top. "In any case, Mr. Lodge is still responsible for whatever damage was incurred." She paused before looking at Press's lawyer. "Could you explain one other thing that seems to be absent from the testimony? Was there a reason the police approached Mr. ah—" the judge looked at her paperwork "—Lodge in the first place?" She looked up over her half glasses.

"If it please the court, I think I can shed light on the reason." A magisterial male voice spoke up from the back of the room.

The judge raised her chin. Everyone else turned around to gawk at the source. Press didn't need to turn to know who had spoken.

Conrad stepped forward. "I'm Conrad Lodge III."

"Certainly we all recognize our former mayor," the judge responded.

"And the reason the police were at Lion Inn was because they had brought me there. I was intoxicated and in no shape to drive. I informed them that I'd be able to get a ride from someone in the building. It was quite late, and it was clear that Press had been working very hard all evening. The last thing he needed was to be his father's babysitter."

The judge pressed the tip of her tongue against her top lip, then spoke to the prosecutor. "Do you have a recommendation?"

The prosecutor suggested serving forty community service hours in lieu of any fines or incarceration.

The judge raised an eyebrow. Then she shuffled the papers in front of her and raised her pen. "That all seems more than fair. Can we set a date of six weeks to complete the community service? That would allow us to have the follow-up court appearance on—" she flipped through her calendar "—August 4. That's a Thursday, in the morning?"

She looked up.

Press spoke softly to his lawyer, who turned to the judge. "My client is currently working at an internship in New York City at the American Museum of Natural History, and that is the last week of the program when the participants make their presentations. Is there any way we can move it to a later date?"

"Unfortunately, I will be on vacation from the end of August. But given that the recycling bin in question appears still to be in perfectly fine working order..." She slanted a narrow glance at the policeman involved in the case. He seemed to have shrunk into his swivel chair. "I'm more than happy to have you as his counsel present written documentation on the August 4 date. Do we have agreement?"

Press nodded to Bruce.

"That would be most generous of you, Judge," Bruce said with just the right touch of politeness that could no way be mistaken for sarcasm.

"One other thing, though." The judge lifted her face after she had written down the information and passed it to the court clerk. "Mr. Lodge, Conrad Lodge III, that is?"

"Yes, Your Honor." Conrad stood at attention.

"In light of the fact that you appear to have been involved in the circumstances, I think it only fair that you participate in the community service along with your son. Naturally, the court cannot force you to do so since you were not charged with any crime, but as a gesture of goodwill and as an example of parental responsibility, I highly advise you to take note of the court's suggestion." She waited, putting Conrad on the spot.

Press was ready for some condescending rejoinder, putting the judge in her place. Which was why he was totally surprised when his father said humbly—well, just a bit humbly, "I think that's only fair, Your Honor." Then he turned to Press. "And I mean it."

LILAH COULD HARDLY TAKE it all in. "I wonder how he found out. It looks like Press was as surprised as everyone else—maybe more so."

"I'm sure Mimi will be able to clue you in when we

get out of here." On the sly, he was looking at his emails on his iPhone, frowning.

Press's case ended quickly, and Lilah had been glad that the punishment wasn't too harsh. She watched him turn and approach the couple from Hoagie Palace. The woman was insisting he talk to his father, and she was not taking no for an answer. As a group, along with the lawyer, they left quickly. First thing after she finished here, Lilah would definitely text Mimi.

Then she heard the bailiff call a case, using a name that was familiar to her. She quickly realized it was the name of the man who had rear-ended her rental car. He and his daughter moved forward to the judge, who questioned the man about the events. He muttered something about not really knowing what happened.

Lilah felt a pit in her stomach. If he suddenly started blaming her…

The prosecutor leaped up and explained, as he'd done numerous times that afternoon, that the defendant had pleaded guilty and the charge had been reduced to a fine plus court charges.

The judge nodded as she listened, then glanced at her notes. "I see that there's a Lilah Evans listed, as well?"

Lilah sprang up. "I'm Lilah Evans."

"Would you come forward?" the judge instructed.

Lilah scooted in front of Justin to reach the aisle—he gave her an encouraging smile—and she stood next to the others.

"I gather that your car was the one rear-ended?" the judge read without looking up.

Lilah agreed.

"And you were the one to call the ambulance? No, a passenger in your car?"

"No, I believe it was the defendant's wife. She was in his truck," Lilah answered.

The judge knitted her brows and looked at the man.

His daughter spoke up. "That was my mother. She just got alarmed. There was nothing wrong as it turned out. That's just the way she is," the young woman said, offering a smile.

The judge blinked and nodded her head dubiously. This seemed to be a common reaction on her part, Lilah had noted.

"But, Ms. Evans, you're all right?" the judge asked Lilah.

"Fine, Your Honor."

"Do you have anything further you'd like to say?"

Here was Lilah's opportunity to rail against the gross waste of her time and the taxpayers' money, and the cocksure attitude of the young Grantham policeman who seemed more interested in feathering his arrest record than providing justice and keeping the streets safe. She opened her mouth. And thought about it. But when the words came out it was to say, "No, Your Honor. I think my statement to the police at the time of the accident was complete and accurate. All I can say is that I've learned a lot here today."

The judge handed down the reduced sentence and announced the fine, and after all of Lilah's anxiety and inconvenience, the...whatever it was...was over. She blinked and turned.

Justin rose and collected her shoulder bag. He joined her in the aisle and they headed out to the lobby.

"I was right not to say anything else, don't you think? I mean, it's not like I want the man to suffer. And I think it wasn't fair to make other people wait any longer." She held out her hand for her bag.

Her phone started ringing inside. She fumbled for it and looked at the screen. The number wasn't one she recognized. "Hello."

"Lilah, it's Noreen."

"Noreen." Lilah gave Justin the news with a smile. "What's up? You and Matt got in with no problems?"

"The Air France flight from Paris was pretty much on time and we're at our hotel in the capital, Kinshasa, now. I'm glad you warned me about the faded glory of the place. Frankly, I think you were being generous."

"The sight of dilapidated 1980s concrete high-rises doesn't really do much for tourist brochures. And you got a taxi all right from the airport?"

"Thank goodness you arranged for a representative from your office here to accompany us. The whole taxi–little bus system appears to be a mystery. In fact, calling it a system would be a gross overstatement. Anyway, we even had our first meeting at their office."

"That's fantastic." She covered her other ear to muffle the sound of the people mingling outside the courtroom. "Listen, hold up a minute. I just want to move where it's quieter. I've just finished my court appearance—a total no-brainer and a complete waste of the taxpayers' money. What can I say?"

She pushed open the heavy glass door to the stairwell, trotted down the few steps of the hallway until she reached the outer door. She leaned into the handle to push it open, then found a calm spot away from the parking lot and near the brown stone wall of the municipal building. "So it all sounds like it's going smoothly. Do you have your itinerary set for visiting the villages?"

"Actually, that's what I'm calling about." There was hesitation from Noreen's end of the phone line.

"Oh, no, don't tell me the rains have washed out the

local roads? Sometimes even four-wheel drive vehicles can't get around for days, even weeks."

"Lilah, it's not the roads."

Lilah suddenly felt her excitement fade. She turned to see Justin catching up to her. She leaned against the wall and hugged her middle with her free arm. "What's wrong, then? The usual bureaucratic hassles? Who wants a bribe now?"

"We haven't encountered anything like that. It's the rebels. There've been some new attacks." There was an echo coming across the line, which gave the news a certain surreal quality.

Lilah hugged herself harder. "Please tell me that you and Matt are okay."

"We're fine, absolutely fine. It's not us. It's out in the eastern villages."

"Which villages?" Lilah could feel fear rise in her throat even an ocean away.

Noreen named some villages near Kilembo, including one last one—the one very familiar to Lilah.

"Tell me everything," she insisted.

Noreen gave a detailed account of the bloodshed, including the number of fatalities.

Lilah didn't say anything.

"Lilah? Lilah? Are you still there?" For the first time Noreen's voice was frantic.

"She's dead, isn't she?" Lilah couldn't bring herself to say her friend's name.

"Yes, Esther was one of the casualties."

"I should have been there." Lilah closed her eyes to fight off the tears. For Esther's sake she would not cry. She had to be brave.

"Lilah, there was nothing you could have done. No

one saw this coming. And if anything, you could have been another tragic statistic," Noreen argued.

Lilah rubbed the back of her neck, trying to shut out the pain. "Listen, I'll get the first flight out and join you. Please don't leave the capital before I get there. And, Noreen?"

"Yes?"

"Thanks for calling me right away."

"There was no point in delaying the news. Besides, I thought you might want to hear about the funeral arrangements." Noreen explained the plans, gave the details then said goodbye.

Lilah turned off her phone. She was aware for the first time that Justin had his hand on her shoulder. Only instead of feeling comforting, it was somehow annoying. She turned and faced him.

"There's been some bad news from Congo," she announced to him in businesslike fashion.

"Matt and Noreen?" he asked. Concern was etched in his face.

"They're fine. Still in Kinshasa. No, there were raids in some of the outlying villages. Rebel forces. They killed Esther." She spoke like she was dispassionately reading a telegram.

"Oh, my God, that's terrible." He went to give her a hug, but she retreated.

"While I was here enjoying myself, playing teacher's helper and going to stupid traffic court—instead of doing my job, she was killed."

"You can't possibly think that you're somehow responsible?" Justin asked with a shake of his head. "I mean, that's just crazy. Not to mention outright hubris. You alone can't stop these maniacs."

"Excuse me. Who just preached to me not two weeks

ago how one person can make a difference despite the odds? For that I'll always be grateful."

"Grateful?" he shouted. "You think I want gratitude? I want much more from you. And if you don't know that, then…I'm not sure what's going on here."

"What *is* going on around here, Justin?" She looked at him inquiringly. "What are we playing at? I mean, you can't tell me that you intend to follow me on my travels? You've got your own life, your own job that ties you down."

He rolled his eyes. "I could tell you things about that job, but I told myself I wouldn't."

"Why not? You're afraid that I won't understand?"

"No, it's not that. It's just that I didn't want anything to get in the way of this…this…special moment we were sharing. I mean—" he looked around as if to find the right words "—it was all so good, I didn't want to break the spell, the magic. Back in school, all these years since, you've been my ideal of someone to look up to—idealistic, principled, disciplined, achievement-oriented—a crusader for just causes."

"Who just caved in the face of Judge…whatever her name is." Lilah shook her head.

"Judge Freyman," Justin supplied.

Lilah breathed in deeply. "You know, I don't like what's happening here—to me, to us. This pretend world, like the real one doesn't exist. This compromising."

Justin frowned. "What are you really getting at?"

Lilah swallowed with determination. "I'm saying that Reunions are over. It's time to get on with reality."

"And us?"

"There is no 'us' in the real world."

He paced around in a circle before stopping in front of her. "So you're saying that's it? You're just calling it quits? You're not willing to try to give it a go? Wait out this difficult patch and...and—"

"And what? Wait for good things to happen? Maybe that's just too naive? After all, didn't you say that was the advice of children? I mean, what do they know about the real world? Good things don't always happen in the real world. Just ask Press." She pointed toward the front door where Press had exited. "Or ask Esther."

Justin narrowed his eyes. "Ah, the trump card. The pathos of your work."

"Are you blaming my work now for our...our..."

"Relationship," he supplied. Again.

"Okay, for want of a better word, *relationship*. Are you blaming my work for the end of our relationship? Because if you are, that has a certain déjà vu quality about it. Let me see." She tapped her chin melodramatically. "That's right. Didn't you criticize your old roommate and my ex—Stephen—for using the exact same rationale when he broke off our engagement?"

"I'm not Stephen and that's not what I meant about your work," he said, his voice barely audible. "Of course Esther's death is tragic, and I know how close you were. But it still doesn't justify running away—even for a good cause. Dammit, Lilah, I love you. And I think you love me, too, if you'd only admit it. We just need time."

"Which is something I don't have at the moment. I need to collect my stuff and find out the train schedule and catch the first plane to Congo. I want to be there for Esther's funeral."

"And after that?"

"I can't think after that right now," she answered stubbornly.

"And what am I supposed to do?" he asked. "Sit around and wait for your call?"

It was on the tip of her tongue to say, "Why don't you fly with me?" But she didn't say it. If he couldn't figure it out, couldn't take the bull by the horns, jump up and down and declare he was willing to fight for her—show some outrage at the world instead of—

She growled. "That's so bloody like you to talk about something like sitting around and waiting. It's just so passive. I'm not surprised your bully of a principal picks on you, you know. For that matter, maybe your aversion to testing is because it puts the kids—but mostly you—on the spot. So much nicer just to live in denial—the same way you avoided facing down your dyslexia in college by partying. Or the way you still let your father get to you. Why don't you just tell him what a rotten job he did as a parent and then move on, huh? No, because that would require a confrontation, and you don't do confrontations. You'd rather feel sorry for yourself."

Justin looked down and shook his head. Finally, he raised his chin and stared at her solemnly. "I guess there's nothing more to say." He fished his car keys out of his pocket. Then he gave her one more steely eyed gaze.

"What?" Lilah asked.

"You still haven't answered my question."

And she never did.

CHAPTER THIRTY-ONE

One week later

OF COURSE SHE LOVED HIM.

She didn't talk about it to anyone in Congo. She'd spent all of her energy just to get to the village for Esther's funeral, where she hugged everyone and everyone hugged her. Where she grieved for the loss of her dear friend who had been so brave. And while she worried what would happen to her children, she saw that despite their obvious sadness, the other women in the village immediately adopted them into their families. So, really, there was nothing for her to do but marvel at the resilience of those who'd survived. And maybe feel sorry for herself.

She tried shifting her nurturing instincts to Matt, who truly had joined the organization under fire. "You can go home, if you want," she encouraged him. True, she had arranged for armed guards for them, even before she landed. But that protection was no guarantee that trouble couldn't happen again.

But he'd shrugged his shoulders in his loose T-shirt and acted very logical. "I'm not sure what exactly I thought I was getting into when I signed up. But I certainly can't go back now. We have the next traveling clinic to work on, and the doctors and nurses are really cool."

She could see she wasn't needed there. So she sought out Noreen. Somewhere in the shift of continents, Noreen had abandoned her designer duds and taken to wearing old Grantham University T-shirts and cargo shorts. Still, the statuesque redhead cut a dramatic figure as she made her way through the villages, the children running after her, shouting, *"La Rousse. La Rousse."* "The redhead, the redhead," and waiting for handouts of sugarless gum that she always seemed to have in supply.

"You're sure this isn't too much for you, Noreen?" Lilah would ask. "It's not exactly Grantham."

"It's scary and incredible all at the same time. I can't take it all in," Noreen would respond.

"But if you need to go home early?"

"I'll stay the two weeks that I signed up for. I've heard from Mimi and Conrad, and they're managing to hold the fort. Besides I'm just starting to talk to the women about the limited schooling possibilities. I really think it's an area where we can make an impact with our donors." She'd look inquiringly at Lilah, her hair a frizzy mound but somehow glamorous anyway.

How does she manage that? Lilah wondered as she pushed her own bangs out of her eyes. She knew she looked exhausted, circles under her eyes, her skin pasty, her heart and soul aching.

"That sounds very exciting. I'm glad you came then so that you can see it all in person," Lilah answered. And she was excited, she really was. Only...

"It will require someone to organize the effort, someone who is an expert in early education, and who could spend a lot of time traveling," Noreen noted.

"I agree. Perhaps the village elders might have some ideas," Lilah answered.

"Perhaps." And then she paused. "You haven't spoken with Justin lately, have you?"

Lilah shook her head. "No, not since coming over here. I'm sure he's busy though." And then she purposely avoided the topic, even later when Noreen brought up his name in conversation.

And she really wasn't fishing for information when she called Mimi on Skype. "How are things holding up?" Lilah asked.

"We're managing. Now that school's out, it's more time-consuming. I now know every park, playground and petting farm in a ten-mile radius. By the way, if you ever go to Broward Farm, avoid at all costs getting a cider slushee *and* a bag of cinnamon donuts. Your stomach will never tolerate the mix—trust me."

Lilah looked down, her own stomach more concave than usual. She just couldn't work up an appetite these days.

"And your father?" Lilah tiptoed into dangerous waters.

"We tend to limit our communications to text messages, but at least they're civil. Anyway, he's acknowledged he owes me for letting him know about Press's court mess, so I can hold that over him for a while, at least." Mimi had seen the court summons in the mail after she'd arrived to help with Brigid, and when she'd confronted Conrad about it, he'd claimed he didn't know anything. And then, the proverbial lightbulb had apparently gone off, and he'd made some inquiries.

"He fessed up to me about how the whole thing started, and when I heard, I had the mother of all fits. If he hadn't sworn on a stack of Bibles that he would go to court for Press I was going to personally blackball him out of the Grantham Club of New York."

"What did Press say about the whole thing? About your involvement?"

"I think his reaction was one of shock and awe. Anyway, it's not like our relationship has suddenly gotten all soft and fuzzy," Mimi admitted. "Though Press did allow me to drive him to his dorm at Columbia, where the museum is putting up the summer interns. And get this, since that meant I wasn't in Grantham, I forced my father to take Brigid to Yoga and Me. I have this sneaky ambition to make it part of his weekly schedule now that I've commandeered Noreen's whiteboard and felt-tip pens. I mean, it's not as if I'm about to go. Really. Can you imagine me at a yoga class?"

"No, I can't say that I can." Lilah found herself laughing, even if most of what Mimi was telling her didn't really make any sense from halfway around the world.

"So tell me, have you spoken to Justin at all?"

Why did the whole world seem to want to know? "No, but I know he's been busy with the end of school." She repeated her well-worn and unconvincing mantra. Lilah had yet to break the news to Mimi that the two of them were no longer an item, or whatever parlance was appropriate for the end of a spring fling. She had left the States so abruptly, with so many other things preoccupying her, that she had never found the time to tell anyone.

Yeah, right. It was more like she'd chickened out. She just hadn't been able to face a Mimi-type rehashing of events. "Any reason you ask?" was about as nonrevealing as she got.

"No, somebody mentioned him to me the other day. I'm not sure who. Maybe one of the moms waiting to pick up their kids after school. And did I tell you how vicious it is out there? If you want to be toward the front of the line, do you know how early you need to get there?

And I ask you, how can they drive these monster SUVs while talking on their phones? It's a miracle someone doesn't…"

Lilah tuned out the nonessential bits and eventually said goodbye.

But that call had been a few days ago. In between she'd spoken with her parents several times as they offered their love and support.

"We think you're doing great things, pumpkin," Walt had said in their last call.

"No one could ask for a better daughter," her mother had added before filling her in on the graduation traditions that Lilah knew so well from her family's little island.

"And have you talked to your friends?" her father had seemingly innocently asked.

But Lilah had heard some scolding in the background before her mother joined in, "And when you speak to Mimi, tell her how much she's welcome to visit anytime." Mention of Justin was left hanging. Her mother must have sensed from an earlier conversation that that discussion was verboten.

But today she was left by herself. Matt had pulled out with the medical crew and one of the traveling clinics, on their way to two neighboring villages. Noreen had tagged along to talk to the village women about schools. A Jeep followed, full of bodyguards riding shotgun.

Lilah had been prepared to go along—Sisters for Sisters was after all her initiative. But they had all insisted that she still needed some time after Esther's death to just stay and soak in her memory of Esther, talk about her with the other women. Hug her children.

And she did. But she couldn't help feeling empty.

Empty from grief. Empty from love lost—Esther's and Justin's.

As she sat on a stoop at the open door to Esther's empty hut, Lilah contemplated just how lonely she felt. Yes, she was embraced by friends who treated her as one of their own. She had achieved recognition for her efforts, a successful reward after ten years of backbreaking work. Esther was gone, but her children lived on, including her youngest daughter, Lilah—yes, a special gift bestowed on her by her late friend.

And if she was truthful, she didn't need to do a damn thing today if she wanted it that way. She could sit and soak up the sun that had been absent for days. Listen to the birds calling, the insects buzzing, the children playing, the women going about their chores, the two remaining guards trading good-natured insults as they played cards near the village well. In fact, just enjoy a moment of living.

She closed her eyes, but try as she might, her muscles remained tense. Maybe that was her trouble? She shouldn't try so hard? Maybe she needed Yoga and Me classes?

The sound of a sputtering car engine broke the humdrum noises. Lilah opened her eyes and with her hand shadowing her brow, peered down the winding road that led to the village. Clouds of red dust kicked up, announcing the vehicle's entrance. And the noise brought a few of the smallest children out of their huts to investigate.

Their mothers quickly ran out to snatch them back inside. Lilah rose. She thought of the shotgun she had left by her cot. They were all tense from the recent brutalities.

The guards abandoned their game and readied their rifles. "*Arrêt!* Stop!" they ordered.

A single Jeep came to a stop. There were none of the volleys of gunfire that accompanied a raid. Instead, a dusty man rose from the passenger seat, his hands raised. A hat covered his head, hiding his features, and he wore the ubiquitous T-shirt, cargo pants and hiking boots of all aid workers. But there was something different. It was his gait, his loping stride.

Lilah turned quickly to the guards, who were still at the ready. *"Tout va bien. C'est un ami."* "Everything's all right. It's a friend," she said, directing them to stand down.

She took a step, then another. "Justin," she called out, but her voice hardly carried.

It was enough, because he immediately turned and strode in her direction.

"You're here? Not in Grantham?" she said when he stopped several feet away. He looked tired and grimy and sunburned and incredibly...right.

"I took an unpaid leave-of-absence from my teaching job next fall. There was no way I was going to keep compromising my principles with that jackass. You made me see that." He dropped his rucksack on the ground. "You were right to say I was a coward, that I ran away from confrontation."

She grimaced. "No, I never should have mouthed off like that. What do I know about teaching and testing? I was in pain and I lashed out—cruelly—in a way that I knew would hurt you. And the things I said about you and your dad? I feel so bad. I mean, I have a great relationship with my mom and dad. I don't know how I'd act if I had a father that didn't support me."

Lilah replayed his words over in her mind. "Wait a minute. Unpaid? What are you going to live on, then?"

"Noreen had been emailing me for advice about establishing a more modern curriculum for local schools and the pros and cons of long-distance learning, and I decided to make her a preemptive offer to head up the schools program for Sisters for Sisters."

"And she accepted?"

"Not yet. She said she's run the numbers, and they look good. But she wanted to talk it over with you when things had settled down a little."

"Yes, everyone has been walking on eggshells around me. They think I'm some fragile piece of porcelain that will crack."

"No, they just love and respect you and don't want to overburden you. Accept help when it's given—okay? It makes other people feel good to give it."

She nodded. "I'll try. You're right. But I still can't get over that you're here. Wait a minute. If you took an unpaid leave and we still haven't worked out the terms of your contract—" she gave him a once-up-and-down "—how did you afford the plane ticket?"

"Well, I was ready to charge it, but I didn't have to. I made a sale instead."

"A sale?" She looked quizzical.

"My car. I sold it."

"Oh, no, your pride and joy, I can't believe it. Who bought it? Don't tell me your father?"

Justin shook his head. "That would be too unbelievable. No, Penelope, my sister. It seems she's taken a job at the rare book library at Grantham and, having never owned a car in Chicago, was in need of wheels."

"But it's more than wheels. It's…it's…"

"It's a car. And you…well…you are you."

Lilah smiled reluctantly. "Are you sure I am who you think I am? I mean, back in Grantham, even though we said we weren't ruled by the past, I can't help thinking we were somehow still caught up in memories."

"And memories can be less than accurate?"

"Well, that's why I've flown all this way to get reacquainted—no, acquainted. Call me crazy, but I think there's this amazing possibility that if we actually get to know each other under normal—well, normal for us—circumstances, we may just have a long and very happy future together."

Lilah smiled wholeheartedly. Who wouldn't? She held out her hand. "I don't think we've properly met. Allow me to introduce myself. I'm Lilah Evans, founder of Sisters for Sisters and a terrible softball player."

"And I'm Justinian Bigelow, an unemployed schoolteacher."

"Justinian?" Lilah interrupted. "I never knew your real name was Justinian."

"There're a lot of things you never knew about me." He held out his hand, looked at it, then withdrew it, swearing softly under his breath.

Lilah watched his actions then looked at his face, confused. "You don't want to shake hands?"

"We're done with the introductions," he said and pulled her close and kissed her. Really kissed her. And it wasn't like friends.

And when they finally broke apart he searched her face. "I know it's early goings, but would you be offended if I said I loved you?"

"Only if I didn't love you back."

And he was about to kiss her for a second time when she held up her hand.

"Recite the lines," she said with a grin twitching her lips.

"What lines?" He angled his head and tried again.

But again she pressed her fingertips to his lips. "Recite the lines from Shakespeare's sonnet that you used to use on all the women at Grantham."

"I thought we'd moved beyond college?"

"We have. But that still doesn't mean I don't want to hear it.... C'mon. 'Shall I compare thee to a summer's day?'"

He took her in his arms. His long legs straddled hers. He whispered the love poem by heart.

The warm vibrations from his mouth close to her ear tickled her skin.

And then he finished with the familiar words, "'and this gives life to thee.'"

Lilah sighed.

"This is the moment, of course, when I kiss the girl."

"By all means," she agreed.

And he did—with a vibrant love that touched her heart.

When he ended the kiss, she pulled back and exclaimed, "My hero."

"No, you're *my* hero. *And* my love."

This time, she was the one kissing Justin Bigelow.

* * * * *

HEART & HOME

Heartwarming romances where love can
happen right when you least expect it.

COMING NEXT MONTH
AVAILABLE MARCH 13, 2012

#1764 FROM FATHER TO SON
A Brother's Word
Janice Kay Johnson

#1765 MORE THAN ONE NIGHT
Sarah Mayberry

#1766 THE VINEYARD OF HOPES AND DREAMS
Together Again
Kathleen O'Brien

#1767 OUTSIDE THE LAW
Project Justice
Kara Lennox

#1768 A SAFE PLACE
Margaret Watson

#1769 CASSIE'S GRAND PLAN
Emmie Dark

REQUEST YOUR FREE BOOKS!
2 FREE NOVELS PLUS 2 FREE GIFTS!

Harlequin

Super Romance

Exciting, emotional, unexpected!

YES! Please send me 2 FREE Harlequin® Superromance® novels and my 2 FREE gifts (gifts are worth about $10). After receiving them, if I don't wish to receive any more books, I can return the shipping statement marked "cancel." If I don't cancel, I will receive 6 brand-new novels every month and be billed just $4.69 per book in the U.S. or $5.24 per book in Canada. That's a saving of at least 15% off the cover price! It's quite a bargain! Shipping and handling is just 50¢ per book in the U.S. and 75¢ per book in Canada.* I understand that accepting the 2 free books and gifts places me under no obligation to buy anything. I can always return a shipment and cancel at any time. Even if I never buy another book, the two free books and gifts are mine to keep forever.

135/336 HDN FC6T

Name _____ (PLEASE PRINT)

Address _____ Apt. #

City _____ State/Prov. _____ Zip/Postal Code

Signature (if under 18, a parent or guardian must sign)

Mail to the Reader Service:
IN U.S.A.: P.O. Box 1867, Buffalo, NY 14240-1867
IN CANADA: P.O. Box 609, Fort Erie, Ontario L2A 5X3

Not valid for current subscribers to Harlequin Superromance books.

**Are you a current subscriber to Harlequin Superromance books
and want to receive the larger-print edition?**
Call 1-800-873-8635 or visit www.ReaderService.com.

* Terms and prices subject to change without notice. Prices do not include applicable taxes. Sales tax applicable in N.Y. Canadian residents will be charged applicable taxes. Offer not valid in Quebec. This offer is limited to one order per household. All orders subject to credit approval. Credit or debit balances in a customer's account(s) may be offset by any other outstanding balance owed by or to the customer. Please allow 4 to 6 weeks for delivery. Offer available while quantities last.

Your Privacy—The Reader Service is committed to protecting your privacy. Our Privacy Policy is available online at www.ReaderService.com or upon request from the Reader Service.

We make a portion of our mailing list available to reputable third parties that offer products we believe may interest you. If you prefer that we not exchange your name with third parties, or if you wish to clarify or modify your communication preferences, please visit us at www.ReaderService.com/consumerschoice or write to us at Reader Service Preference Service, P.O. Box 9062, Buffalo, NY 14269. Include your complete name and address.

HSR11

There came a time in a man's life when he knew he was well and truly caught. Devon Carter stared down at the diamond ring nestled in velvet and acknowledged that this was one such time. He snapped the lid closed and shoved the box into the breast pocket of his suit.

He had two choices. He could marry Ashley Copeland and fulfill his goal of merging his company with Copeland Hotels, thus creating the largest, most exclusive line of resorts in the world, or he could refuse and lose it all.

Put in that light, there wasn't much he could do except pop the question.

The doorman to his Manhattan high-rise apartment hurried to open the door as Devon strode toward the street. He took a deep breath before ducking into his car, and the driver pulled into traffic.

Tonight was the night. All of his careful wooing, the countless dinners, kisses that started brief and casual and became more breathless—all a lead-up to tonight. Tonight his seduction of Ashley Copeland would be complete, and then he'd ask her to marry him.

He shook his head as the absurdity of the situation hit him for the hundredth time. Personally, he thought William Copeland was crazy for forcing his daughter down Devon's throat.

Ashley was a sweet enough girl, but Devon had no desire

to marry anyone.

William had other plans. He'd told Devon that Ashley had no head for the family business. She was too softhearted, too naive. So he'd made Ashley part of the deal. The catch? Ashley wasn't to know of it. Which meant Devon was stuck playing stupid games.

Ashley was supposed to think this was a grand love match. She was a starry-eyed woman who preferred her animal-rescue foundation over board meetings, charts and financials for Copeland Hotels.

If she ever found out the truth, she wouldn't take it well.

And hell, he couldn't blame her.

But no matter the reason for his proposal, before the night was over, she'd have no doubts that she belonged to him.

What will happen when Devon marries Ashley?
Find out in Maya Banks's passionate new novel
TEMPTED BY HER INNOCENT KISS
Available March 2012 from Harlequin Desire!